Praise for *Recall*

"David McCaleb has a real winner here. *Recall* is a smart and well-plotted thriller, a fantastic read that I could not put down. Red Harmon is a guy I'd want on my side."

—**Marc Cameron,** *New York Times*
bestselling author of *Brute Force*

"If you're looking for suspense, nonstop action, and a hero you can root for, The Red Ops series will clean your X ring."

—**David Poyer,** *USA Today* bestselling author
of *Tipping Point* and *Onslaught*

Recall
A Red Ops Thriller

DAVID MCCALEB

KENSINGTON PUBLISHING CORP.

www.kensingtonbooks.com

LYRICAL UNDERGROUND BOOKS are published by

Kensington Publishing Corp.
119 West 40th Street
New York, NY 10018

All Kensington titles, imprints, and distributed lines are available at special quantity discounts for bulk purchases for sales promotions, premiums, fund-raising, educational, or institutional use. Special book excerpts or customized printings can also be created to fit specific needs. For details, write or phone the office of the Kensington sales manager: Kensington Publishing Corp., 119 West 40th Street, New York, NY 10018, attn: Sales Department; phone 1-800-221-2647.

PUBLISHER'S NOTE
This book is a work of fiction. Names, characters, businesses, organizations, places, events, and incidents either are the product of the author's imagination or are used fictitiously. Any resemblance to actual persons, living or dead, events, or locales is entirely coincidental.

LYRICAL PRESS, LYRICAL UNDERGROUND, and the Lyrical Underground logo are Reg. U.S. Pat, & TM Office.

First Lyrical Underground edition: August 2016

ISBN-13: 978-1-60183-862-9
ISBN-10: 1-60183-862-X

First trade paperback edition: August 2016

ISBN-13: 978-1-60183-863-6
ISBN-10: 1-60183-863-8

To Dorie
For encouraging me to dream

Chapter 1
Three Seconds

Tony "Red" Harmon yawned as he rubbed burning, fatigued eyes with a palm. His cuff slipped back from his watch. 9:47 P.M. Too late for the family to be out. Nick dragged his feet on concrete, cheeks puffy, hand gripping Red's index finger. So tired he didn't even ask for a treat as they walked out of Walmart, past the candy machines. He looked up, snot glistening under a pink nose. Red winked at him, surprised yet again how his son looked like he'd cloned his mother's eyes.

The shopping cart was full of things they needed, but didn't want. School supplies and vegetables. A wheel with a flat spot clacked a steady cadence as Red pushed it under a rush of warm air blowing from above, into the January chill outside. How'd he always end up with the broken ones? He pushed with one hand, straining his wrist to keep the thing straight, pulling Nick with the other. He stepped slowly, careful not to slip on the frozen pavement. Just ahead, little Penny held Jackson's hand so tight his fingers were turning blue. Her head was high. She was obviously pleased Dad thought she was mature enough to guide her younger brother through the perils of the parking lot.

Hope his fingers don't go numb, Red thought.

"Look for reverse lights. They're the ones that'll run you over," Lori told them. She reached for Penny, then tucked her hand back into her peacoat, as if trying not to be too controlling. Narrow hips swayed as she kept pace with the kids.

Red looked back down at Nick, who was yawning again. "Tired, buddy?"

"I wanna go bed."

He laughed. "Me too. Been looking forward to it all day."

Lori glanced back, smiling, and lifted her chin.

They passed through a fog of exhaust from an old Ford pickup, the decal of a deer and crosshairs on the back window. The smell of gasoline stung his nose. Their SUV was parked far out, under the same pole as always, the lamp casting a cone of brilliance like a stage spotlight. A few snowflakes whisked through its beam like mayflies in summer. They passed a red Nissan Armada, just like the one their petite Filipina neighbor drove, the vehicle's tires tall as her shoulder.

The Armada was running, but without lights. Penny waited, watching the bumper, then scurried behind it with Jackson in tow. No more parked cars, so she skipped the rest of the way to their new Ford Explorer. Somehow it already had a dent in the quarter panel, and enough fruit juice in the carpet to make your soles sticky as a lint roller.

Penny had just pulled Jackson around the far side when Red heard two thumps—doors shutting. He glanced back. It was the Armada. Three people were following them through the dark, hands in pockets, heads down.

Red passed through a warm pocket of air rising from the pavement. He put Nick's hand into Lori's and reached for the keys. The horn beeped, the door locks snapped up, and the interior lights glowed. "Kids, get in."

He pushed the cart to the rear bumper, leaving it sticking into the traffic lane. The kids jumped into the back and slammed the door, smiling, glad their once-a-week shopping torment was over. Red grabbed Lori's shoulder, opened the passenger door, and pushed her in. The three men stepped past the shopping cart. Red locked the doors and tossed the controller into Lori's lap, relieved as the door slammed shut.

All three wore black jeans low on the hips. Two were tall and sported matching red sweatshirts, hoods pulled up. A tight-fitting blue one covered the third, a short, slender man. He came close while the others stood back. When he lifted his head, the pole light illuminated a Roman nose and light brown skin. The hood shadowed the rest. He pulled a long knife with a serrated blade from his pocket. Its sharpened edge glinted in the brightness. His voice was young and scratchy. "Your wallet, bitch!"

Sure. Take the damn thing. Red glanced to the SUV. The kids were bouncing in the backseat, blowing into cupped hands, unaware. Lori had pulled out her phone and was dialing. She could drive them out if she had to. Red reached to his back pocket and pulled out the wallet, staring at the gangbanger's eyes. They were empty, soulless, like his nephew strung out on meth when his sister had called for his help last year.

Red held the wallet next to his hip for a second, then took a step back. He slipped it into his pocket. What the hell was he doing? His life wasn't worth risking over a couple maxed-out credit cards. His vision blurred, then focused on the glinting edge of the blade. It was as if he were watching his own body from above. His arms spread, hands still as steel. Words surged from his chest, from someone caged inside him, forcing their way through his voice box. "Come and get it . . . bitch."

"Tony!" Lori said again. Only now did Red realize she'd been screaming it. Her eyes were wide, pleading. She pointed to the ground. One of the gangbangers lay on his belly, blood running from his legs and a small pool forming under his head. Red was bent over, knuckles clenched in the man's hair, pulling him off the pavement. His forearm was bloody and he pressed a snub-nosed revolver at the mugger's brain stem. Where'd the pistol come from?

The thug's eyes were closed; he wasn't moving. Dead? Resisting the urge to let go, Red laid the guy's head on the asphalt.

"Tony, you don't have to kill that one." Her voice was shrill.

He backed up, pointing the pistol at the still body. Red licked a metallic taste from chapped lips, breathing fast and shallow as a panting dog. What the hell was going on? A tall man an aisle over held up leather-gloved hands, backing away. He ducked into a Dodge Charger, tires squealing as he accelerated out of the parking lot.

Red slowed his breathing, then turned to Lori. "The kids?" Where was the Explorer? He spotted it a few spaces away. The shopping cart lay to one side, three boxes of number two pencils scattered across the pavement like pickup sticks. He jumped over the mess, landing next to two bloody heaps, the bodies of the other muggers. He squinted as the light reflected off one of the scarlet pools and stifled a retch.

The SUV's rear window was broken. High-pitched crying blasted from inside. He ripped open a back door and saw all three kids in the seat, huddled.

"You guys okay?" No answer, just more crying. He grabbed Nick's shoulder. The boy's frail body was quivering. "You hurt, buddy?"

Penny looked up. "Is it over?"

A smear of blood was across his daughter's cheek, tear tracks streaking through it. He cradled her head, trying to wipe her face with his thumbs, only making a bigger mess with the blood from his hands.

"I'm okay," she said, wiping her nose with a knuckle. "The— the blood. It's not ours."

The debrief room was gray, cold, and Spartan. Detective Matt Carter had designed it to look more like a morgue than a police interrogation chamber. "Three seconds!" Carter said. "Hard to believe." He sat in front of the stainless-steel table he'd bought when the seafood plant across the street went out of business. The shiny, sterile slab and knife slots of the tabletop fit the mortuary theme perfectly.

He felt in the pocket of his tan d'Avenza herringbone sport jacket for the pack of Wrigley's gum. "That's all it took . . . three seconds." He unwrapped a stick, then checked the time on his titanium Tag Heuer. No clocks in his debrief room. It hadn't been a long night yet, he thought. Two delinquents dead. One all but. They'd deserved it, murderous punks. Feeding their habit. If all three were gone there'd be less paperwork. The commonwealth attorney perched, buzzard-like, next to him at the table. Pencil-neck politician. Probably resented being woken up this hour.

Wasn't long ago that Carter had left Chicago's mean seventh district to become a detective in the sheriff's department of his sleepy hometown in New Kent County, Virginia. He still did homicide investigation, but at nothing like the one-a-day burn rate his team had done for years. The whole bloody confusion was still too familiar.

The killer sat across the table. His reflection in the stainless steel was distorted, fuzzy from a surface scarred by years of filet knives. Carter threw the green pack of gum on the slab, then stood and paced, neck back, eyes closed. So, what's wrong here? Stupid question. The killer, Mr. Harmon.

Guy has a good job. Nice family. No record. Acted in self-defense. Video from the parking lot cameras proved it. Even pencil-neck said they couldn't charge him. But Harmon's story didn't make sense. Experience told Carter when a piece didn't fit, something was hidden. But he had to be careful not to overstep legal bounds.

"Mr. Harmon?"

"Yes, sir," he said, scratching his neatly trimmed beard. Eyes were bloodshot, starting to sag underneath. He'd been to the bathroom to wash blood from his hands, but still picked at what was dried under his fingernails. That sweater would never come clean.

"Mind answering a few more questions?"

"Sure. Can I talk to Lori first?"

"Absolutely. No problem." Carter peered through the small bullet-proof window in the gray steel door at an empty hallway. "Looks like Sheriff Jenson is still talking with her. Mind if we go through this now? It'll get you out faster. I appreciate your cooperation. You've heard about the gang problem we've had?"

"I can wait. Rather not come back." The killer took a deep breath and pushed his fingers through tight red locks. "But I don't know what else I can add. Been through it twice. Can I see that parking lot video? I don't understand why I can't remember more."

Never answers my damn question. Knows exactly what he's doing. Poker-faced. "Don't see why not. Maybe it'll jog your memory." Carter slipped out and grabbed the DVD off his desk. Walmart's security manager wasn't there tonight, but the store supervisor gave it over when Carter promised he'd bring it back the next day. Yeah, right.

"Your vehicle was parked near a light. Surveillance camera had a perfect view." Carter slipped the disk into a player at the end of the table and fast-forwarded to 9:49, then pressed *Pause*. "If you honestly don't remember this, well—it's graphic. As graphic as a black-and-white security video can be."

Harmon shrugged. "If I did it, I need to see."

Pencil-neck pulled his chair closer to the TV. "Okay by me," in a nasal voice, as if speaking through a pipe.

Carter put it on slow motion. The closest gangbanger lunged at Harmon with the knife. He deflected the attack, grabbed the man's wrist and locked his elbow, then snapped that arm and pushed the guy's head through the rear window of the Explorer. He slammed a fist onto the back of his neck, slicing it open on the sharp edge of the broken window seal. As the body dropped to the pavement, one of the other thugs pulled a pistol from the front pocket of his sweat-shirt. Harmon pushed it away, the gun firing three times into the air. He punched the attacker's neck, grabbed the pistol as the body fell limp, and took aim at the last one sprinting away. That one knocked over the shopping cart in his haste. He was at full speed when Harmon shot twice with his left hand. The gangster fell, only his feet remaining inside the view of the security camera. *Pause.*

Harmon stared at the screen.

"Three seconds!" Carter said. "You killed two people, almost three, without a weapon of your own, and don't remember. Sure you're not a black belt or something?"

Harmon rubbed a knuckle. "Building manager. Like I said."

Time to press. Carter sat and pointed at the screen, rewinding a few seconds. "Look at this. The guy who pulled the pistol. You punched him in the neck. Look at your hand just before that. You're not making a fist. It's flat, like a blade. I saw this guy's body. You didn't hit him. You stuck your hand *into* his neck, grabbed his throat, and yanked it out. That's why you've got all that crud under your nails. That's only second number two. A building manager, buddy, you're not. The last guy, the smartest of the bunch, runs. Just not fast enough. Two shots. You plant one bullet in each thigh of a moving target. Three seconds."

Carter stood, tipping his chair so it crashed to the floor. Harmon was lying. But what could he charge him with?

Pencil-neck shook his head, as if anticipating the question.

Carter had nothing. Hell, he should thank Harmon for cleaning up. "You can't see the rest in the video, but you scrubbed his face on the asphalt. According to our only witness, the guy in the Charger, you were swearing like a sailor. That's saying a lot coming from a house framer. He thought *you* were the assailant. Thank goodness no one else was packing or they'd have shot the wrong guy."

No reply.

Carter picked up the three-page witness statement from the table and pushed it toward Harmon. "I don't get this. He said you kept yelling, 'Who are you? Who hired you?' as you beat the perp's head against the blacktop. Why were you asking him that?"

Red stared at the video screen and blinked. "I still don't remember any of this. I'm sorry. Wish I could be more help."

Yeah, sure he did. He knew Carter had nothing. "That must've been when your wife got your attention. If she hadn't, you would've been guilty of manslaughter. The first two were self-defense, but this guy was running away. Good thing you didn't kill him. . . . For your sake, that is. NHI."

Harmon furrowed his brow.

"NHI. No humans involved," Carter said.

Harmon squinted, and rubbed the bridge of his nose, as if to clear away disturbing thoughts. "Can I see Lori now?"

Hell, this wasn't going anywhere. Might as well order cocktails. "Yeah. That's enough for now. Let's get you home." Carter turned the doorknob. "I'll see if the sheriff's done with her."

He shut the door behind him, making sure it didn't slam. What was missing? Harmon was evasive for certain, but displayed no signs of it. Carter, if anyone, could read signs. He knew people, personalities, and when the two didn't fit. Could tell when he was looking at the wrong pieces, or when some were missing. Oftentimes, like tonight, he couldn't put it together right away. It all had to bounce around in his mind until the parts formed a meaningful whole. The other detectives in Chicago had called it *women's intuition*. All the time jealous of his clearance rate.

He walked down the hall, head down, thoughts bouncing. Turned the corner and bumped into Sheriff Jenson's belly.

"Oof," said the portly man. "What you find out?"

Jenson's long, skinny legs led up to an ample middle, capped by skinny arms and neck. If he didn't know where something was on his gun belt, he'd have to feel his way. Country boy, North Carolina type. Once Carter had settled in, this hillbilly first impression faded. The sheriff was slow spoken, but highly intelligent. Nothing got past him without notice.

"You mean other than don't get on his bad side? Nothing. Just like he said on the ride here, he doesn't remember anything after he pulled his wallet, till his wife started yelling. Can't figure out why I don't believe a word of it. You pull his record?"

"Yep. Nothing in it. Didn't 'spect to find nuthin', nohow. Hell, known his father for years. 'Nam vet, his daddy was. Tony played football with my boys. Get one hand on a pass and he'd bring her in. Not a single fumble, no matter how hard he got crunched. Back then he was small, but you had to add thirty pounds for meanness. Nasty as a boar hog on the field. One time some poor linebacker got between him and the end zone. Bastard woke up four minutes later, five yards back, and six points down."

Carter shifted his feet. "Sheriff. Uh, I've got to—"

"Sorry. Other than a speeding ticket, clean. Talked to his wife. *Damn*, she's a hot number, isn't she? Real upset. Still shaky, so I didn't ask too much. Said he works as a building manager at Varneck's."

"What does she do?"

"Some exec at a think tank, whatever that means. 'Process improvement,' she says. Sounds like bullshit to me."

Carter leaned an arm on the gray-painted cement block wall. "No reason to keep him. Mind if I let Red go home?"

"Who's 'Red'?"

"The killer. You know—Mr. Harmon. Said everyone but his wife calls him Red."

"Huh. Wouldn't have thought he went by that. Once got in a fight with my youngest for calling him 'Carrottop.' Get him. I'll let his wife know they can go."

Carter slipped back into the debrief room. Harmon was still sitting, arms on the fillet table, eyes focused nowhere. "Okay, been a long night. Thanks for sticking it out. Stay in town till we contact you. Go home, get some sleep. Try to put it behind you. Remember, we've got counselors on retainer who can help you guys talk through things. Especially the kids."

"Thanks. I'm sad they saw it, but glad no one got hurt—well, you know what I mean. We'll keep an eye on the kids. They're at my parents' now. Always sleep good there. At least tomorrow's Saturday. We can all sleep in."

The chair screeched as pencil-neck stood. "I'll let you know when a suit's been filed."

Harmon stared at him, blank-faced.

"We're not charging you," pencil-neck added, scratching a blotchy red cheek. "But this is America, so you'll be sued by someone. Probably the house framer, for emotional distress. I advise getting a lawyer."

Carter rolled his eyes. "Mind signing the incident report?" He pushed the form toward Harmon. The killer signed quick as a doctor, pen clicking over the knife-marks, and pushed the papers back.

"You ambidextrous?" Carter asked.

"Not that I know of. Think I do pretty much everything right-handed."

Chapter 2
Psych Visit

The hard black vinyl chairs of the waiting room squeaked as Red fidgeted, loud in the otherwise silent space. His legs kept falling asleep. He stood and stretched tense calves. The blue polyester drapes with scalloped edges that covered the single window smelled of cigarette smoke. Probably from a patient who couldn't stand the delay, Red mused.

"I should've been a doctor," he muttered. "Make you wait past the appointment, ask nosy questions, ignore your answers, then demand payment before you leave."

Lori smiled and kept turning pages in *Cosmopolitan*, looking comfortable in the short chair though she was several inches taller than he. She always looked graceful, even on a Monday morning and with no coffee.

"The county's paying. Relax." She flipped another page and glanced up, raising eyebrows. "We've all known for years you're half crazy. Good excuse to get you free help."

Red's lip turned up in an edgy half-smile. Her cheerful cynicism put him at ease, disarming the issue. A button on her blouse had come undone, revealing the black lace bra he'd bought last Valentine's Day. That had been a night to remember.

Following his gaze, she pursed her lips, looked down, and buttoned up. "You must've slept good last night."

A cloud passed and the sun shone through the window, warming his face. Two weeks and he still hadn't remembered anything new. They'd talked about the Walmart incident often. Detective Carter called daily. Not a bad guy, outside the interrogation room. They'd almost become friends, despite the rough start. Carter seemed to believe his lack of recall. Last week Red had been resigned to everything blowing over, but not Lori. He'd made the appointment with the shrink at her urging.

Voices approached from behind the reception desk. "Next week," said a female in a jumpy, Eastern European accent he couldn't place.

A brown-haired woman tugged a young boy sucking a red Blow Pop behind her. Her face hung tired; her hair half tangled. "Next week," she replied, trailing the kid in her wake like a tugboat.

A short woman with a round face and fair skin stepped into the waiting room. Her eyes were lively, set close together behind thick-rimmed glasses. She was trim, maybe even prim, sporting a pressed black pantsuit, like a miniature pallbearer, and the owner of the accent. "Good morning. You must be Mr. Harmon. I'm Dr. Christian Sato."

Red shook her hand. Her fingers were too short to wrap around his. And cold. "Yes, ma'am."

She closed her eyes and bobbed in a slight bow. "I see you brought your wife." Head inclined toward Lori.

"Actually, she brought me."

Her cheeks rounded even more as she smiled. "Please, follow me."

So she was Japanese. He was never good with accents, not like Lori. But how'd she get a first name like Christian? Chinese maybe, or—Dr. Sato looked back and stopped. "I'm sorry, Mrs. Harmon. Please wait for us out here. Today will be with your husband alone."

Red frowned and gripped Lori's elbow. "Doctor, I'd prefer her with me. She saw the whole—"

Sato's cheeks tightened. All the unassuming humbleness drained away. Eyebrows rose to pointed triangles, as if the doctor were possessed by an evil twin. Red didn't know whether to laugh or turn and run. "As did *you*," she said, looking past him to the empty waiting room. Her smile returned. The demon must have decided to move to another host. Another bob and she continued down the hall.

Lori rolled her eyes, then smacked Red on the ass. "Go on, then." She went back to her chair.

Sato opened a black walnut veneer door, its deep purple iridescence caught by sunlight beaming through a window. She almost needed to reach up to grasp the handle. Red stopped on the threshold. His shoulders drooped when she pointed to a short black chair like the one he'd just escaped. She pulled out a high-backed wooden stool from behind a '60s-vintage metal desk, drab green, picked up a pen, and flipped open a pad. "So. Tell me why you're here."

"I'm doing very well, thank you."

Sato's pen tapped the paper.

Red squirmed, glancing at the door, making sure it wasn't locked. She reminded him of Aunt Susan's rat terrier, the one that used to snarl and bite at his calves when they visited every Christmas. He'd kick the mutt away, but it just kept coming back, growling and nipping like a rabid chipmunk.

She smiled again. "Tell me about yourself."

Maybe if he played along, with short answers, he'd get out faster.

No such luck. Sato kept firing questions back. About family. His parents. Then his brothers. Did they fight? What the hell kind of question was that? "Of course we fought. If either son of a bitch was here now, you'd probably see a fight."

More questions. As if she liked to hear him talk. After half an hour, she took off her glasses and rubbed two red dots on the bridge of her nose. "You'd make a lousy dance partner, Mr. Harmon. I can't help if you don't cooperate."

"I don't see how all this talk is gonna do anything."

"Hmm. Denial."

The narrow armrests dug into his elbows as he pushed himself upright. "What?"

She set the glasses back on her nose, peering over the rims. "That's what we call it. Denial. You recently killed two men. Almost three. Out of character, wouldn't you say? Yet, you're not concerned with figuring it out. Why?"

Red clenched his jaw. He detected a faint whiff of cigarette smoke again. "Yeah, I wanna do that. But what if you write down on that pad that I'm crazy? Maybe a danger to my family?"

Her tone was gentler now. "I'm here to help, Mr. Harmon, not disrupt your life. I realize you may be worried."

"You think?" he exclaimed.

"If I am to help, we must trust each other. The only way that'll happen is if you open up." She slipped off her stool with a hop. Didn't stand much taller than when she was sitting. She walked around the desk with folded arms, hands clasping elbows, heels clicking the floor, pen snapping in and out. Her shoes had three-inch spike heels. Red smiled, though he tried not to.

"If I give you a clearer picture of where I'm going with the questions, would that help you open up?"

He tilted his head. "Uh—sure."

She walked behind him. "At first, when you called, I thought maybe *brain tumor*. Or head trauma. Your file says medically discharged from the Air Force. Almost crushed to death when a bank of shelves fell down on you. So, could be, I thought. Then I received the Walmart video from Detective Carter."

Red sat up. She'd already studied his case. "What about the video?"

"Let's do some deduction. About the way you killed those men. I would say you've been trained."

His nails dug into the armrest. "I told you, I've never been trained for anything like that. Maybe it was some sort of adrenaline overload. A reaction to—"

"No." She stuck out her lip. "Adrenaline can't teach you how to do a task you don't know. What you did was skillful—violent." She stood next to his chair now, leaning forward, flaring her fingers before his face. "Even . . . beautiful."

He snorted. "You're nuts. You oughta be the one in this chair."

Sato's cackle startled him. She strutted back to her stool. "Ah, yes. Three ex-husbands would agree."

Maybe she wasn't such a bitch after all. Least she could take a joke. Red got up and went to the window, stretching his legs to get the blood flowing again. Felt like needles in his skin.

"Back to deduction," she said. "I see a lot of military in my practice. In a situation like yours at Walmart, a civilian does what he's told. But if you've been trained, well—that's where it comes out." She thrust her palms toward him. "So, you didn't do what you were told."

"Maybe I panicked."

"The video doesn't support that theory. Only other option is trained."

He scratched the cowlicks on the crown of his skull. "Whatever."

Sato leaned over the desk, fingers flat on the top, the tips white. "So. We've accepted that you were trained. Now, don't you want to know why you can't remember that? Are there other things you aren't remembering? *That's* why the questions. *That's* why you need to open up."

The chair squeaked like nails on slate as Red slid himself back into it. He pushed his legs straight out in front and clasped his fingers behind his neck. "Okay. I'll quit being a jerk."

"How do you feel now, about the killing?"

His eyes studied the ceiling. "Don't know. Try not to think about it, I guess."

"But now you can."

"When I do, it seems surreal. Like watching a movie. I really don't think it's hit me yet."

"I see." Sato scribbled a note. "Sleeping okay?"

"Like a baby."

"What about dreams? Any strange ones? Nightmares?"

"None I remember. But . . ."

"Yes?"

He closed his eyes, trying to think back. "Okay. Had one. In it I was tied to a chair with piano wire. The punk, the one I didn't kill, he was beating on me. Hurt like a bitch. I was in a hospital, bandaged up, just like after all those shelves came down on me in the warehouse. Then I woke up. That's all."

She underlined something. "Feelings of guilt? For doing what you did?"

He yawned. Why should he feel badly? "No. They were trying to kill me."

She hopped up. "Let's dance, Mr. Harmon. I want you to act something out." She grasped his wrist, grip firm now, and pulled him to his feet. She pushed his chair toward the door, then sat on her desk with a jump. "You saw the video. Pretend it's happening again. Tell me what you feel. Ready? Okay—one guy lunges at you with a knife."

This lady was nuts. But why not go along? He slipped his hands from his pockets, wedding ring snagging on the seam. He closed his eyes and swung an arm. "Yeah. The video showed—"

"We know what it shows. Quit thinking about it. Put *yourself* back there, two weeks ago. Just pretend. What do you *feel*?"

His eyes burned as he shut them tight. Okay. If he was crazy, he needed to know. This shrink might testify if the lawsuit filed by the dead guys' families ever went to court. What can it hurt?

He envisioned the gangster holding the knife again, sharp edge gleaming. The last thing he remembered before the forgotten time. "I feel . . . relieved."

"Explain." Her voice was calm, almost seductive.

Keeping his eyes closed, he pointed to the side, where Lori would've been sitting in the truck. "Lori has the keys. The doors are locked. She's already calling 911. Even if they kill me, my family's safe. So, I'm relieved." He tilted his head. Another thought appeared in his mind, as if a spotlight had just shone upon it. "But those other two. If they've got a gun, they could still hurt them."

"How does that make you feel?"

His heart beat heavy, but slower. The cadence you'd use to work a sledgehammer on a wedge to split an unyielding piece of firewood. "I'm angry."

"Not scared?"

He huffed, surprised. "Uh—no. So the first guy lunges at me and I—" The sledgehammer swung faster now, harder. A presence, a ghost, distantly familiar, was knocking to be let in at his mind's door. He licked salty perspiration from his lip. "*Now* I'm scared."

Sato's voice was deadpan. "Now, as at Walmart? Or now, as in this room?"

He strained to pull his thoughts back to the present, to this office. What had that been? Maybe he *was* crazy. He opened his eyes. "Nothing. Just scared then . . . at the idea of being robbed. I guess."

She dropped her head, as if disappointed. Then hopped off the desk and climbed back onto her stool.

"Mr. Harmon, you're a terrible liar. I realize you're scared, so we'll take it as slow as you want. Before you go, here's something to think about: You say you have memory problems. Yet clearly you knew what you were doing when you killed those men. Handling yourself with adept violence." She pointed her fingers to the ceiling. "You pulled out a man's throat! I never even knew that could be done bare-handed. The fact that only two are dead is not by chance. Three seconds later, you're interrogating a prisoner." She leaned forward, staring with too-close eyes. "You don't *remember* training. You don't *remember* a fight in a parking lot. The two may be connected. It may not be the first time this has happened. You see? Let's find out together, shall we?"

She slapped the pad with her pen and leaned back. "Or, you could possibly have past brain trauma. I'm going to ask your doctor to order an MRI. Either way, next visit I *do* want your wife in here with you."

She smiled again, the devil back in her eyes. "By their wives, ye shall know them."

Chapter 3
Crawler

Seven years earlier

Major Jim Mayard leaned away from the passenger-side window. Tires on the narrow Afghan dirt road blew fine dust over the entire convoy trailing behind them. Calling it a road was an exaggeration. By most standards it was a dilapidated mountain trail. His sight followed it as they rounded a corner. He needed to stay sharp, though his last sleep had been two days ago, and stimulants were a last resort. He checked his watch. Only been riding an hour. Still six, maybe seven hours till Bagram Air Base. He spread open a jagged tear in the knee of his trousers, inspecting a dirt-encrusted scab the size of a quarter.

Sergeant Crawler yanked the Humvee's steering wheel, narrowly missing an orange rock outcrop. Three-day stubble dotted the driver's tanned leather cheeks, splotchy from sunburn. His frame looked like that of a linebacker, retired a few years ago. Jim rubbed his own beard, itchy in the heat. It had been two weeks since his last shave.

The gunner squatted below the turret. "I swear I'll haunt you if you kill me on this mountain." Sweat dripped off his chin, wetting his kneepads. Goggles were fogging up. Jim leaned back toward the window, trying to find relief from the locker-room stench.

"How long I been driving ya?" Crawler asked with a Brooklyn accent. The gunner said nothing. "This is your second deploy here. Been with me for the both. All that time, I ever run you into anything?"

"Do fence posts and guard shacks count?"

Crawler huffed. "The post only took off the mirror and the guard shack was shooting at us." He wiggled upright in the ripped tan seat and rubbed his sweat-stained lower back.

"Whatever. Keep your damn eyes on the road. You wreck anything else and they won't let your crazy ass drive. Not even out here."

The two had been jabbing at each other like a couple of sisters ever since Jim had sat down. Had they been doing this all the way out? He could put an end to their bickering, but they wouldn't care. What was he going to do? The pair were already in Afghanistan, driving convoys. Even Hell looked like a promotion. Jim and his team were cargo and at the end of the day they'd be delivered.

Crawler turned, facing the gunner. He draped one hand over the wheel and removed an unlit cigar with the other. He steered without looking at the trail, as if he knew it all too well. His eyes were focused on the reflection in the gunner's goggles. Jim thought he'd let him have his fun.

"What you think of them Yankees?" Crawler asked.

"I don't give a shit. Look at the road," the gunner said.

"You see the game they had against the Orioles?" He turned the wheel and circumvented a VW-sized boulder outside Jim's window.

"The road, Crawler. The road."

"Nine to one. Almost a shutout."

"I don't care what the hell they did. Watch the damn road!"

Crawler smirked, then turned forward again, winking at Jim as he jammed the cigar back between his teeth.

Around the next turn the trail narrowed, running laterally across a steep ridge. On Jim's side rose a sharp hill and to the other was a steep drop-off, several hundred feet to a dry ravine.

Jim pushed the cover back from his watch, then grabbed the radio and held the mic close. He pressed the button and a shock wave swept over the Humvee with a deafening boom. He turned to see the front end of the M35 transport behind them on fire. He looked at the mic button. Had he triggered the explosion?

The M35 crunched into the hill and came to a stop. Fire billowed from the engine compartment and the driver was slouched back in his seat. Automatic fire crackled from the hill above, stitching holes in the hood near the wheel. The gunner stood upright into the turret and the fifty cal boomed.

Jim shouted into the radio, "Transport down! Suppressing fire!"

Men leapt from the burning vehicle. Several scrambled behind a Cougar mine-resistant truck while another pulled the driver from the burning wreck.

The Humvee peeled away, tires spinning, pressing Jim back into his seat. "What the hell you doing?" The truck continued to accelerate. He aimed his M4 at Crawler's head.

"I ain't going nowhere," Crawler said. "Point that at the guys shootin'."

Ahead the trail widened. Crawler turned hard and slammed the brakes, locking all four wheels. They slid sideways, almost all the way around, then accelerated hard back toward the burning M35. Jim stuck his head out the window, then leaned away as if it were on fire. The wheels were riding on the edge of the drop-off.

The gunner ducked from the turret. "Son of a bitch! You can't make it past that truck! I can cover from here!" Crawler said nothing, keeping the accelerator down. They plowed down the side of the burning transport, tearing off the open door where the driver had been pulled out. Jim felt the tires beneath him slip down toward the ravine, but they held.

Red Harmon was in the middle of the trail, M4 aimed high and returning fire over the unconscious driver. Crawler headed directly for them at speed, then turned hard and slammed the brakes. This time, the skid was graceful. Red dropped to his belly and the Humvee came to a stop, straddling the pair. The fifty cal echoed from the turret as Jim helped lift the injured driver into the back.

"Get the rest into the other trucks," he shouted at Red. Jim ran back to the cab and aimed his weapon up the hill through the open window. No enemy in sight. Only dust clouds along a ridge where the gunner was concentrating the fifty cal. Tracers from the combat mix ammunition snapped like lasers every fifth round.

The burning troop transport blocked their escape. Crawler sped up, slamming into the back of it and pushing forward. Gravel clinked against the floorboards as all four wheels on the Humvee spun. The transport wandered toward the cliff, the road curving away. After a few seconds, it rolled down the side and the convoy sped past. The sulfur stench of burning gear oil filled Jim's nose. He pressed one nostril closed and blew onto the floor. A quarter mile later the landscape leveled somewhat.

Loud groaning and white smoke came from the Humvee's engine compartment, but it kept running. The sweet aroma of burning antifreeze filled the cabin. Crawler leaned over and shouted above the engine noise. "Round the next curve's a bitch! A red zone, maybe half mile long. 'The Gauntlet' we calls it. Tell your guys to get low till we're through."

"Ever have trouble there?"

"No shots. But they ain't friendlies."

Crawler slowed around the sharp curve. Several small white rocks the size of a man's fist were in the middle of the road, as if newly fallen.

"See those?"

"Nothing. We checked 'em on the way out," Crawler said, speeding over.

An orange stone-walled town stood ahead, the road running straight through the middle. Situated on a ridge, it offered no way around. A burning car blocked the entrance. Jim put the radio down and shouted, "We can't go back. Our tail's got a vehicle in pursuit."

Crawler leaned back his head. "Keep your eyes on the rooftops!" he shouted to the gunner. He slowed and slammed into the burning car, crunching it into the wall, clearing the road. Heads emerged atop a two-story home, peeking over the mud-brown parapet, like jack-o-lanterns on a wall. A man stood and an AK-47 clattered. The gunner spun and the fifty cal roared, blowing chunks off the low wall, puffing dust clouds that floated slowly away like they had on the ridge.

The engine revved higher as the truck accelerated. Jim smacked into the doorpost when Crawler yanked the wheel avoiding potholes. The turn made the gunner stitch the entire side of the home, shattering a second-story window. The AK stopped, but a block later a short bespectacled man stepped into the road in front of them. He raised a pistol and opened fire. Crawler swerved toward him, catching him square in the chest and bouncing his head off the quarter panel, spraying blood on Jim through bullet holes in the windshield.

The mad driver almost looked like he was smiling as he leaned over and shouted above the still-ringing fifty cal, "They's high on all kindsa shit. Don't even move!"

A few hundred feet ahead, atop a yellow adobe building, a

brown turban peeked over a knee-high wall. The last tall structure before they were through.

"RPG!" Jim shouted, pointing to the rooftop. The gunner spun and fired. The turban sank back down.

Crawler slammed the brakes and stopped ahead of the building. Jim leaned out his window. Barely enough room for the convoy to pass.

The driver opened his door. "Keep that guy's head down!" he shouted, then drew his pistol and ran inside.

"What the hell," Jim said, dropping the radio and jumping out. Dumbass just ran through the door. Didn't even clear it.

As Jim followed, gunfire broke from inside, the racket of a single AK mixed with a sidearm.

Shit. Now I'm gonna be driving us home.

Jim stooped and ducked through the door, M4 raised. The room was dark and broiling, a concrete floor and dirty yellow walls. He blinked, adjusting to the dimness. The smell of mold was heavy. He knelt past the entrance, keeping aware of anything that may move in his peripheral vision. Ahead was an open room with rotting wooden crates stacked around, half of them caving in. Crawler's silhouette was a few paces forward, squatting beside a corner wall, sidearm pointed toward a body lying facedown on the concrete.

"Got one," he whispered, then dropped an empty magazine to the floor. The clatter echoed off the concrete.

Dumbass.

Before he grabbed a second magazine, a skinny, thin-bearded man in brown kameez ran from behind a crate a few feet away, charging Crawler with a knife. Jim leaned to get a clear shot around him, but Crawler stepped into the line of fire, readying himself for the attack. He dropped the sidearm and snatched his KA-BAR, pushing it through the attacker's belly on the upstroke till it stuck out his back. The blow lifted the skinny man from his feet. Crawler threw him backwards on the cement, pulling the knife out and returning it to a scabbard without wiping the blade, then stooped and wrapped the sidearm in a hairy fist. "That's the other."

Jim inhaled the heavy scent of entrails, like an eviscerated deer after a successful hunt. "Stupid shit! I could've gotten him! Next time get the hell out of my way!"

Crawler turned and ran up gray-plank stairs that bent under his weight.

Runs like a damn elephant. Gonna kill the both of us.

Jim followed, weapon and eyes focused behind them. Crawler was almost at the roof access when a shower of wood splinters exploded. Bullets riddled the door from the outside, stitching the rafters. Crawler pulled a grenade from his belt and tossed it across the jamb, the door flapping on its hinges, smacking the munition, almost sending it back down the stairs. Footsteps pounded above, running in opposite directions, one cracking the thin wooden roof. A second later the grenade blew a crater where the crack had been, spraying splinters and dust against Jim's goggles. Crawler barreled up through the door and turned toward the RPG, halfway blocking the opening, back to the other soldier.

Son of a bitch was gonna get shot. Jim pushed his shoulders between the doorpost and Crawler, slicing a neat line in his arm on a sharp nail. Crawler fired twice.

Across the crater, Jim saw a soldier with a green bandolier lying facedown. The enemy rolled over, pulling a pistol from under his leg, bleeding in gushes. Jim squeezed a double tap, stapling his head to the roof. He checked the rest of the area. Crawler started toward the door. Jim stepped in front and went down first, angling his rifle into the darkness. Sweat dripped into the gash on his shoulder, burning. The last truck in the convoy was passing as they closed the doors of the Humvee. Crawler pulled out and took up the tail.

The radio was alive with chatter and a headcount confirmed no one missing. Only serious injury was the driver of the M35, now stretched in the back of the Humvee, a doc wrapping gauze around a charred face. Then silence. Precious silence.

Jim glanced at Crawler. His shoulders were hunched. Splinters stuck to one forearm like the whiskers on his cheeks. "Didn't have a clue what you were doing, did you?"

The driver squinted. "Nope!" He winced as he pulled out a bloody sliver. "But I wasn't gonna let that sonofabitch hit my train."

Jim grabbed at the slice in the shoulder of his fatigues and gave a yank, tearing the rip-stop fabric with a *snap-snap-snap*. The gash in his shoulder ached as he pinched the flesh together. "For a dumb shit, not bad. You got lucky. Do that again and you'll be going home in a C-17, zipped in a body bag."

"That's what the Army's hopin'."

"What?"

The driver rubbed his forehead, squeezing dirty sweat droplets down his cheeks. "Long story."

"Know how to drive anything other than a Humvee?"

Crawler smiled for the first time. "Only if it's got wheels . . . or tracks."

Jim glanced back at the medic, who'd jumped from his own transport into the Humvee as the convoy had passed. He was sticking a fentanyl lollipop between bandage strips into the injured driver's mouth. "Sergeant Crawler, thought you'd kill us squeezing past that burning truck. Interested in getting stateside?"

Crawler frowned. "Love to, but I gotta finish my tour. Volunteered. Third one. Some tickets need to drop off my record stateside. Trucks out here is the only thing the Army is letting me do."

"Drive like that for me, and I'll have you licensed tomorrow. Don't care what your record says."

Crawler's forehead wrinkled. "You fuh real?"

"I make one call and you're mine. We leave in the morning. Your choice."

Chapter 4
Leak

The cool six a.m. air stung the back of Red's throat as his breath came harder. Approaching the end of the morning run, he pushed himself down the ice-packed street, startling a neighbor wrapped in blue-plaid flannel bending over to pick up a paper. Winter was like death—the skeletons of leafless trees against the cold sky. At dawn everything seemed to bleed gray. Gray houses, gray cars, sidewalks, and lawns. However, this morning held some warmth, a little light, as the rising sun cast deep-pink streaks beneath black clouds.

Since the Walmart incident, morning runs helped clear his head. The time to himself, enjoying the heavy morning frost that held the beloved crisp scent. This was what he imagined the expanse of the Arctic must radiate when there's nothing around but frozen emptiness. He pictured himself running across the tundra, alone, breathing the heavy air. It had been six years since his discharge from the Air Force, but he kept fit. Just didn't feel right if he didn't push himself.

He settled into a slow jog, the warm-down, no faster than a brisk walk. Around the corner a white Chevy Malibu was parked in front of his house. It was not out of place in a middle-class neighborhood, but he didn't recognize it. He stalked up from behind to the driver's side, sliding his feet flat across the slick, packed snow, then peered in. A closed laptop was mounted in front of the armrest, an empty shotgun stand next to it. A clipboard was bungeed to the passenger headrest.

Unmarked police car.

Red ran across the clean snow on his front lawn and bounded up the porch steps, then stooped to grab the house key he'd laced in his

shoe. Muted voices bled through the mail slot. The knob was unlocked. He trotted through the warm living room, trailing melted
snow.

Lori's voice floated from the kitchen. "Sounds like him now."

Matt Carter was leaning against the kitchen island. He straightened when Red came in, but said nothing. Red extended a hand.
"Good to see you again."

The creases on the detective's forehead disappeared, his countenance softening as they shook. "Sorry for the intrusion. Thought
it'd be best if, well, there's been a turn of events."

Red pulled a stool close and all three sat around the black granite counter where the family ate breakfast. Carter took Nick's usual
seat. Where were the kids? Shouldn't they be up by now?

Red slowed his breathing, catching up from the jog. The warm
air caused his pores to open further, sweat rolling down his beard,
dripping to the counter. He took off his sweatshirt. The granite was
cool as he leaned on an arm. The other he slipped under and
squeezed Lori's knee. She tossed her hair over one shoulder, looking ready to give one of her sales pitches to a group of execs.

Carter's face reddened in anger. "The Walmart surveillance
video went viral."

Lori stared. "What does that mean?"

"It was leaked."

"Great!" She looked at Red, grimacing. "Just great."

"We don't know how or who, yet. Maybe someone from Walmart, or could be in our office. Yesterday it had half a million hits
on YouTube. We found out when a friend of my deputy posted a
link. The deputy recognized it and let me know yesterday. Around
two o'clock."

Red stared at him. What? How could the cops let that happen?
Would the family be in danger? But Carter had said they didn't
know who leaked it. Courteous, giving bad news in person.

The deep lines returned to Carter's forehead. "We don't have
the resources to track those things electronically. Going to figure it
out the old-fashioned way. I've put in for warrants. Hopefully get
us past the gatekeepers at YouTube. The video should be pulled
soon, but that won't matter. It's out there."

Red leaned in toward Carter. "Do we need to be worried? Was
any of our info leaked with it?"

"No. Not as far as we can tell. That's what put fuel on the fire. There're threads out there on a couple blogs where folks are trying to figure it out. Where it was. Who it was. The only detail we can see is the time-date stamp from the surveillance camera. I've put the fear of God and a gag order on the guys at Walmart. They won't be saying anything."

"Won't someone connect the dots?"

"They could, but not without effort. We've kept the incident out of the papers for two weeks. The feds could figure it out, but no one on some random blog. But there's always Murphy's Law working against you. Someone from town could see the video and notice it looks like our Walmart. Could be as simple as posting, 'I was at Walmart that night. There's my car.'"

Lori's cheeks reddened till they matched her lipstick. "But even if they figure out the location, they can't pin it to us. Plus, it's not like we did anything wrong."

Red leaned back. "Yeah, but I don't want the headache. Father Ingram only lives two doors down. He'll be wondering why I haven't been to confession. I can have some fun for a while, but if it gets out, our friends will keep us at arm's length."

"We've got great friends. They'll stand by us." Lori lifted her chin. "On the other hand, my family has been waiting for you to accomplish something big. Now you have."

Red rolled his eyes. Hadn't told her family yet, waiting for a more opportune time. He turned to Carter. "Sorry. Inside joke. You see, my wife is perfect. The youngest of three girls. Straight A's. No trouble. Never drank till twenty-three. Drop-dead gorgeous. Stiff-armed every guy that asked for a date. Ivy League college. Grad school at U Penn." Red patted his chest. "Meets me at a bar. Way out of my league, but I trick her long enough to get married, then discover it was actually *she* who pulled one over on me. She'd hidden me from her parents . . . till rehearsal dinner. My self-esteem gradually gets chipped away as I get introduced around the table. Hell, I was the jock in high school. Did okay in college football. Big fish in a small pond. Only didn't have sense to know how small. Lori grew up in a much bigger pond."

Lori put her hand on Red's leg and rubbed the inside of his thigh. It always turned her on when he bragged about her. "You're exaggerating, but that's okay," she said, squeezing.

"Her father's a three-term state senator. Used to play for the Colts. Mother, concert pianist. Rest of the family just like 'em. Me? Building manager, two inches shorter than my wife. They call me *Lori's husband*. Keep me because we make cute kids."

Lori's smile was contented. The way her hand was rubbing his leg, she was well pleased. Tonight would be a good night.

"Don't let him fool you. My family loves Tony despite his shortcomings."

Red grimaced. "Thanks. Now back to reality. The guy in ICU, still there?"

Carter nodded.

"If we get ID'd on the video, reporters might show up for a few days. I'll go on the talk show circuit and admit I don't have any recall, and we make a few dollars off the deal. Maybe write a book. It'll be forgotten quick as it started. Awkward with the neighbors, but I don't see any big deal. Though I appreciate you stopping by, the heads-up."

Carter's stool screeched on the wood floor as he stood. "Just wanted you to hear it from me. Never know which way these things will turn." He lifted the tip of one toe, then squinted at Red. "What did Dr. Sato say?"

"She thinks I'm a brain-damaged assassin."

Carter's lip curled in a sneer.

Red laughed. "Yeah, the same look I left with."

"Least the brain damage part made sense." Lori bobbed her head playfully side to side.

Carter glanced at his watch. "Well, that's Sato. Anything else?"

"Said she does psych work for the military. Mainly PTSD."

"Military? So she contracts with them, too. . . . She told me CIA. Makes more money in a week than I make all year. Moonlights for the county in her extra time. That's how we got you in." Carter's eyes were bright as he looked back, walking to the door. He grabbed the knob as a loud knocking came from the other side.

Red put his hands into warm pockets. "Probably from next door. Post office gets confused. Neighbors get our mail. You can let 'em in. We'll talk again soon."

Carter's grip on the doorknob tightened. He squared up and took a breath, focusing on the jamb. The paint on the door's edge was cracked and a chip revealed bare metal beneath. Why was an alarm sounding in his head? It was as if some random piece of the puzzle had fallen into place, but he didn't know which.

He resisted the temptation to throw the door open. Instead, he forced a smile and slowly pulled. The cold frost pushed into the warm room, bringing with it the fragrance of Givenchy.

Atop a snow-encrusted doormat stood a man in an Air Force long coat. He was as tall as Carter but more muscular, and had silver eagles on his shoulders. MAYARD was engraved on his blue name tag. Closely trimmed gray hair jutted below a flight cap. Sharp-jawed and steel-eyed, he could have been a recruiting poster in his younger years. Water beaded on his patent leather shoes and the hems of his well-pressed pants were wet.

Carter stood in the opening like a bouncer and scanned the front yard. Nothing moved behind the blue-coated man. A blue Ford Taurus was parked ahead of his squad car, bumpers almost touching. Fresh footprints slogged in a straight line from it to the front door, despite the walkway being shoveled. The colonel's gaze seemed to pierce Carter and focus on Red. The man raised an eyebrow. "Red! Long time, old friend!"

The blue-coated colonel stamped his feet hard, knocking the snow from his shoes. "Pardon me," he muttered, brushing against Carter, as if noticing him only now, forcing his way into the living room.

Red's mouth drew into a grin. "Jim!" He extended a hand and, after a firm shake, they ended up in that awkward yet manly hug that happens when one encounters a close friend from the distant past. Red's body language seemed at ease. Carter studied Lori, but her smile was only slight, nothing he could qualify as an unconscious signal.

Red made the introductions. "Jim, this is Matt Carter, a detective from the sheriff's department. New friend of mine. He stopped by to let me know I'm about to be an Internet star."

"What?"

"Long story. Tell you later. Carter, Major Jim Mayard, a very, *very* old friend, from a previous life."

"Colonel," Carter said, glancing at Jim's shoulders. "Full bird."

"Has it been that long?" Red asked.

"Four years. Just pinned on. Only three as a light colonel."

Mayard's words were clipped, but his smile revealed the pride of his accomplishment.

"And still haven't figured out you're a waste of oxygen?"

"Only rumors."

"I can speed up the dishonorable discharge. Remember what we made you do when you couldn't hold your liquor against that female staff sergeant?"

Jim laughed and slapped Red on the shoulder hard enough to make him stumble. A subdued warning entered his voice. "You haven't changed. The prodigal returns and it's like I never left." He leaned close to Red's ear, but spoke loud enough for all to hear. "The only thing that said *female* about her were the dog tags."

Lori cleared her throat.

Jim turned to her with arms outstretched. "The *real* reason for my visit—this sexy lady. How's the woman in my dreams?"

"Still waiting for you to ditch your wife." Lori gave him a hug, standing on her tiptoes. His embrace lifted her from the floor, her frame dwarfed by his. He put her down and straightened his back as if called to attention, gray eyes aimed at Carter. There was a story behind that look, Carter sensed. Jim was smiling. The mood of Red and Lori, bright. No distrust he could discern. But Jim's eyes . . . their whites were cold and the irises, hard as granite.

"What's this 'Internet star' thing? Red's got me curious," Jim asked.

Carter extended his hand as he took a step toward the door. "I'll let Red fill you in, sir. Nice meeting you. Gotta run. You two catch up. Red, we'll be in touch."

Carter stepped outside and shut the door behind him, forcing himself to not look back. His mind was unsettled, thoughts bouncing.

He'd grown fond of Red over the last couple weeks. Harmon was the kind of guy you could only say good things about. Everyone in town knew him, even the grain farmer with the dental bridge at the diner. He'd sat next to him when Carter had met Red there for lunch. The farmer had pointed to one of his front teeth, explaining how Red had knocked it out in a football game. The guy had even slipped out early and paid for their lunch.

Fresh snow was frosted over a rough layer of ice on the handle of Carter's cruiser. He tried it, but it held fast. He pulled up harder and it broke loose with a *crunch*. His grip slipped off and the handle smacked back down.

"Son of a bitch!" He cradled throbbing fingers with his other hand. Two nails were folded backwards in the middle. The blood seeped into his cold palm. A snowflake dropped into the middle of the red pool, its pure white contrasting with the steaming deep red. Apart from the pain, a beautiful, delicate sight. The blood pushed its way up between the flake's crystals, which melted it as quickly as it had appeared.

An idea floated to the surface. He stared at the blood, just a few drops now, hitting the perfectly white snow beneath the car door. He tried to hold the thought, not wanting it to slip away. What had eluded him about Red? How did such dissimilar pieces fit the same puzzle? He now realized he'd been distracted. The mystery wasn't the pieces, but the material from which they were made. Seeing Red with the colonel . . . within Red, then, Carter sensed—*danger*.

He hunched over, cradling the thought. Had he been sensing his own fear, his own reaction to what he'd unconsciously perceived? If so, why hadn't he seen it before? Yes, because Red didn't even know it was there. Other killers had thin facades. But Red had no such thing. He was, indeed, both killer and family man.

Carter winced as he pushed his fingernails back down. He shook the last blood onto the snow, then got into the Malibu. As he pulled away, the skeletons of winter trees stood in the foreground of a bright orange eastern sky. The sun warmed his face.

Danger . . . Good to see it there.

Jim Mayard eyed Carter through the living room window as his tires crunched over packed snow. The icy ruts seemed to be hanging around forever on the streets. Unusual, this heavy snow. Moist, like in North Korea during last month's snoop and poop. He pulled his finger back from the curtains and turned to Red, scrunching his nose. "Seems like a nice enough guy."

Red smirked. "You're just turned on because he called you *sir*."

"Beats the treatment I get from you. Still curious. What's this 'Internet star' thing he said?"

Red waved his hand. "Plenty of time for that. Hope you're hungry. My one day off and I'm cooking. You're a full bird now, so no one notices when you don't show up to work. Right?"

"Gotta get to Hampton Roads. But I'll stay if you're making pancakes."

Red lifted three small pans, one cast iron, from the pot rack above his head. The iron one went on the counter while he held the other two by the handles. His blue eyes shone. The tip of his tongue stuck out to one side. He tossed one into the air and then the other, handles spinning, almost smacking the ceiling. As the second left his hand, he grabbed the iron one from the counter and tossed it in turn.

Red had the best coordination of any team member Jim had ever known. Could throw a knife spot-on at thirty feet. Did he still remember nothing? Dr. Sato's warning call hadn't been a surprise, but she'd said not to ask direct questions.

Jim glanced up at the wrought-iron pot rack hovering over them like a bomb rack ready to drop its ordnance. He selected a fourth pan. Red was in a steady rhythm, even with the iron one that wobbled clumsily.

Lori scowled. "You break it, you fix it."

Jim returned an ornery smile, then lobbed the fourth to Red, its handle looping.

Red dropped to a knee and caught it, speeding up the rhythm. He managed a single round, then one of the pans crashed to the floor, followed by another.

Never could handle that fourth one, Jim mused. "Hope the 'cakes are better than your juggling."

Red leaned over the stove. In short order the kitchen smelled of coffee and hot bacon. Jim sat across from Lori as she told him about the Walmart incident. He tried to act surprised. There were no hints Red remembered anything. Red pulled some blueberries from the freezer and Jim's mouth grew wet—his buddy still remembered his favorite.

Jim told them he'd spent two of the last four years in South Korea, but was reassigned to Hampton Roads. At least that much was the truth. "It gets harder to make an honest living the higher in rank you go. They keep trying to put me behind a desk at the Pentagon. I keep telling them to go to hell." He glanced over a sticky plate at Lori. He'd always been jealous of his friend in several ways. Red lived gracefully, even as an operator. So intense on an op, but turned it off like a switch at the end. Those years together, Jim had depended on Red's spirit to balance him out.

"Remember how the squad would play basketball at lunch?" Jim asked. "You were such a son of a bitch on—" He hunched his shoulders. "Sorry. Kids aren't up, are they?"

Red laughed. "Won't be long, though."

"You were such a son of a bitch on the court. Ran circles around me."

Red shoved a triangular three-stack into his mouth. "Yeah. You'd lay me out for a while once you'd had enough."

"I'd call it your *cooldown*."

The lights glimmered off Red's eyes. "Funny. Ref always called it a technical foul."

Jim missed that about Red—he never held a grudge. Not like the backbiting political pansies trying to put an end to his squadron. Jim dreaded the conference room full of them in Hampton Roads. He checked his watch. Better be late, to make sure the mood of the room was ripe. He twisted the band on his wrist and stood. "Got to get moving. Thanks for breakfast. You haven't lost your touch."

As he walked to the front door, Penny came downstairs in pink Disney princess pajamas, the bottoms pulled halfway up her calves.

"Remember Uncle Jim?" Lori asked. "You were only five last time you saw him."

Penny looked up and smiled, then hugged his leg without a word, rubbing the sleep from her eye with a knuckle.

Jim lifted her. "Damn, I mean, you're all grown. Too big to pick up."

Penny smiled, then wiggled herself down and sniffed the air. "What's for breakfast?"

Jim's shoulders drooped, but he leaned on the wall to mask it. "Don't know why it's been so long."

"Road goes both ways," Lori said. "Our fault, too."

He gave her a quick hug and moved toward the door. "Watch your back, Red. Might not be so lucky next time."

His buddy laughed. "I've punched that ticket. Shouldn't run into it again."

Jim stepped down the shoveled sidewalk. He sniffed the familiar welcome of the morning cold. He stood next to his blue Taurus and raised a hand to shade his eyes, squinting eastward toward the sun. Funny. It was cold on his face. Nice getting caught up. Even better was Red's innocence—he still didn't remember. But with what had happened at Walmart, those memories couldn't be buried too deeply.

Chapter 5
Professionals

Red woke to a splitting headache. A hangover? He tried to recall last night, but it took too much effort. Hadn't had anything to drink. The house was pitch black, but then he liked to keep the room dark at night. The mattress felt like a plank. He pushed up. *Not a mattress at all.* Carpet. Red snickered. How had he fallen out of bed?

On his knees, he lifted his head, scanning for the faint glow from the bathroom night-light. Turned completely around, but couldn't find it. Maybe the bed was blocking his view. He reached out to grab it and hoist himself. Instead, his hands landed upon something unfamiliar, hard. There was a dim luminance around the doorway, but from the wrong side. Had Lori moved the night-light to a different socket?

He straightened, almost lost his balance. Why such a headache? He'd get dizzy with a cold, but didn't feel one coming on. Looked for the night-light again. He wasn't in the bedroom, but the hallway. The faint glow came from the clock on the kitchen microwave. Must've been sleepwalking and fallen. He'd never done that before. As a bolt of pain jolted his senses, he ran his fingers through hair soaked from night sweats.

Taking a deep breath, he stumbled downstairs for water, bracing himself with a hand to the wall. Why was the air so cold, but the floor still warm? Have to check the thermostat on the way back up. He pulled the microwave open, casting light over the counter, and reached for a glass. Even that dim glow was too bright. He winced and let go. A big dark smear ran the handle's length from the kids making hot chocolate before bed. He licked the stickiness from his fingers. Tasted of metal and salt. He frowned and held his hand to the light. Blood, not chocolate. Then a memory shook him—the nightmare before he woke.

He bolted upstairs and slammed on the light switch in the boys' room. Jackson was down from his bunk bed, huddled with Nick, eyes huge. He didn't even squint at the brightness, just got up and ran to Red, hugging his leg. "What's going on, Dad?"

Nick's chest was rising and falling. The boy could sleep through the Second Coming. Red broke free of Jackson's grasp and sprinted to Penny's room.

She, like Nick, didn't move. His daughter slept so soundly he'd put an ear next to her mouth to hear her breathe. As he knelt at the bed, she frowned and rolled over. *Thank God.*

He ran to his own bedroom and flicked on that light, too. Lori should be up by now, asking what was going on. She wasn't in bed, so he turned to the bathroom. Door closed. "Lori, you in there?"

No answer. He yanked it open. No Lori.

Ripped back the shower curtain. Nothing.

He pulled his hair and paced the bathroom floor.

Something inside tried to take hold of him. A feeling, distantly familiar, from another lifetime, the same as at Sato's office. Fear, the gut-felt kind like when he was a kid after a bad dream. Knowing he was awake, but too scared to move, eyes searching the darkness. Only this fear was even more gripping. It held weight, possessed substance. This nightmare was real. His teeth cut into his tongue.

Footsteps stalked behind him. Too heavy for the kids. A nightstick grazed the doorjamb, then the faint tinkle of handcuff chains. How'd he know what they were? The fear began to crawl within him, but he pushed it back down. Turned and stared down the barrel of a 9mm Sig Sauer.

"Freeze! Police!"

Red leaned on the cold metal skin of a police cruiser in his driveway. Carter stood next to him, arms crossed, looking well put together considering how quickly he'd shown up. Red looked down at his wet slippers and wiggled frozen toes. Morning would come in an hour.

A backup cruiser had arrived minutes after the first officer found Red. Soon it seemed half the police force showed up, then reporters. Red had called his parents, who lived across town. They were both sitting with the kids now in the back of an ambulance, on the way to the hospital to get checked out. Thank God the kids left before the news agencies showed up.

The cold felt like sandpaper under Red's feet. "Sorry you had to get up so early."

Carter smiled, but said nothing. Frozen air pressed Red's skin, like he was back in the debrief room. The cruiser across from him was pocked with bullet holes, its metal skin riddled with automatic weapons fire. All windows were shattered. He wrinkled his forehead and pointed to it. "What happened?"

"That's the cruiser from my officer that found you," Carter replied. "Wasn't like that when he left the station."

Red stared, breath frosting in the morning air. Was he kidding? Hadn't been any shots. Had he forgotten something again? He looked to a black sky. "Anyone hear from Lori?"

Carter took a step closer and put a hand on Red's shoulder. "No. Remember anything?"

A sharp pain stabbed his gut. Was he losing his mind? He wasn't angry at Carter, but himself. He took a few steps toward a holly hedge at the edge of the yard. Hands on hips, he looked up, groaned, then doubled over and heaved pizza chunks and broccoli into the bushes. *Sounded like a good combination at the time.*

After his arms stopped shaking, he raised himself and breathed deeply, staring at the side of his neighbor's Pepto-Bismol-colored house. He struggled to gather his thoughts.

Carter broke the silence. "You okay?"

Red blinked. It was all he could manage at that second. "I've got a problem not remembering. You know that. If I had anything to do with this, lock me up. If not, I'm gonna kill 'em." It was done. He was certain how it would play out.

Carter squinted. "Red, I told you. This wasn't you. Someone else did it. That's why the cruiser's shot up. The officer came on someone carrying Lori from the house. Only thing that kept him alive was ducking behind the cruiser's steel rims. He saw them take her. Remember me telling you this? Know who they were?"

"No."

"You or Lori have any enemies you haven't told me about?"

"No."

"What about the families of those guys at Walmart?"

Red managed a step away from the hedge. "Maybe. Listen, I don't know how much good I'm going to be. I don't trust myself anymore."

"You're all we've got. We need you on this."

"What do you mean I'm all you've got? Your guy saw them. How'd he get here so quick?"

"Got a call from your security system. But your neighbors already phoned a few minutes earlier. Saw two people in their backyard, so we had a cruiser on the way."

Made sense, sort of. "The officer that got me in the bathroom, he did a good job. Pass that on to his boss."

"You just did," Carter said.

"One problem, though. We don't have a security system."

Carter frowned. "No?"

"You're the detective. Figure it out."

A man with bed-head kicked snow as he approached. Green plaid flannel pajama bottoms were too short, exposing bare ankles in Nike running shoes. A grease-smudged Carhartt jacket bulged at the pockets. A badge hung loosely from his neck. He stared at a pad of paper in his palm. "Boss, we found something."

"Sulley, you look like hell," Carter said.

Sulley lifted his head, one eye closed against the flashing red and blue from the cruiser's light bar. "You said get here on the double. I did."

He led the pair across well-trampled snow, through a side garden gate. Tracks were everywhere in the backyard. One detective was cursing as he tried to pour plaster into a footprint. Sulley stopped beneath the bedroom window and stepped into the flowerbed where Penny had planted Easter lilies in the spring. Sulley lifted a small metal canister with a gloved hand and held it out to Red.

"Found this on the ground right here, under the bedroom window."

Red went to grab it, but Sulley yanked it back.

"Don't touch."

"Okay. Looks like helium. We've got a can like it in the garage for birthday balloons."

Sulley lifted it over his head, studying a white sticker on its bottom. "Same idea, but not helium. Feels empty, but take a sniff near the valve."

Red stared into the distance and inhaled. It was a familiar scent. "Smells a little like ... citrus? Kind of like oranges. Not exactly, but something close."

Carter took a quick sniff. "Knockout gas. Of some variety. Have it tested, but for now let's assume that's it. Get any prints?"

Sulley waved to a portly woman in a black police uniform as she walked by, and held the canister out to her. "Wiped clean. Not a trace. If this tank says anything, the perps didn't leave any." He pulled a quart-sized plastic bag from his jacket. Inside was a large needle. "Looks like the perps slid this between the seams of the window. See those gouges there? That's what I don't like about these sashes that tip in. Not secure." He pointed to the heat pump next to him, hidden behind low hollies, clusters of red berries topped with snow like whipped cream on cherries. "They cut the power feed. That's why it's cold inside. I figure to keep the air system from coming on. Got enough gas in the room that way. Once the tank was empty, they smashed the front door."

Carter started out the gate. "Got anything else?"

Sulley led them up the front steps. The house was full of people, some uniformed. The air stood cold, the room lifeless, despite everyone milling about. A detective with blue neoprene gloves was pulling prints off the black granite counter where they'd met with Carter a few days before. Another was picking at something with tweezers from the blue oriental rug that Lori had picked from an open-air market in Morocco. Sulley led them upstairs, past the knob at the top of the rail he had to reattach at least twice a year after Lori'd given birth to two boys. Would he see her again? He'd better give his mother a call—they would be at the hospital by now.

"Red, anything else coming back?" Carter asked.

He stumbled across the top step. "You know those nightmares where you try to wake up, but can't? That's what the dream was like. Seemed everything was in fast-forward."

"Sounds like gas. Probably a chloroform derivative. Get a look at any faces?"

"No. I was lying in bed, awake, but couldn't move. One threw Lori over his shoulder. She flopped like ... she was dead." Red's eyes started to tear but he tensed his stomach so his voice held steady. "All this rage inside, but couldn't do anything. Not even scream. The other picked me up and started out the bedroom, then dropped me. I don't remember anything after that."

Carter nudged Sulley's shoulder. "Why would he drop Red? Why leave him if he wanted him?"

"Maybe that's when our first responder showed up. He said there were three perps. One on the street in the car. That guy opened fire right away. The other two shot at him from the house." He grimaced. "The extraction team."

Red felt lightheaded. He leaned on the wall and rubbed an eye with his palm. "You're making it sound like these guys were professional."

Carter squatted next to a hall table, inspecting something on its surface. "They gassed you, breached the door, and made off with a hostage. All in . . . maybe four minutes. Professional."

"Why?"

Carter straightened and motioned Sulley to the table. "Don't have a motive. Just going by what I see. These guys were good."

"Then why didn't they get both of us?"

"Remember the cruiser out front? Lots of holes."

Red took a step down the hallway toward the front of the house, then leaned onto the wall again.

"Bullet holes are all over the side facing the house," Sulley said. "The guy probably dropped Red and helped cover while they all got away. Our guy tried, but he's lucky to be alive."

Carter pointed Sulley to a splattering of blood on the table and dots of crimson on the carpet beneath. "Our officer couldn't pursue. Car was shot up. He called in the situation, then went inside. That's when he found you," he said, pointing to Red. He tapped the hall table. "Hit your skull on this when the intruder dropped you. Explains the gash in your head and the reason you don't remember shots. You were unconscious. Woke up after the firefight, but before our officer came in."

"What about the getaway car?" Red asked. "Anything on that?"

Carter rubbed eyebrows. "Might have a license plate if the memory stick from the cruiser's camera is okay. Even if we run the plates, won't turn up anything. They'll be stolen. It was a newer model Toyota Camry, silver. Thousands of those out there. Not an accident." He lifted his chin toward Red. "No, this isn't the family of those guys you killed. Think hard. Who would *want* to do this?"

Red squatted and stared. He'd never noticed how narrow the hallway was. He glanced at the scuffed paint next to the bloody handprint left as he'd steadied himself earlier. Nomadic desert, the name of the shade. Lori was so proud of it. Sounded like such an elegant color. Now it was empty. Dry. The whole home was bare, pressing, cold as stainless steel.

Something bubbled within his belly, like nervous butterflies. A resolve. "I need to get some air."

When he passed through the front door, he paused. Pressed his fingers against the rough, freshly splintered wood where the lock bolts had been rammed through the doorjamb. He trod out to the cruiser, riddled with bullet holes, and pressed his pinky into several. The metal was cold, hard. Flecks of paint stuck to his finger. He brushed them off into the snow.

He craned his neck backwards, the black sky a backdrop for frosted breath in bitter air. Tree skeletons stood gray against a faint glow, low in the east. Soon be time for the morning run. He chuckled at the absurdity of the thought. But that's what he wanted to do. To run, to clear his head, to remember, and understand.

He started toward the other cruiser. Carter and Sulley were huddled next to it. Halfway, he stopped. Turned toward the police barricade, then squinted into a flashlight shining on his face. A dark figure stepped out of the background of the night, silhouetted by police car headlights. How long had he been standing there?

The visitor took another step forward. He heard Jim's familiar voice. "Red. We need to talk."

Chapter 6
Reunion

Red squinted. What the hell? Why was Jim here? The Air Force officer stepped into their company, frozen breath streaming from his nostrils. The trouser seams of his blue service dress uniform broke perfectly above his ankles. He eyeballed Red. "You look like hell." Stuck a hand out in greeting.

Red lifted an arm, but Carter stepped between and grabbed Jim's hand instead. "What you doing here, sir?"

Jim's eyes stayed fixed on Red. "I need a word with my friend. In private."

"Not now. Something's happened. I need to—"

"This crime is beyond the capabilities of your office. It's in Red's best interests to come with me."

"You've got no jurisdiction here," Carter said. "I appreciate your concern, but—"

Jim's eyes narrowed. "Detective, it's for his own good."

Sulley stepped forward, looking like a mall cop in pajamas. Carter squared up. "I'm in charge of the scene. You've got no authority."

Red forced himself between the two and shoved each in the chest. "Stop the pissing contest and act like you give a damn!" He leaned into Jim, jabbing a finger at his nose. "Don't try to pass off this visit like the last one. Why're you here? Lori's gone. Come clean or I'll beat it out of you!"

Carter leaned against a cruiser, arms crossed. Sulley put a hand on his Taser. Jim said nothing.

Red took a step closer. Jim glanced at the reporters behind the yellow tape. "Can't talk here. Not in front of the detective, either."

"Why not?"

A snowflake landed on Jim's shoulder, then melted. The tiny bead of water ran off.

Red grabbed the collar of Jim's blue coat. "Well?"

Still nothing.

"It's classified," Carter muttered, staring at Jim.

"What is?" Red sneered.

Carter aimed a crossed elbow at his friend in blue. "Ask him. You were doing fine."

Red frowned. "How you figure?"

"Easy. These kidnappers were professionals. As in well-funded, ex-military types. A wet team. Your buddy here can't say what's going on because it's restricted."

Jim's gray eyes were in shadows. Red couldn't make out his expression. Jim could never lie well. "That true?"

He turned and started away, slipping to a knee on a patch of ice, but straightened up. "I'll fill you in at my office. Let's go."

"What the hell? Just like that?"

Jim looked back over his shoulder. "Not here, Red. Come on. We're wasting time."

Red stepped back. "Not without Carter."

Jim frowned. "Why?"

"Because I don't know who to trust. You want me? Then Carter's coming, too. You've got info on Lori? He needs to know."

Jim clenched his fists. "You don't want the detective in on this. Trust me."

"Trust you like what? Like I don't see you for five years and you show up when the video goes viral? Like you show up again this morning when Lori's been taken? Maybe you're behind this crap. Carter's coming."

Jim mumbled.

"What?"

"Whatever! The detective can come. Now let's go." He turned and started again.

Carter pushed off the cruiser, stance wide on a patch of slick ice. "I'm not going. I've got charge of the scene. Can't let you go, either."

Red turned back. "You're in charge of investigating Lori's kidnapping. Jim says he's got answers. You got no choice. Delegate."

"Red, I should stay here. Same goes for you."

Red's head throbbed. "Get in the damn car, Carter!"

Carter grabbed Sulley's arm and turned away.

Ice crackled under Red's feet as he followed Jim in the shallow snow. A cold dampness numbed his toes. He pushed it to the same part of his mind where he crammed other distractions to be ignored. He stood, knees close to the headlights, welcoming their heat on his skin. His friend's presence was warm, though his manner was cold as always. A figure of strength. Genuine. But now . . . How the hell had Jim known to show up this morning? Red shook damp snow from his slippers and leaned in to his old friend. "I'm gonna kill the guys who did it. Even if Lori's alive, they're dead."

Jim slapped Red's shoulder so hard his feet slid on the ice. "Only if you beat me to it."

Lori searched for a bridle from the tack room. Where was it? The new one with blue padding across the nose. No, she hadn't bought that one, or had she? Tony wandered down the center of the barn between stalls.

Why is he wearing those awful work boots?

Dark, hand-hewn timbers, well over a hundred years old, stood on either side of the aisle like sentinels, supporting a massive hay loft. Dizzy, she leaned on one, fingers running the gouge made by an adze near the time her great-grandfather was born. A century of horses scratching their necks made the heavy post smooth with a dark, shiny finish. The stall was neat and mucked out, as always. She inhaled air heavy with moist hay and sweaty saddle blankets.

Which horses to tack up? Tony shook his head as he leaned into every stall. Each seemed skittish, spooked at something. "Maybe bad weather's coming," he said.

When they reached the end of the aisle, he grasped the thick, black handle of the heavy wooden door. He set his feet, and metal wheels squeaked from the rail above as it slid open. A pale green light flooded the barn.

Lori gasped, awake, eyes opening to the same light. So heavy with sleep, she couldn't fight the sedation. They closed again. When she awoke once more, the same pale light washed back in.

Why did Tony leave the lights on? He never does that.

She tried to wake herself, to get some water for her dry mouth, but she could barely move.

So tired.

She lifted her head but hit something soft, a few inches up. Leaning into one shoulder to see if Tony had come back to bed, she realized something was in her mouth. It was . . . what was it? Terry cloth?

Where was Tony?

She tried to shout his name, but nothing came through the gag. She looked down her cheeks and puckered. Her lips were covered with silver-gray tape. She tried to sit again but hit the same invisible softness. Tried to move her arms but they were tied to her sides— legs bound as well. Turned her head and looked down past her shoulder. Shackles clamped her wrists with a chain running under her back. Frilly lace hovered a few inches above her face. She squinted in the pale green glow.

Shit. It was the inside of a coffin.

"Tony! Tony!" she screamed, trying to push her muted voice through the gag. Straining, she twisted her arms, but the shackles only slipped down her wrists. They stopped at the base of her thumbs and dug in. The hardest kicks produced little noise. She tore at padding beneath her, then scratched at the metal skin under it, abrading her fingers on welded seams. She tried to sit, beating her forehead against the lid of the coffin until blackness descended.

Some creature snorted and kicked in its stall. Devil's Delight, her Appaloosa mare. Why was she so spooked? Lori pulled a green apple, the favorite treat, from a warm, black wool waistcoat. Devil refused. Lori walked to the metal trash can they used as a feed bin and lifted the lid. Pale green light spilled out. She blinked hard and saw white lace.

Still in this wretched coffin. Stabs of fear churned in her stomach, overshadowed only by her throbbing head.

Don't panic. Not again.

She turned her head side to side, up and down. This prison smelled of a dirty fabric shop: new polyester and stale body odor. She saw now the light came from a glow stick hung next to her shoulder, like the ones she gave the kids when they went trick-or-treating.

The kids.

Where were they? Safe? Was Tony okay? Were they all in coffins, too, buried alive, with a rag choking them? She wept.

What's going on? Who the hell is doing this? She tried to sit again, slamming the thinly padded lid so hard she saw bursts of light before her eyes. Was she buried alive? If so, why the handcuffs?

Think. She remembered tucking in Jackson under his blue Batman blanket. His eyes had already closed, his breathing deep—like the purring of a tomcat. He could fall asleep faster than anyone. Some nights he'd crawl in and be snoring before she even made it upstairs.

Must be drugged. Focus, Lori.

She'd gone to bed. Tony followed sometime after that. Had woken her with those ice-cold feet. That's the last thing she remembered.

A horse snorted outside the coffin. A short, sharp sound.

Thank God I'm not buried! Dreaming again? No—it snorted a second time. A sign of anxiety. Hooves clattered on metal.

Must be on a steel floor. Maybe she wasn't underground, but in a horse trailer?

A dog barked, then a different one, higher pitched. The coffin bobbed up and down slightly, with the vibrating hum of tires on a road. She listened. No seams in this pavement, no jolting potholes. The ride was smooth, the hum steady, shrill, like moving at high speed. On an interstate, but which one? Couldn't be I-64, which was bad enough to put you in a coffin all by itself. Which interstate would be this smooth?

Her ears popped, but she hadn't felt the coffin tilt up or down as if going over hills. Then she understood.

I'm in an airplane! She lay back on the thin pillow.

Where was she? The kids? Would she ever see any of them again? How had she let this happen?

Hold it together, for the kids, for Tony.

The padding on the underside of the lid was smudged red. Like . . . blood? She strained her farsighted eyes. Yes, blood. But . . . on a piece of paper. A dark scrawl indicated writing. She lowered her head to one shoulder like she was holding a phone, giving herself a few extra inches of distance. Typed, in sans serif font were the words, *"Relax. It will be a long ride."*

Maybe Tony or the kids are close.

She kicked again, rhythmically, then waited for a reply. Nothing. She bent her knees so they smacked the lid, louder. Beat them steadily, trying to make the noise obvious over any others. Footsteps approached.

Saved. Someone's close.

They stopped over in the direction of the horse. Hooves clattered as it apparently tried to rear once . . . twice . . . then nothing. She held her breath, straining to hear. Only the faintest sound came, as a whisper, and a couple muffled slaps.

"Help! Help!" she screamed, banging her knees against the lid. The steps drew near. She held her breath again. Now someone would help. Would open the—

The visitor rapped the lid, a deafening tone inside the coffin. "Shut up! No one will hear you! You're scaring my horse. I'll put a bullet through your skull and dump you in the ocean if you frighten him again!" The voice was male, middle-aged, with maybe a hint of a German accent. The visitor's steps moved away, toward the horse again. A few more whispers, then the footsteps faded into the distance.

Lori dropped her head back, feeling the cold metal skin of the coffin through the thin pillow. He'd said they were over an ocean. Couldn't have been drugged that long. Probably the Atlantic. Wouldn't have made such a scene if they weren't alone. He'd want her to at least think she was by herself. So, if Tony wasn't close, where was he? Dead?

How wonderful their last six years had been. She'd actually had time with him, enough to conceive Nick and Jackson. Their life had been perfect, the way it was.

She pressed back sobs. Choking on mucus, she turned her head and blew yellow snot onto white lace.

All good things come to an end. Tony may be dead, but what about the kids? *If he's still alive, maybe he'll self-recall. He'll know who to contact. If not, my office will get him. Won't be long. Either way, I have to stay alive to see it happen.*

Chapter 7
Home

Red leaned against the vinyl headrest in Jim's car, tensing his shoulders. The engine whined a high note near his feet. They were well over the speed limit, headed east on I-64 toward Hampton Roads. The interior smelled of cigar smoke and pine air freshener. A wheel bottomed out on a pothole, as if it wanted to break loose.

"So, why am I here?" Carter asked from the backseat. His olive complexion and jet-black hair seemed to push his figure even farther away, blending with shadow, beyond Red's reach. Only his silhouette kept him from slipping away.

Red turned in his seat. Trees flashed by the side window in a blur of brown and white. "Because I insisted."

"That's not what I meant. I was asking him."

Jim looked into the rearview mirror.

"If the military's somehow wrapped up in this," Carter continued, "I've got no need-to-know. The colonel can't tell me anything."

"Maybe," Jim said. "Or maybe *I've* got the need."

Red scowled. "What the hell does that mean?"

"It means never underestimate the locals. We may need intel from his office for the op."

Red's mouth curled. "What the hell are you talking about? You're base supply. You sound like a spook. Where's Lori?"

"You honestly don't remember? The team? The Det?"

Red massaged a knuckle, bewildered. "What team?"

Jim grabbed his phone and pressed a key. "Grace? Jim." He paused. "Redeye. Remember Detective Carter? Matt Carter. Put him on the roster."

Red pointed to the side of the road. "Pull over and let me drive. Then you can talk to your girlfriend. You're too damn slow."

Jim waved him off and the engine spun higher. "We're inbound. Be there in eight. Call the good doctor and have him meet us." He hit end.

Jim glanced at Red. "You're bizarre, know that?"

"Yeah. And you're still slower than my mother. Let me drive."

Jim smiled and gunned a finger at Carter. "If you call Carter and me friends, you need help picking 'em. The kind detective told you who he is, right? You know he's spent time at the Bureau? Not long ago, either."

"We've all got secrets, Jim. Apparently, you've got 'em, too. Where's Lori?"

Jim straightened himself and eyed the rearview again. "I've agreed to temporarily sponsor your clearance, Detective Carter. However, all information about my organization—everything from now on—is classified top secret. I don't waste time with leaks. They get plugged. Do I make myself clear?"

"Perfectly," came from the backseat.

Jim settled back down, glanced sideways at Red, then back to the road. "Lori's been taken by the Iranians."

"By the who?" What the hell was Jim saying?

"They didn't want Lori, they wanted *you*," Jim said.

"You're nuts. Why would Iranians give a damn about me?"

"Even so, she's the daughter of a senator. A bargaining chip. Your father-in-law swings some weight. I got orders twenty minutes after she was taken."

"Jim, how do you know? And why would the Iranians want to kidnap either of us?"

"Damn it, Red! Try to keep up."

Red gripped the seat. "Fine. What orders?"

"Get her back, and the guys holding her. Assuming we don't kill 'em in the process."

"You're doing a military strike against Iran?"

"*We're* doing an op. Yes, the military is involved—maybe several branches. The op's not planned yet. Against Iran? We don't know where Lori is, but that won't take long. Once we have her pinned, we'll have wheels up in twenty-four hours. I've called the rest of the team."

"Wheels up? She's only been gone a couple hours. Can't be outside the U.S." Red pushed at a split cuticle on his thumb. They were in the left lane, flashing cars a quarter mile ahead to move over. Their speed still seemed too slow. "How does Base Supply fit in? You're helping get a team ready?"

"No. I'm executing the op."

"I'm not in a mood to joke, Jim."

Nothing.

Red leaned closer. "You're serious?"

Jim raised an eyebrow. "Yeah."

Red aimed his thumb at Carter. "I'd rather have the sheriff's office on this than you guys. What, op's tempo so high they got fatass supply sergeants doing HALOs?"

Jim's lips creased, like when Red had used to strip the basketball from him time and again. "It'll clear up once we're at my office."

They passed Langley's main gates and drove to the far side of the airfield, stopping in Base Supply's parking lot. The drab concrete building abutted Langley's security fence. Functional, no flair. Low in the front, rising four windowless stories in back. Several semis were parked with trailers sealed tightly to loading ramps. The gum tree on the edge of the lot seemed twice as big as he remembered. A dirty gray heap of snow stood beneath it, stubbornly refusing to melt.

They pulled into a spot with a blue sign that read SQUADRON COMMANDER. Red slapped the door handle and stood. His head throbbed.

Carter took his time, as if he were being escorted to a prison cell. "Where are we?"

Red pushed his palm to his forehead, then pointed at a faded brown sign near the roof. "Base Supply."

"Bullshit," Carter said.

Red winced, head down. "What?"

Carter took a half step backwards. "Supply wouldn't be all the way out here."

"I didn't design the place, just worked here. It's got some hazardous materials. That's why it's separate."

Carter crammed his hands in pockets. "We'll see."

Jim stopped at a gray metal door with a card reader. "Smile for the camera." He waved and drew an ID through. The door buzzed and Red yanked. It was slow to open, heavy. From the front it looked like a standard metal door, like so many at work. But the edge showed quarter-inch steel plate welded front and back. Security locks fastened all four corners. Inside lay a tight square room with an identical door opposite. A single round light on the ceiling, turned off or burned out.

Jim followed them in. "Face left."

That wall was smooth, almost shiny. The room had a new car scent so strong it stung Red's eyes. Jim shut the door and all went dark. Red twisted his neck, but saw no light, not even a leak around the seams. The air was stifling, choking, a companion to the darkness in his mind. Like when the family had toured a gold mine in Colorado and the guide had turned out the lights to show how dark it was that far below the surface. An electric servo buzzed somewhere near the door and locks clicked at the corners.

"This'll just be a minute," Jim mumbled.

The light came on and Red barged through the opposite door. He stopped, squinting in bright light. Through slit eyes he could make out a spacious foyer, polished Carrara marble crisscrossed with stainless-steel expansion joints. Dark wood paneled the walls. "You guys remodeled."

An office space lay beyond, full of green-gray cubicles. It was only six a.m., but at least twenty staff were in view, a dozen around a maple conference table. Ahead stood a single marine, in Kevlar jacket and helmet, thumb on the safety of an M4, one ear missing a lobe. *Déjà vu.*

A woman at a mahogany reception desk spun in her chair and stood, tall, nodding to Jim. Salt-and-pepper hair, physically fit, pin-striped skirt-suit.

Jim took her hand and escorted her into their company. "Red, my assistant Grace. Known around here as Moneypenny, in honor of my favorite franchise."

She extended her hand to Red. "A pleasure to finally make your acquaintance, Mr. Harmon."

Red shook. Firm grip for a prim lady. Her smile was pleasant, but guarded.

Jim continued. "Grace, Detective Carter. Thanks for getting him on the roster. Don't turn your back on him."

"Yes, I know," Grace purred. She proffered her hand to Carter. "Nice to meet you, *Detective*."

Jim laughed. "He's a married man. I'll bring you a single one next time." He eyed the guard. "Are we clear?"

"The detective has a Glock 9mm, left arm, extra clip. Also got a 32 auto in a wallet holster, and a five-inch boot knife on the right calf. Major Harmon is clean, just the collateral inside, like you said."

Red tilted his head. What did that mean? Why'd the guard call him by his old rank? Nothing inside was the same, yet somehow it was as it should be. "So we need to check weapons or what? Let's get going."

Jim started toward double doors. "Everybody in my office. Moneypenny, where's the good doctor?"

"Inside." Her tight smile revealed deep satisfaction. "He was on his way for an appointment across base. I cancelled it."

"You're a bitch, gal. Get the other one here, too—Dr. Ali. Red's scalp needs stitches."

As in the car, aftershave and cigar smoke seemed to bleed from the air inside Jim's office. Dual widescreens were pushed to one end of a deep mahogany desk.

A gaunt man with hollow cheeks and white goatee stood, holding a cane, though he didn't lean upon it. Dark complexion, he looked Indian. He gave an unenthusiastic smile to Jim, then took a hard look at Red. His voice held power, though his frame lacked it. "Mr. Harmon? You're the reason my appointment was cancelled?"

"He is," Jim said, walking away from the man, around the opposite side of his desk. He sat in a retro wooden swivel chair, its reclining spring *urrrrrching* a protest, listing under the strain of its cargo. Jim massaged his temples and forehead with fingertips. He punched a button on the phone. "Grace, be a doll and get me a cup of Mr. Frank's brew. Two more for our guests. Thanks, love."

He released the intercom and pressed fingertips together. "Mr. Frank's been in clandestine circles since diapers. His coffee makes espresso taste like apple juice—only reason I keep his worthless ass around. You're gonna need some for what I'm about to unload." He pointed to a brown leather armchair. "Sit."

Grace strode in without knocking, taking long steps, carrying a tray with three cups. "Already on it." She gave Carter's to him with a wink, then left silently, as if without touching the floor.

Red winced. "This guy gonna fix my head? It's starting to throb."

"In a way. Another doctor's going to stitch it up. Genova here's a head doctor. A psychiatrist."

"Why's a shrink here?"

Jim smiled and swallowed hard. He leaned forward, breath like the burnt bottom of a coffeepot. "Red, you're my friend. But today, a fellow soldier. Here's the truth. You were never in Base Supply. You're sitting in Detachment Three of Special Operations Command. We call ourselves the Det for short. Six years ago you were an operator, assigned here. A damn good one."

Red lifted a finger and made a swirling motion. "You can call this place the Bat Cave for all I care. When I was here, it was Base Supply."

Jim slapped the desk, then stared at Genova. "Get his ass through recall."

Genova leaned forward, eyes narrowed. He opened his mouth as if to ask a question, but remained silent.

"What's that mean?" Red asked. "You can do whatever you want. All I care about is getting Lori back. You said you knew something. Come clean."

Jim yanked one of the flat screens to face Red. "At oh-four hundred we received this video from intel."

Jim punched a key. The screen lit up, then faded to reveal a blurred face.

"We can't undo the censorship. No matter what movies say, can't be done."

The blur revealed only an olive complexion and black hair. A female voice came from the speaker. She was the censored image and wore green fatigues with no rank, no insignia. Behind her stood a blank concrete wall, orange rust stain running down. The room was dim and echoed. A single overhead bulb hung by a pair of wires. No clues as to the time of day or location. She spoke a foreign language with no emotion. After a minute. she raised two fists toward the camera and shouted a word Red recognized: *Moses.* The video faded and cut off.

"It was e-mailed to your father-in-law, Senator Moses, an hour *before* Lori's kidnapping. We got our CIA liaison to get his best hackers on it, but so far nothing. Whoever sent it knew how to cover their tracks."

Carter was leaning over Red's shoulder. "Was it sent anywhere else?"

"Don't know. You're the detective. I wanna kill the bitch. Waiting for intel to tell me how. I didn't even know Senator Moses knew the Det existed. He still may not. My guess is that whoever sent the e-mail doesn't know who owns us, who's a player. But they knew if they sent it to the senator, we'd get it somehow."

"What'd she say about Lori?" Red asked.

"My interpreters said the lady in the video was speaking Farsi. She claimed to have 'The Red One and the daughter of Senator Moses.' Her demands were that the U.S. disclose all member countries of the Det. If not, they'd kill the prisoners. Gave seven days. Must've anticipated having Red and Lori in their hands when they made the video. Accused the U.S. of undermining Iran's nuclear program."

"What's that about?"

Jim laughed. "We've been in Iran, but not only us. Israel has a good system, especially adept at setting up and managing networks of human intelligence. Humint. The U.S. doesn't do that very well anymore. We rely on technology, satellites, communications monitoring. But those can't see into a person's head, what he's thinking, what he's planning. With our tech and Israeli humint, we've kept Iran below the red line. But depending on Israel is like sleeping with a rattlesnake.

"Humint says Iran is pursuing nuclear weapons. No surprise. The kidnap is an attempt to compromise the Det, get us off their backs. Once compromised, all the agencies, all the co-ops will pull out. It'll cease to exist. Because that's all we are, a hub of cooperation. A fusion cell on steroids."

Jim stood, the wooden chair squeaking as it rolled away. It thumped into a file cabinet. "We've got a hostage to find. Then I've got an op to plan."

Red's eyes followed him. This made no sense. What about the video? He couldn't even understand what the lady had said. This could all be Jim's pipe dream. "So, what are you saying?"

Jim raised an eyebrow. "Get you into recall, get the real Red back, get your wife back. Take a couple dune rats prisoner, kill the rest, leave behind no trace. Intel's scrutinizing it now. Should have

Lori's location by the time you wake up. We may need some info that's buried in that thick skull of yours."

Red wrapped fingers into a fist, but his grip felt empty. "Jim, I listened, but you've lost your mind. I worked in Base Supply. Don't know what recall is. Carter and I are leaving."

Carter pushed out a lip. "I think you need to listen to the man, for a little longer at least."

"What?"

"He's got the video," Carter said. "He knew something had gone down before the news announced it. I didn't think I'd be saying it, but he's got answers. Let's hear him out."

Red turned back and squinted, pain searing an eye. "I think he's crazy."

"I don't care if you believe me," Jim said. "But do you trust me?"

"Used to. But right now you're short-sheeted."

"Trust me for another hour. Then, if you still want out, I'll drive you both back."

Red scratched a rough beard. His head throbbed like a farrier was mounting a shoe to it. What a waste of time. He ran fingers through his knotted hair, recoiling at the matted blood.

Lori was everything to the kids, and in their innocence they'd look to him to get her back. He couldn't face them without seeing this through. He'd been shivering all morning, but now sweat beaded on his brow. "If I do this recall thing, will I have a chance to kill these guys?"

"Like I said, only if you're faster than me."

Red looked at Carter, then nodded.

Jim rubbed his hands like a boy scout trying to use a fire stick. "Good!" He jerked open the double doors and stepped halfway into the foyer. Glancing back with narrow eyes, he yelled, "Do I need Ms. Grace to write an invitation? Follow me, damn it!"

Chapter 8
Recall

Red glanced at Carter, then hopped up. Dr. Genova moved slowly, deliberately. They followed Jim through a cubicle maze, making their way toward the back of the building. What was everyone staring at?

Jim dropped his head and snorted. "Yes, folks. Red's back from the dead. Now get to work."

They walked past a glass-walled conference room, one side covered with large flat screens. Each displayed satellite images of different regions of the globe. The pictures were splashed with small multicolored shapes: a triangle, square, or stars. Some seemed to move. Maybe an air traffic system? But why for Moscow and Riyadh? Red turned to ask, but Jim was almost at the end of a hallway.

Red hustled after him. The gray hall was like the one at the sheriff's office, except this had a polished marble floor. The tap of Jim's shoes echoed a cadence that resonated inside Red. Jim ducked into a doorway near the end. Through a small window Red glimpsed the tail of a helo. He paused to study it, but Jim pulled him into another room, office-sized, furnished with only a couple of brown folding chairs. Photos were pinned on the walls from floor to ceiling, as if it was one huge bulletin board.

"Wall of fame," Red whispered.

"You remember this?" asked Genova, strolling through the door, hand in pocket. Carter rolled his eyes.

"Saw something like it in a dream," Red muttered. "Actually, several."

"Nightmares?"

"No. Not really."

Red stood before the montage, noting the tail numbers of a C-17 in one of the photos, but his mind was unable to grasp...what? Something about the picture, or the wall itself? He ran a finger across it. He could see the plane clearly, but the memory was blurry, beyond reach. Tapped another photo, he said, "I know this one."

Jim stepped next to him and leaned close to the wall, squinting. "You're in it. So am I."

The photo was dark. Jim's jawline was unmistakable, though his face was smeared with black out. He wore dark fatigues and a helmet like a skateboarder's. The flash on the camera glistened off sweat, or maybe he'd been for a swim. In one hand he gripped a bearded man by the hair. Blood smeared across the lid of the prisoner's eye, swollen shut and purple. In the other hand, Jim gripped a black knife. Red was the only other person in the picture, tipping up a canteen. The caption under it read, "Major Mayard reading Miranda rights." Red laughed out loud, surprised he found humor in the brutal image.

"You remember?" Jim asked.

"Just the photo. That's all. From my dream, I think." He pinched the thumbtack and yanked it out, holding the image beneath an overhead light. "It's frustrating. Like I want to remember, but can't. All I've got are memories of being bored out of my mind, filling purchase orders." He glanced at Genova and lifted his chin. "Doc, let's get going. We're wasting time."

Jim grasped his shoulder. "There's a lot of things I'd love to forget. After this, so will you."

Genova led them through a purple side door into an examination room. Over the jamb hung a rough-hewn wooden plaque: THOUGH I WALK THROUGH THE VALLEY OF THE SHADOW OF DEATH, I WILL FEAR NO EVIL, FOR I AM THE MEANEST SON OF A BITCH IN THE VALLEY. Genova pointed to a blue vinyl exam table like the ones in a family practitioner's office.

Red hesitated, but took a seat when Carter stood in the threshold. Jim pulled up a folding chair, scraping the legs across the floor, sending a chill up Red's spine. Dr. Genova offered a glass of water, but he waved it off.

"Drink it. You need to be hydrated before recall."

The doctor's hands shook slightly, creating small ripples on the surface of the water. Red took a deep breath and drank. It didn't taste like plain water. What was in it?

"You'll start to feel relaxed," Genova said. "Questions?"

"What the hell *is* recall? Do I just sit here?"

The doctor wrapped a latex tube around Red's arm above the elbow and assumed a professorial tone. "It's mental and medical. Before you entered the Det, we established a restore point in your subconscious through *in-processing*—using light sedatives and something like hypnosis. In the Det you were assigned a job in Base Supply to work once in a while, as a reservist. We book-marked those memories through verbal cues, assigned during in-processing. When we decommission someone, *out-processing* brings the bookmarked memories forward, and pushes the others back. Your brain fills in the rest."

"I don't remember any of that."

Genova's lip curled. "Huh. Must've worked. However, you were never out-processed."

Red propped himself on his elbows. Blinking hard at a sudden head rush. "What?"

"Remember your discharge?" Jim asked.

"Yeah. Some damn airman backed a forklift into a shelving sys-tem. It toppled on me."

"You remember the accident?"

Red closed one eye. "No. Just waking in the hospital with a feeding tube."

Jim smiled. "See, it never happened. Actually, we never figured out what did. An op went bad, you were caught. We got you out, but it took a couple days. You woke up like you'd been out-processed. Life's a bitch."

Genova held up a hand. "It will be clear if the recall works."

Red gaped at him. "*If* it works?"

Genova smiled. "Restoring your memory isn't like working on a car."

There were two of Carter now. "Buddy, stay here. Make sure these yahoos don't screw me up." The detective's mouth moved, but no sound came to Red's ears. The throbbing in his head sub-sided. Were the kids okay at his parents'? Of course, they were. What about Lori? Had Jim known this would happen? Had he allowed it? Red was putting his life in Jim's hands. What if he screwed that up, too? *I shouldn't have agreed to this.*

Red gripped the side rails and sat up. The IV bag seemed to bob around, as if he'd been drinking. Jim leaned over him with a scowl, jaw tensed and moving. But there was only the sound of a conch shell in Red's ear. He managed to grab Jim's collar. Then Carter stepped close. A flash of stainless-steel watchband as his arm came across Red's chest. *Damn, I never knew Carter could swing like that.* Red scowled as a nylon strap tightened across his chest.

"Trust us," Jim's voice broke through the fog. "You're a special case."

The faint metallic *twang* of feet descending metal steps pierced the coffin walls. It pulled Lori's mind from its haze and reminded her of what she was supposed to be doing. She held her breath, listening, sending her senses out beyond the casket. A muffled voice, then another, too faint to make out. The pitch of the plane's engines dropped lower and she was pulled to one side. They'd started a descent.

She listened, though her mind was still foggy. Maybe she would hear something that might tell where she was landing. Steps sounded near the horse again. This time two sets, one behind the other. The first had the same pace and weight of the man who'd threatened her earlier. The intruders stopped and spoke in low whispers. Then there were several slaps, pats on the animal's neck. The second set of footsteps was heavier, but came with the same number of strides as the first.

Probably male.

The two walked to the side of the coffin, opposite the hinge. Were they going to let her out?

The German accent again, speaking low. "Ready?"

"I don't like this," said a British voice, male. "This is your cargo. We just move it. Take care of your own bloody problems."

A snicker. "You picked up the king's shilling and expect to keep your hands clean? If she makes any noise when we unload, you're as guilty as I. Now get ready."

Fingers wedged beneath the coffin lid and it was flung open. Two men leaned over her, one above her head. That one was neatly shaved, with short black hair, fair complexion, expensive aviator

Ray-Bans—probably the copilot or navigator. She sat up but he grabbed her by the shoulders and pinned her down. Light grip. Apprehensive. He wasn't a killer. She could take him if she wasn't cuffed. She tried to scream and turned to the other. She froze at his smile. His well-tanned skin creased like seams in a saddle as the corners of his mouth turned up. His teeth were bright white, but crooked. He flung his head sideways to get a few strands of black, oily hair out of his eyes. *Probably gay.* He reached into the coffin and squeezed a pressure point near the collarbone.

"Quiet, bitch!" he said, raising a hypodermic with his free hand. He held it upright and gave a final squirt. "This won't hurt, unless I snap the needle in your arm. No noise when we refuel. Sweet dreams."

He stuck her shoulder and discharged its burning contents. He stared at her chest. *Maybe he wasn't gay.* Then down her arms and wrists. "You've got a long way to go. No chance of getting out and no one can hear you. They're all dead," he said smiling, pointing the needle to a silver coffin next to her, "so quit hurting yourself or I'll put you under the entire trip." He licked sweat from his lip. "They dock my pay if you're cut up, but don't think I won't do it." At least five more coffins were in her periphery. Some wood, others stainless steel.

She closed her eyes and strained against the gag. What did he mean, *they're all dead?* Who's in the other coffins? Where's my family? *I will hunt you down.* His bloodshot eyes, dimpled chin–she seared every detail into her waning mind. Only a few more seconds till she would be out.

The two released her in unison. The lid slammed in her face as she sat up. One last scream, but nothing made it through the gag. Her wrists ached, though she wasn't straining against the cuffs. He was right. No hope of getting out, not now. The best she could do was listen and remember, just like field training had taught her.

Heavy steps pounded away, pausing again near the horse. A total of eight *twang*s on metal stairs, then only the faint hum of engines and her breathing remained, slowing. The drug started to take her down. *Not such a bad thing right now,* she thought.

Red opened an eye. A bright white light blinded it. His other was slow to respond. He closed them both and lay motionless a few more minutes. He tried again and was able to focus. Dr. Genova sat in a corner. But this wasn't the same place. More machines surrounded the bed. *Maybe a hospital room.* The vital signs monitor read 58 beats per minute. The last blood pressure reading was 110 over 68. An IV bag hung overhead. The bed was inclined. He tried to sit but flopped back, fatigued.

Genova turned and his white goatee crinkled as he spoke. "Relax. The sedative takes a while to wear off." He picked up a phone on the wall. "Tell the colonel that Mr. Harmon is coming around."

Red blinked, then Jim was standing over him. "You're still ugly. Doc says we can't do a damn thing about it."

Red smiled. "Great to see you, too." Jim tugged at the blouse of his desert fatigues. "Changed your uniform?"

"It's been a while. The protocol took longer than Genova said. Had someone stitch up your head while you were under."

"How long?"

"It's noon on Tuesday."

A day and a half? Thirty-six more hours for Lori to be missing? To be raped, tortured, killed? Why had they taken so long? "Found her?"

Jim stroked his head, as if pushing hair out of his eyes. Little to move; his short gray stubble held fast. "Think so."

"Why so long? You said mild sedatives."

Genova snapped a pen on a low wooden counter. "Maybe an understatement. It holds you at the edge where both your conscious and subconscious are available. Your system will work it out over the next couple hours. You may start recall as the effects wear off."

Red's arms were heavy, like after a set of pull-ups. He sat motionless and thought back to his job at Base Supply. "Waste of time. I don't have any new memories."

"A necessary step," Genova said, lifting a skinny, crooked finger. "Plus, memories are only one of the things you need back."

Break that damn finger off and shove it up your . . . Red closed his eyes. Next time he opened them, Jim was sitting in the opposite corner. Red's scalp tingled. A presence—a heaviness, as if spiritual—moved over him, asking for possession, to be let in. "Jim!"

Jim shot up. Dr. Genova grasped Red's ankle. "It's normal. Recall only works if you let your defenses down. Don't fight it."

Red scowled. "Like hell if I'm gonna believe the same idiot who put me under for a day and a half."

Jim leaned over, shadowing Red from the dazzling brightness of the overheads. "It's true. Just go with it." One of his eyes was dark, white tape below it.

"Where's Carter? What happened to your eye?"

"You've come this far. Don't mess it up now."

"Let it come," Genova pleaded.

Red leaned back. Fear was an enemy. It always stood between him and everything good. He had to get past that wall. The presence had disappeared earlier when he'd resisted. He tried to let go of his defenses, to let his mind drift, but couldn't. It was as if he was hanging from a rope over a canyon and Jim was telling him to let go.

Red leaned his chin to his chest and drew a slow breath. The scent of Dune made him open his eyes. Lori's perfume. Probably still on his clothes. *No. Not for Jim. But for Lori, for the kids.* He had to go through with it, to face whatever was knocking at the door of his mind. He let go of the rope.

The presence returned and entered him. The room—the same one where he had stitches in his forearm after a knife fight. A raid on one of PCC's drug compounds in Brazil. The Cartier on Jim's wrist—a gift from a grateful Italian model turned spy.

Warmth grew at the base of Red's neck, spreading up from the rear of his skull to the top of his head. Then it flowed down past his ears and jaw. Down his spine, along his arms and legs, all the way to fingers and toes. It shot inward, as if filling his entire being. His body tensed and straightened in the bed. The warmth subsided.

Jim was pinning his shoulders to the bed. "You in there, buddy?"

The handle of Jim's KA-BAR stuck over the side of the bed. He'd always carried one on his hip. Too damn predictable. Red grasped a wrist and twisted hard, pinning the arm behind. He dropped a knee over Jim's bicep, locking it in place. Jim swung with his other, but Red dodged the blows. A couple fell on his ribs, but from the awkward position they were mere taps. The IV bag hit the far wall. Blood sprayed in quick bursts from the puncture in his arm. The vital signs monitor landed on the bed. Dr. Genova cowered in the corner, elbow over his head.

Jim grasped at Red's hair, but he pinned that arm as well and slipped the knife from its scabbard. Red was piggybacked across Jim's shoulders now, one hand gripping his forehead and a knife across his throat. Jim turned toward Genova, who glanced at the panic button on the phone, but Red tightened his grip on Jim's skull.

Jim smiled wide. "We got him back!"

Red dropped off his shoulders, then tossed the knife and caught the blade, handle toward Jim. "Like your mother, slow and sloppy."

Jim was busy working his arms loose. "Damn. Arms went numb. You almost dislocated a shoulder."

"And still a bleeding whiner." He flipped the blade again, grabbed the handle, and slid it into its sheath.

Genova stuttered as he pushed off the floor, black leather loafers slipping beneath him.

Red put his thumb over the puncture in his arm, stemming the oozing flow. "Just playing, doc. Never seen a couple guys wrestle?"

Genova pushed on a shaking knee and straightened, sweeping flat his white lab coat. "I had two brothers in Chennai. We wrestled. Not with knives." He stooped and brushed his calves. "'You won't see any combat. We'll pay off your med school bills,' they told me. Wish I never signed that paper. I could be making just as much in a legitimate practice." A brightness returned to his eyes as his goatee turned up again. "What do you feel?"

"Hungry." Red grabbed a white square and tore it open with his teeth, then pressed the cloth to his forearm. "Anxious to get going. The op planned?"

"No," Genova said. "What I mean is do you remember anything?"

"Yeah. Jim owes me a hundred fifty bucks in winnings."

Genova scowled. "We have a lot to go through before I clear you." He made a note on a pad, then snapped on a glove and wiped a drop of blood from the page.

"That'll wait." Jim reached to his belt and snapped a leather strap around the handle of his KA-BAR. "We don't have time. He's on the op."

Genova scoffed. "Colonel, you don't even know if—"

"The first two went fine. Red'll be just like 'em."

"I had two months before I cleared them."

Jim rolled his shoulders forward, wincing, then slapped Red's chest, hard enough to be a right cross. "A lot's happened since you went under. Intel has some solid info. Wheels up at 0830 tomorrow. Got to get you briefed."

On the op? Could he do that? "I kinda agree with the shrink," Red said. "Sure, I feel good, but you can't yank me out of retirement and expect me to be operational."

Jim stomped to the door. "You're coming. Always been a quick study." He turned back with a smile wide enough to reveal a gold molar. "What you did at Walmart, that was gorgeous. You're ready."

"Not till I see the kids. I've played by your rules, but I've been gone two nights. They're scared. I'm seeing them before wheels up."

Jim dropped his head, as if looking at his boot strings. "I'll allow it. Be back by 2200," then he stepped out the door.

Chapter 9
Home Base

Red pushed through a heavy, blue-painted door with Armory bolted overhead, the letters protruding from a thick steel plate in shiny welded beads. He stepped through a bathroom-size entry with a checkout log splayed open on a metal machinist's table, into a tight room with tall blue and green equipment lining a wall. He stood behind a wrinkled, white-haired man twisting a clamp below a drill press. He tapped the mechanic on the shoulder. "Gunny, I need to check out a sidearm."

The operator's head jerked up. He turned with a start, grasping the bold assembly of an M4. He shook metal shavings from his hands, like chopped tinsel at Christmas. He pushed up jeweler's goggles and blinked. Then again.

"Red?"

"You look like you saw a ghost."

"They told me you were dead." He stared into Red's eyes, then shook his head as if coming from a daydream. "I'm sorry, what did you want?"

"Just a sidearm."

"Jim said there were two new guys coming in. To get them fit with Det issue. He didn't tell me one was you. I'd have gotten your weapons set up the way you like 'em."

"Just a sidearm for now."

"I can do better than that."

Here we go. Gunny hasn't changed.

"I've got something special." Placing the bolt beneath a silver fluted bit, he shuffled toward the armory door, a four-foot-wide steel slab, hinged open. His feet slid across the floor with a hissing sound, like a mini-locomotive struggling down tracks. One hand steadied his wobbling body as he stepped over an extension cord. He fidgeted with a combination lock to a metal cabinet in the far corner.

"Come on, Gunny. I'm not going to be gone long. There're three over there on the table." He pointed to a low shelf with three SIGs, slides removed. If Gunny wasn't there, he'd grab one and leave. But the man had been a father he'd never had in Tom. His old, strong hands struggled with the dial.

"Gunny, you're inside a vault. Why another locker?"

The white-crowned man gave no reply. The lock gave way and he withdrew a spotless SIG Saur housed in a worn, bottom-access, concealed carry holster. "Here you go."

The weapon was light, but the barrel fatter. "You guys switched to 45 cal?"

"No. 9mm like always. The barrel's made of laminated ceramic and steel. That's why it's so thick."

"Ceramic?"

"Awesome stuff. Need it for the new propellants. Corrosive and got higher temps. Plus, it doesn't wear."

Red pulled his sweater over his head and strapped on the weapon. The fit was perfect. "You kept my holster?"

"They turned it in and said your sidearm was taken. I couldn't get rid of it, and it didn't seem right to be empty. I made the pistol years ago. Just like your old one, but with a few new tricks." His feet scooched closer. "I never believed what they said. That you were killed."

Red stared at the weapon, barrel resting atop two fingers. His eyes started to tear, so he laughed. "You're still a senile bastard."

"You're welcome," the old man huffed.

Red strapped it in, then turned and started out of the vault. "I'll bring her back."

Gunny pointed a fat finger at him. "You better not. She's yours. Got a dual stage recoil spring so you can—"

Red held up a hand. "I've got to run."

He didn't know how he'd connected with Gunny, but there it was. Maybe because everyone else just saw a weapon. He tried to see it through the old smith's eyes. A life's passion, a creative outlet, an art. To Red, it held purpose, a reason for being, an instigator of momentum. Maybe that's where they connected, in the art.

"One more thing," Gunny called back. "I've kept a box for you."

"What?"

He leaned in. "I don't know. That one in your locker. I left it there."

Red tried, but couldn't remember, so he walked to the cabinet from which Gunny had just pulled his sidearm. A small white cardboard container about the size of a paperback book sat on the top shelf. It seemed vaguely familiar, but contained only a single page, folded in half, with Lori's handwriting. *Pick up the leaf on your way home. Mount one over the headboard. Burn the rest.*

It made no sense. He stuck the paper in his pocket and walked out the door.

Gunny followed him again. "Don't forget to name her."

"I won't." He smiled at Gunny's superstition. The machinist believed operators kept better care of weapons if they named them. That much made sense. But he also claimed a named weapon took better care of the operator.

Walking to Jim's office, he felt the pistol's bulk under his arm. It seemed to balance his stride, as if he'd been nursing a limp without knowing it. Jim pulled a lockbox containing several stacks of IDs and passports from his desk drawer. "While you're stateside, use this. U.S. Marshal. It's one of your old ones, but you haven't aged much. We'll get new photos for you later. May need it to get around with a weapon."

He pointed at Red's shoulder. "Almost scared to ask, but what'd you name her?"

Red checked the lock strap under his armpit. "Same as always. Lori."

"Why always after your wife?"

Red's hand slipped back into his pocket around the paper. "She'll kick your ass when you're not looking."

Red swiped his phone's screen: 14:28. He'd told his parents to let the kids know he'd arrive around three, so he had a few extra minutes. He set the parking brake in front of St. Andrew's Catholic Church and jogged up the stairs, through black double doors, beneath an aged-white steeple. Father Ingram was in his office, bent over a legal pad filled with blue ink scrawls. Guess the padre still couldn't type. He lifted his head, stood, and stretched out his arms. "The prodigal returns! To what do I owe the pleasure?"

Red admired the priest's humanity, but never understood his reserved nature. After a two-handed shake across the desk, Father Ingram came around and sat next to him.

"Anyone told you what happened to Lori?" Red asked.

"No. Saw it on the news. You doing okay? Kids?"

"I'm going to be gone for a few days, father. I really need God on my side right now."

Father Ingram tapped a pen on his knee, mouth open. "You know God doesn't work like that. The most important question to ask isn't of Him, but of yourself. Are you on God's side?"

The priest always had a way of pointing out the one thing Red had overlooked. "I guess so."

He clapped his hands together. "Well, then there's nothing else to be said. You already have His blessing. I will pray for your faith and Lori's safe return." He bowed his head and prayed quickly, never one to mince words.

At the *Amen*, Red shot up. "Sorry for the brief visit." He pushed back his cuff. Still had fifteen minutes. "Mind if I have confession?" he asked, walking out of the office toward the booth.

Funny, really. Why did he feel comfortable with confession in the booth, but not Father Ingram's office? Something about the concealment, the anonymity, a division between sinner and saint, made it easier.

Growing up, Red had never considered himself religious. But Lori attended mass and took the kids. She invited him, but didn't hold it against him for not coming. Three years ago he'd gone with them once, then again, and eventually joined the church. Now he looked forward to unloading at confession every once in a while.

He closed the dark-paneled door and sat on a thin-legged wooden stool. Father Ingram's shirt rustled from the other side of the screen. The moving shadow meant he was crossing himself. Red did the same.

"Bless me, Father, for I've sinned. It's been three weeks since my last confession."

"There is forgiveness and grace from God for those who ask."

"I've killed two hundred and thirty-six men."

Silence. Red looked down and brushed his foot in a circle on the sandy floor. Looked like the last person in the booth had stopped by on the way back from the beach. "Father?"

"I . . . What did you say?"

"I've killed two hundred and thirty-six men."

"Since your last confession?"

"No. That's not what I meant."

A sigh of relief came through the screen. "Good. I was thinking that was a bit much."

"It's only been two since then."

Silence again. The booth *rreeek-reeekkk*ed as Father Ingram shifted in his seat. His knee slapped the divider wall. "I . . . You pulling my leg?"

"No, Father."

"I don't understand."

"It was several years ago. Probably eight by now."

"Why haven't you confessed this before?"

"I didn't remember."

"You forgot?"

"Yeah."

"You forgot to confess the killing of over two hundred men?"

"No. I forgot I'd killed them."

"How?"

"It didn't happen all at once. I did it over a couple years."

"Well shit, Red . . ." Father Ingram's shadow waved across the screen as he crossed himself again. "I mean . . . that doesn't make it any better."

"I told you before that I was in the Air Force, right? I'd cross-commissioned into the Marines before. Volunteered for a special assignment. Ended up getting involved with . . . exceptional people. I think it was two hundred and thirty or so. But I didn't do it all my-self."

"That's a bit much for one man."

"I did my share. Their blood's on my hands."

"But you were ordered. It was part of your job. Right?"

"Yeah." With his foot, Red drew the sand on the floor into a line.

"And it was to save lives of others, I hope?"

"Yes, Father. But since then I've joined the church. You've said you're not supposed to kill. 'Blessed are the peacemakers' and all that shhh . . . stuff."

The shadow leaned forward. "Listen. God didn't make Christians to be limp-wristed."

Red kicked, cutting across the sand line. "Father?"

"There will always be wars, till He puts an end to them. In the meantime, He doesn't expect you to roll over and play dead. He's given you a family and expects you to protect them. If He puts you in the military, He expects you to obey your authorities best you can."

Red tried to straighten the sand line back out, but it was jagged, like a serrated edge. "I'm back in. On a team to get her. You saying it's okay if I kill to do it?"

"Red, I can't tell you what's in your heart. That's above my pay grade. But if you've got to kill to get Lori back, be good at it."

Red pushed his cuff back again, then slapped his knees and stood. "Thanks."

"Not so long between visits."

Red was out the door. Halfway down the nave Father Ingram called, "Tell Jim I said 'Hello.'"

Red stopped. *How does he know Jim?* He continued down cement stairs striped with grip tape. Maybe his memory wasn't all back yet.

Penny was the last one to tuck in. She had her own room at Red's parents' house. The two boys shared another, like at home. Red couldn't help but smile at the pink walls in a pearlescent sheen, painted two-tone in a large diamond pattern. His mom had it done when Penny was only five, a special paint applied by air gun in multiple layers, the whole effect costing far too much for Tom's taste. "They grow too fast," he'd complained. "In a couple years she'll be too grown up for it."

Penny gazed up at Red now, eyes wide. "You're going to pick up Mommy tomorrow?"

"Going to try, sweetheart." He stroked her fine blond hair.

"Did the police take her?"

"No, peanut. They're trying to find her. Someone else did."

"Did they take her because you killed those bad men?"

He remembered wiping blood from Penny's face after the fight at Walmart. The enormous relief that none of it had been hers. He pushed back her hair with a knuckle and tucked it behind her ear, against the pillow. "No, nothing to do with that. Some different bad guys took her."

She frowned, as if the thought of how many bad guys there might be in the world worried her. "When will you be back?"

"I don't know. Maybe a few days."

"Will Mommy be with you?"

The nightlight cast small rainbows on the wall through a cut-glass push-pin at the corner of one pink diamond. Lori had stuck it there. A fuchsia band fell across a ballerina music box on the dresser. Last month the entire family had gone to Penny's ballet recital. Lori had glowed for days, pretending to dance around the house to the music in her head, proud of her daughter. "Wouldn't come back without her."

"Will she be okay?"

Wow. How do you answer that one? "I'm going to make sure, sweetheart." He hoped he could keep that promise. "Remember when you lost your watch—the one Grandma gave you that belonged to her mamma?"

Penny's mouth fell open. "That was scary!"

"And how we looked and looked until we finally found it—between your headboard and mattress? Well, Momma's worth more than a million of those. We won't stop looking till we've found her."

"Won't the bad guys try to stop you?"

"Maybe. But we've got more bad guys on our side than they do."

"You mean you're working with Uncle Jim again?"

Red raised an eyebrow. *Just like her mother.* Penny must have something in her youthful woman's intuition that said Jim was only safe on the outside. A good operator was also a good killer. Like a trained attack dog, the feral nature could explode when needed. Some people could sense it lurking under the surface, and like Penny, they subconsciously distanced their trust. But Red knew better of Jim. "Yep. That okay with you?"

She smiled. "Oh, yes. I love Uncle Jim. But he's scary, too." She giggled and pulled the covers up under her chin.

Red stood, then gave the quilt one last tuck. "You're the oldest, sweetheart." He wrinkled his nose. "Jackson and Nick don't understand. Can I trust you? Don't say anything that'll make them scared."

She held up a hand like she was giving the oath of office. "Yep."

He kissed her forehead, then without looking down stepped over Heinz lying next to the bed. He was Tom's dog, a big brute. With his two different-colored eyes, long legs in the front, short in the back, and missing half an ear, the beast looked like he'd been put together by Congress. Tom had named him after Heinz 57 Sauce since it had fifty-seven ingredients. Red called him at the door, but the dog glanced at Penny and put his head back down on the carpet.

Penny patted him. "Grandma lets me keep him in my room."

Red walked downstairs. Mother and Tom were waiting at the bottom. He hugged his mother and gave Tom a handshake. She padded upstairs and went into the boys' room. Red scurried through the living room past the fireplace mantel that held his picture, taken at his pinning-on ceremony; Tom's Purple Heart; and a photo of his grandfather with crew in front of their B-17, the wingtip of an ME-109 still sticking out the fuselage.

Tom followed him outside, leaning on a cane and wincing. The rod made a *thunking* rhythm on the oak floor. Outside, Tom looked back, then shut the door behind them. His smile was slight.

"Don't worry about the kids. We raised you and your brothers well enough. Having your gang here brings some life back to this old place."

Red had routinely bellyached to the kids how it wasn't fair that Tom was more patient now than when he was little. Like two different men, but the kids never believed him.

Tom straightened and pushed out his chest like a parakeet smoothing his feathers after a nervous spell.

"We haven't seen you for a while, son."

"I know. We don't come by enough. But thanks for taking—"

"No. I mean, you're different now. *This* man"—he tapped Red's chest—"I haven't seen him for a while. Truth be told, I like him a lot better."

"What do you mean?" Red knew, he thought. But wanted to know what his father saw.

Tom cocked his head to one side. "Listen, I'm not nearly as senile as you or your mother think. Whatever you've gotten yourself mixed up in, it's none of my damn business. We'll keep the kids as long as you need, under one condition."

Red frowned. Here it comes. Old Tom. "Which is?"

A gust shook a few of the last long, thin leaves from the enormous pin oak in the front yard. They spun and darted like arrows in the breeze. Tom gripped his cane as if wielding a club. It was the look that told a much younger Red and his brothers to turn and run like hell. Tom plugged his fingers into Red's chest. "You gut every single one of those damn bastards. Understand me! I want their mothers to remember how hard it was to recognize their swollen blue bodies."

"I don't know what you're talking about."

"Like hell you don't. Listen, I'm proud of you. Always have been. But they made this one personal. If you don't come back with your bride, you'd better be in a body bag."

Damn. Love you, too, Dad.

The stitches in Red's head ached when he bumped them, stooping into the car. Tom shouted, "And tell your friends to call off the goons. We don't need anyone keeping track of us."

"I'll mention it," Red yelled out the window. Jim hadn't said anything about having his parents tailed, but it wasn't a bad idea. The kids would be safer.

He pressed the accelerator and pulled onto a dim street. His mom had always said Tom was never the same after Vietnam. *Darker* in some ways, she'd said, but *sweeter* in others. The only Tom that Red had known was the one with the twitch in his eye from nerve damage he got from "some bug over there." The one who told him stories he didn't know whether to believe—about Charlie, the blue squads, and cold beer with ground glass. The one that worked him and his brothers all week in the sweaty heat on a two-acre God-forsaken garden, being eaten by mosquitoes and green-head flies.

However, Tom was also the one who had smiled when Red had come home from middle school with a black eye and bloody nose, hugged him tight, then took him to the garage and taught him how to throw a punch on a sand-filled canvas bag. No one tried to bully his younger brother after that.

Red ran crosschecks as he steered toward the Det, eyes never landing on anything more than a second. His mind seemed to grow sharper with time, as if coming down off a drug. Faces were imprinted with high detail. Even license plate numbers. The man with long legs, limping slightly as he crossed at the red light. His tilt indicated the graphite briefcase contained something heavier than papers. Red squeezed his eyelids shut till the car behind him honked. The light was green.

He couldn't turn it off, so he tried to think of Lori. Was she still alive? He'd gone after female assets before and every one had been tortured, raped, or mutilated. Tom was right. The kidnappers had made this one personal. He'd kill every one of them, slowly if he could. Guess that's why they have confession.

Chapter 10
The Team

Lori woke to darkness. To her left only a faint glow from the light stick remained. How long had she been out? She lifted her head and looked around her coffin. Nothing had changed. How long had the kids' light sticks worked last Halloween? She remembered the devices still glowing faintly when she'd tucked them in bed the next night. They'd thrown the sticks into the corner of their room, the novelty eclipsed by an overdose-ecstasy of sugar and chocolate. Lori hated Halloween. The kids were hyped up for weeks. She'd cull their plunder while they were at school, throwing away at least half.

How would they grow up without a mother? Would Red remarry? Would Nick remember her later in life? She clenched her jaw, pulling her thoughts back in. Drugs must still be dulling her mind. She held her breath. The hum of engines was the only sound. Lower now and from a different direction, or maybe they'd moved her coffin around while she was out.

She listened again. No, these couldn't be the same ones. Definitely a different pitch, a different aircraft.

Judging from last Halloween, the light stick looked to be at least twelve hours old, maybe more. When her captor had held up the syringe, it held twenty CCs of something, but what? He'd want her under for two, maybe four hours while they switched planes. She didn't remember being kidnapped, so they must have given her something when they'd taken her. All that time under, plus whatever she'd spent in the coffin, awake, added up to at least fourteen hours. That made sense, considering the dying light stick.

Her captor had threatened to throw her into the ocean if she didn't stay quiet. That was a slip. Assuming it was the Atlantic, then New

York to London would be around seven and a half hours. No. New York was too far away to have been the takeoff. Maybe Dulles, Reagan, or Philadelphia.

She threw her head back. Damn it. Who knows where they landed? London, Paris, Madrid, even Johannesburg.

She was on the second leg of a flight with no idea where it was headed. No way to know what she'd been given, if they'd used a contaminated needle, or if Tony would be able to get her out before they sawed off her head with a kitchen knife.

She couldn't let herself go that way. She strained her ears, trying to hear the horse's hooves on the metal floor, or maybe another bark from the dog. Nothing. When the plane hit some turbulence, she heard metal banging. Maybe cargo crates? There were no smells except her deodorant and the sweat-soaked polyester padding all around her.

She gave the lid a few quick kicks to see if anyone would answer. She didn't care if her captors put her back under. There was nothing else she could do right now. That was the worst part. Worse than smelling her own stink. Worse than needing to pee like she had when she'd been pregnant. Worse than having a spit-soaked gag in her mouth for fourteen hours. Being helpless was despicable. She should have seen this coming. She'd failed the kids. She'd failed Tony.

Red glanced at his watch as he pulled into the Det's parking lot: 21:56. He turned off the car and ran to the entry, swiped his card, and entered the millimeter wave scanner. After a thirty-second exam, the green light glowed and he blew through the warm foyer where Sergeant Ramirez was on duty again. *"Semper Fi."*

He clipped through the offices and down the hallway, past the debrief room where he'd started recall two days earlier. His head was down, thoughts back with the kids. He pushed open the door at the end and stopped, as if called to attention. The hangar ceiling towered over him, high enough it could fit the tail of a C-17. Ahead were two mid-sized Gulfstream VIP transports, a Bell V-22 Osprey, and two MH-60 Pave Hawks. He smiled when he saw an old Sikorsky MH-53J Pave Low. A few years ago he'd read an article saying the Air Force had retired its fleet and replaced the Sikorskys with the controversial Ospreys. Apparently, no one had given Jim the memo he wasn't allowed to have the older model.

Tinted windows capped the high walls. A crescent moon angled through a pane of glass from the south, faintly glaring off the white wing of one of the Gulfstreams. The polished concrete floor below reflected the distorted silhouettes of three Humvees. Even so, the hangar wasn't full.

His breath froze in the cold air that hinted of propane. Someone must be running a tug. A group of seven men in gray-black fatigues was gathered fifty feet away in front of one of the Pave Hawks. Jim's stance was still obvious in the dim light. Red started toward him.

As he approached, Jim jiggled his wrist. "Five seconds short of 22:00. That's a hundred and twenty-five push-ups, captain." Several of the men jeered as another dropped and started pumping them out.

The team was in a circle with gear in the middle. Next to Jim was his set. Lots of Kevlar along with helmet, knee, and elbow pads. The body armor was different—not the Interceptor style. The vest held twelve clips and a KA-BAR, nothing more. Red was studying the weapons when the captain popped back up, breathless. Red glanced around the ring. Good to see a few familiar faces.

Jim put a heavy hand on Red's shoulder. His huge thumb looked more like a big toe. His gaze was distant, toward the closed hangar door. "We've recalled Major Tony 'Red' Harmon."

A flat "HOOAH!" rose from the group.

"See anyone familiar?"

Red eyed the circle of men. "A few. Sergeant Crawler, Marksman, Dr. Ali, and . . . Carter."

Jim raised an eyebrow and pointed to the man standing next to Red. He was young, arms crossed, standing a step back from the rest of the group. A trim black toothbrush mustache framed his upper lip. "This is Staff Sergeant Rich Lanyard. He's—"

"New."

Jim cocked his head. "How you know?"

"Don't. But he doesn't look haggard yet. My shadow for the op?"

"You and Lanyard are a set. Bring him back alive."

Red extended a hand and the two shook. The kid had a firm grip. "Hasn't been a problem before."

Jim frowned.

Shit. He *had* forgotten about that one. Maybe he'd wanted to. Red probed his mind, trying to remember the old team member's name, but couldn't. A rookie to the Det but not to spec ops. It had been in Afghanistan, in the boonies but on the way home. An RPG took out their transport and his partner had gotten a shard of floorboard in his belly under his ballistic vest. The kid hadn't even noticed till a few minutes later when blood filled his boot. He'd made it six hours to Bagram Air Base hospital, but died while they were working on him. Red's eyes focused on the distance, mind weary, to the Pave Hawk near the far wall. "Well, hasn't been a problem lately."

Sergeant Lanyard's eyebrows drew close together, but he said nothing.

Red turned to Sergeant Crawler, the stocky, unshaven man next to Lanyard. His uniform was clean, but that's all that could be said for it. The trousers were worn, with patched knees. Boots looked like they'd been dragged behind a car with "Just Married" written across the back. Red remembered him as a good driver and mechanic, but headstrong and heavy on the trigger.

"Crawler, you still have a driver's license?"

He licked the unlit cigar to one side of his mouth and smirked, holding up three fingers. His Bronx accent was as thick as ever. "I saved yer ass t'ree times. Still no respect." No response from anyone. Not even a chuckle.

He aimed his finger at the next one. "Marksman, still going by that? We got a name for you yet?"

"Marksman will be fine," he said with a flare of his nostrils, like a bull about to charge. He was at least fifty when Red last saw him, but his deep black skin looked younger now. He stood several inches taller than Crawler, and even with his age possessed a more tight, athletic build. Red pointed to his head. "Lost the rest of your hair. Still carrying that M14 from our soiree in Brazil?"

Marksman pointed his toe to the weapon placed on a mat in front of him. "Same one." He didn't like being called a sniper. "I've never earned that title," he'd always say. His kill rate said different. The Det had stuck him with his nickname because he'd never give his real one. Only Jim knew who he was. His connection was probably through the CIA, but it didn't really matter. Why was he on this op? Jim had snipers, but only called Marksman when he needed language skills, too. Maybe Marksman knew Farsi.

"Your eyesight going to hold out long enough to tell which one's Lori, old man?"

"It's holding," Marksman said with a patronizing tone.

Red bit his lip, then pointed to the next, the one who had done the push-ups.

"Captain Matt Richards," Jim said before he could ask. "He's been with us two years. Air Force para rescue. Not as mean as me, but he'll be a fine replacement if I ever kick off."

Marksman and Crawler exchanged glances.

Red continued around, running his fingers through his hair. "Dr. Ali, thanks for stitching up my head." He leaned into Lanyard. "Lesson one. Doc holds a grudge."

Crawler yanked the cigar out of his mouth and pointed it at Ali. "Yeah. My ass still hurts, doc! You kept tellin' me, 'Suck it up. I gave you enough morphine to put a cow to sleep.'" He pointed it at Lanyard next. "It wasn't till we got stateside and they pulled a four-inch piece of rusty iron outta my ass that they figured the damn rag-head gave me the wrong thing!"

Ali grunted. "Pakistani, you thickheaded wop! Pakistani." His grin suggested the shot may not have been an accident.

Red kept going before the banter turned into something more heated. "Carter, I wasn't expecting to see you here."

"Me neither." His eyes flashed to Jim. "The colonel can be persuasive."

Sergeant Crawler bit down on the cigar. "You calls it persuasion. I calls it extortion."

"You would, damn guido." Ali sneered. Marksman laughed when Crawler slapped a bicep in a *bras d'honneur*.

Jim picked up a notebook lying atop his gear, as if ready to go through the checklists. "Carter's intel through his office has been invaluable planning the op. Got more connections than Hoffa." Jim mentioned a few other things about the detective, but glanced at Red when he mentioned *interrogator*.

"Prebrief?" Red asked.

"Soon," Jim said. He pointed to the contents of Red's old locker, vacuum sealed, next to his equipment. The others harassed Red while he stripped and pulled on soft, worn, dark woodland camo fatigues.

Everything still fit, even the insults. He bent and ran his finger across a patched hole in the knee. How could he have forgotten for so long? It had happened during a training exercise. Clearing a doorway, he'd dropped to a knee and fired a double tap at a target of a man gripping a pistol. The knee pad had slipped down and a ragged nail tore a neat hole. Was there anything else he couldn't remember? What else was waiting to surprise him? It all seemed so surreal two days ago, but now fit like his boots. Like the patch. Comfortable. Familiar.

Jim pressed the team through the lists. Each member checked his own gear and then his partner's. They ran through armor, communication, night vision, and enhanced auditory. That was something new. A techno geek had found a way to combine a comm set with something like a hearing aid on steroids. The gadget fit behind his neck and clipped to both ears like a Bluetooth. Red clipped his on and steps approached from behind. He turned to see who it was, but no one was there. Twenty yards distant a crewmember walked toward one of the Sikorskys.

"Takes a while to get used to," Lanyard said. "I swear you can hear a fly fart. Direction can be a bitch, but I'd rather hear 'em than not."

They pressed through the rest. Weapons, ammo, KA-BAR, and all other essentials were in the same place on each member so that everyone knew where the requisites were. Marksman was the only one with a different main weapon. Everyone else carried a Det M4. The "Det" designation meant that Gunny had tweaked them to his liking. Eight of the twelve clips were Det spec ammo. They had rounds loaded in-house, using modified propellants. That must have been what Gunny had tried to explain earlier.

"More constant barrel pressure as the bullet accelerates. Increased muzzle energy," Jim said. The rounds also necessitated the custom barrels or they'd shoot out too quickly.

The other four clips looked like weak subsonic ammo. The subsonic stuff was nice when you didn't want to be heard, but you'd better be close to your target because the slugs were slow. Eight hundred and fifty feet per second, less than one-fourth the velocity of a Det round. They had heavier seventy-seven grain slugs, but at that slow speed the weight didn't help much. If they were supposed to be tactically silent, the MP5 would've been a better choice.

Red shrugged on the ballistic vest and felt for his clips. It weighed on his shoulders and dug into his neck when he reached for his M4. Smelled like the inside of a new car. A variant on the Modular Tactical Vest, Lanyard told him. They didn't carry any food except a couple protein bars and a single canteen with iodine tablets. Wherever they were headed, they weren't staying long.

Gear checked out, everyone stripped it off and put it next to their rack in berthing.

Berthing had been Jim's idea, to control the team before a deployment so everyone would be on time, rested, and focused. Problem was it had a Navy name, was almost as confining as a ship's quarters, and meant more waiting. It was right off the hangar, through a thick insulated door to deaden sound. A Navy squid, built like a brick shit-house, stood next to it. Even Crawler looked at him suspiciously as they filed in with their gear.

Crawler pointed his thumb over a shoulder and said, "Someone needs to screen that guy for 'roids."

No sooner had Red dropped his gear than Jim stepped into the dim room. Holding up his fingers, he said, "Briefing in two!" He winked at Red. "Intel says they know where Lori's at."

Chapter 11
Prebrief

The coffin lid hinged open and white light filled Lori's eyes, blinding her. After they adjusted, she realized she was outside. The sky was overcast, as best she could tell through slit eyelids. A cool breeze chilled her cheek and brought a faint smell of pine. A man with a toothless grin peered in. His face was tanned, weather beaten as a sailor's, and a sweat-stained Orioles baseball cap was pulled low over his head. The asshole with the German accent gazed in over that one's shoulder, then wrinkled his nose and turned away. "She stinks of *pisse*."

They switched to Farsi. Her comprehension was spotty, but she made it out.

"Get her cleaned up. I can't deliver her like this."

"Where?"

"The outhouse. It has a sink."

With a bent finishing nail they jimmied the cuffs from her hands and feet. Cheap pricks didn't even have keys. Then they pulled out the gag, peeling away what seemed like an entire layer of skin from her lips that had dried to it. Her jaw ached as she tried to close it, dribbling drool on her neck. As she moved it side to side, her eyes watered at the pain. They shoved her into a cramped corrugated metal outhouse with a rusted enamel steel sink and a hole in the floor. She tried to punch the toothless man when he grabbed a breast, shoving her into the stinking box. As he raised his hand in retaliation the German gripped a spot near his collarbone.

"Basseh!" Toothless gasped.

"Worth twenty of you, *scheisskopf.* Slit your throat and sell your daughter as a whore in Thailand if you touch her again."

To Lori, he said in English, "Don't. Or I'll let him have his way. Now, clean yourself up."

He handed her a bottle of Dasani and shut the door. Much of it dribbled out her mouth as she drank. She couldn't make her jaw do what she wanted. Where were they? The trafficker spoke in Farsi, so maybe Iran? As she squatted to pee, she peered through a bullet hole in the wall. The outhouse stood next to a dilapidated mechanic's shop with the dented front of a Cessna 210 protruding from it, turbo charger hanging on by the waste gate tube.

Her legs threatened to collapse as she braced on the wall, hovering over the hole in the floor. She rinsed her stinking pajamas in rusty water from the sink, then slipped them back on, shivering in the sodden, cold flannel. They tied her hands with jute rope and thrust her, standing, into a tall wood crate that smelled like tar. She could turn around but didn't have room to sit. Still, a refreshing change from the coffin.

Cold but fresh air swept in through gaps between plank sides. The German and his helper lifted the crate into the bed of a troop transport, something like a deuce and a half, as best as she could see through the cracks. Over it they tossed a musty green canvas tarp that reeked of mold.

After at least an hour of driving, the tires sounded upon loose gravel.

Secondary road. The primary hadn't been full of potholes. It was afternoon and they were headed east, judging by the shadows she glimpsed through wide cracks in the truck's bed. They jostled along for another half hour, then the road became furiously rough. She heard only two vehicles pass, going in the opposite direction. A few minutes and they pulled off, then backed up. The rear wheels bounced over something—a speed bump? A ditch? Then the front. All light disappeared with the screech of dry bearings. The truck's engine stopped.

The German broke the crate open and led her out. Toothless wasn't around anymore. The truck was inside a warehouse in front of a silver galvanized overhead door like you'd see at a mechanic's garage. She turned her head, but he put a bag over it. She smelled a creek, like in New Hampshire when Tony took her fly-fishing, but the scent blew past. He led her along a concrete floor, all she could see past her chin where the bag hung loosely. A strong hand gripped her shoulder, but she ran into the sharp corner of something anyway, rasping her hip. Occasionally, she saw what looked like the bottom edge of a wooden crate lining her path. They paused at the top of stairs, then walked down several flights. It took forever, her stumbling and being jerked upright.

Weren't we already at ground level? Must be a basement or bunker or—

She splashed into a puddle and prepared to step down once more, but it was all flat. She felt ahead with her toes, but the hand shoved her from behind. "Move!" The German.

She ran into a doorjamb twice, hard enough to bruise her shoulder. The German yanked the bag off. He shoved her backwards and she tripped, falling to sit in a metal folding chair. He pulled a large black knife from its scabbard on his hip and held it in front of her chest. Looking down, he smiled and swept his oily black hair behind his ear, then wrinkled his nose again. He slipped the blade between her wrists and cut the rope, then walked out and locked a blue steel door behind him.

A single lightbulb hung from two wires in the middle of the empty, windowless room. Yet, this didn't look like it was meant to be a prison. Some muffled voices spoke outside the door. She cupped her hands around her ear and pressed against it.

"Transport was more," said the German. "Your British friend demanded fifty thousand euro. My fee didn't include additional bribes."

"I know," came a reply. "I told you who to use and I'd pay you whatever he required. We've done business before. He's like you. Invisible . . . till next time."

The heavy sound of booted feet walking upstairs. Then, silence.

She slunk back into the chair. Cold metal chilled through the damp flannel PJs. Her head bent low as she rubbed her legs. Tony always said flannel PJs were why they only had three kids. She grinned and swore to herself she'd get an entire wardrobe of silk when she got back and . . . Who was she fooling? Chances were she'd never make it. *Bait.* Tony'd get caught in it, too. The kids would grow up and eventually forget her. She put her head between her knees, closed her eyes, and concentrated on breathing slowly. Then she fell forward and retched, but the only thing that wet the floor was her tears.

* * *

Red clamped a hand onto his knee, keeping his leg from bouncing as he sat waiting for the rest of the team. The cramped briefing room next to berthing was concrete block with empty walls and contained only folding metal chairs, a laptop, an overhead projector, a blackened document incinerator the size of a small woodstove, and a skinny geek with Ben Franklin glasses.

"What's taking so long?" he asked.

The geek rubbed his hands as the team filed in. Sergeant Crawler hissed as he squeezed his ass against the side bars of one chair, unable to scooch back completely into the seat. Its legs creaked in protest.

Jim stood at the front of the room like a schoolteacher, facing them. His eyes sagged, the whites displaying more of a pink tone, but he stood erect. He was always at his best before an op. Tired, but in charge. A one-sided smile as he lifted an eight-by-ten in the air. "This is a seize-and-extract operation. We believe Lori Harmon is being held in Iran, in Saidabad, east of Tehran. In this warehouse."

The geek walked down the line, handing everyone manila folders. Red tore into his. It contained several photos, including the one Jim was holding. Jim had always liked print better than digital. The incinerator meant no paper left the room.

The first was a satellite image of an old brick warehouse with a weathered steel roof. Judging by a truck parked close by, it was about a hundred feet wide and two hundred long. The other photos displayed the same warehouse from several ground-level angles. All clear, high-quality shots.

Red waved one of the pictures at Jim. "How do we know she's here?"

"Humint. Analysis of the video with the blotched-out face didn't turn up anything. We put word out to our co-ops about what we were looking for. Mossad and CIA came back aiming at VEVAK." Jim pointed to the geek. "Gerry, help me out."

Gerry pushed his glasses further up a long nose and patted a folder against his chest. The white flesh of his neck was cinched in a blue Polo buttoned all the way up. His voice sounded as if his nose was a resonance chamber. "VEVAK's a perverted Iranian CIA. Intelligence and secret service and Mafia all in one."

"Not too much different, then," Crawler said, winking at Marksman.

Gerry stared blankly, then said, "Our first source was humint inside Iran, through Mossad. They won't divulge source details, but they're usually precise. Just like the colonel said, the second one was CIA. Intercept from a cell in the U.S. Placed to a VEVAK coordinator. It was thirty minutes after Lori's kidnap." He shrugged. "The intercept was scrambled, but they confirmed it went to VEVAK."

Dr. Ali leaned forward in his chair. "So we're basing this op on an unknown Israeli asset in Iran, confirmed only by a scrambled phone intercept placed to a VEVAK coordinator?"

"What the hell else you want?" Red snapped, half-rising from his chair.

Jim held up a hand. "If VEVAK was behind the kidnap, they wouldn't keep her in the U.S. Plus, their arms don't reach here. It had to be hired out. If so, they'd require the mercs to bring the hostages back home, no delays.

"Based on the timeframe, four aircraft that left the East Coast early Monday morning were possibilities. We narrowed it down to two—one from Philadelphia and one from Newport News. Our co-op at CIA suggested they'd be cargo, not passenger. The one from Newport News was owned by Aero Global."

Gerry pinched his index fingers, as if counting. "Aero Global is a front. They've been on everyone's watch list for years. Their board's controlled by members who aren't Iranian, but they've got oil interests and are generous to Shi'a organizations."

Crawler shrugged. "What's wrong with that?"

Jim snorted. "Terrorists, Crawler. They're financing terrorists."

Crawler pointed his cigar at Gerry. "Why din't he say so?"

"He did. Just not in Neanderthal."

Gerry rocked from his toes to heels. "Our co-ops at U.S. Customs have nothing." He pointed at Carter and smiled. "He shook the trees at Homeland Security. In ten minutes, we had the manifest in our hands. The plane was headed to London with some billionaire's dressage horse and a couple other exotic animals. At the last minute the crew accepted an order to deliver ten coffins. Destination, UK. We're thinking that's how Lori was smuggled out."

Red winced. "In a coffin?" His face grew hot.

"Yep," Jim said. "The plane went Newport News to London, to

Jinnah in Pakistan, then to Tehran. By the time we had the lead on Global Aero, they'd already taken off for Tehran. All we could do was ask Mossad for a favor. Space Command couldn't task a satellite, the cloud cover was too damn heavy or some other bullshit. Mossad photoed the cargo being moved to a warehouse close to the airport. Except one crate. It went to a known VEVAK location, the safe house in these." Jim tapped his manila envelope. "Not certain this is where she is, but it's a damn good guess. We've submitted the op plan to higher. We've got the green light, pending confirmation from Mossad. Then it's wheels up as early as 0600."

Red stood and paced to the back of the room. "Let's go now. Get approval en route. Iran's twelve hours away. They might move her."

"Mossad's intel has been heavy on the op plan. They're also helping on the exfil. They're using Iranian assets and don't want to pull the trigger till they can confirm. That's the way it is."

Red clenched his fists. "Wouldn't hurt to be on the way. We'd be that much closer."

"Too much at stake if we're wrong."

"Damn it! We've got—"

"Break. Be back in five," Jim snapped, pursing his lips. "Not you." He pointed a finger at Red.

The team filed out. Gerry stayed behind, shuffling papers on a table. "See you back in five," Jim said, almost a shout. The intel geek looked up, as if finally getting the cue.

The debrief room's door clicked shut behind Gerry. "This is going to be a one-sided conversation," Jim said.

Shit. Red squared his feet and braced.

"You've made it clear you want to get the hell on the road. I understand. But what good would it do to be over the Atlantic and find out VEVAK set up Mossad with bad intel? We'd all be halfway around the world, ready to squash the wrong bug. Lori could still be here. We can't outrun our intel."

Red could feel the blood pulsing in his head. Was Lori still alive?

Jim placed hands on hips and turned away. "The team doesn't trust you. A couple asked this morning if you should even be involved. Pressing to move before we've got good intel doesn't help. Hell, Red, skills are perishable. Even you said you had doubts. Glad you're eager to go, but quit acting like you've got a hard-on."

He turned back, jabbing a finger into Red's chest, "Higher specified you for the team. They never tell me who to use. Don't know whose fingers are in the pot, but I've bucked orders in the past and they looked the other way because I get results. Now I'm telling you, as your commander, pull it together or I'll yank you. But as your friend, I'm saying that if you want to save Lori, then think about it like any other op. Separate yourself. Understood?"

Red muttered through stiff lips. "Permission to speak?"

"Denied."

He closed his eyes.

"Good. You're back on the team. Don't worry, the time line is under control. After confirmation we'll be on station in seven hours." Jim called the team back in.

Captain Richards raised a hand, as if he was addressing his geometry teacher. "How'd Mossad get ground-level shots of the safe house so fast?" Marksman grunted and shifted in his chair.

"It's a known safe house," Gerry said. "Israel keeps current photos of all locations considered high importance."

"So, we don't know what's inside?"

Gerry walked to the front of the room, hands clasped behind his back. His narrow chest was thrust out, as if he'd finally found some confidence. "We know a little, just not the layout. The outside is a shell. Somewhere inside is a bunker, probably several stories underground. Political prisoners have been brought there for torture. All that makes it a logical holding area for a high-value hostage."

Red looked up from his photos. "For *Lori*."

Gerry's chest sunk again. "Sorry, right. For Lori. Other than that, it's storage for small arms."

Crawler lifted a photo and waved. "Am I the only one thinks it's odd there's arms storage in a nonmilitary area? Look. It's industrial."

Gerry smiled. "VEVAK doesn't trust the military, and it's their equipment. Our source info is thin because their main defense is secrecy. I don't anticipate much security on-site. At least not from what we've seen in the past."

Jim stepped in front of him. "That's what we're hoping, but still prep for the worst. The warehouse is next to the Pardis River." He pointed to another satellite photo. "Not more than a hundred feet across, less at spots. However, one mile north, upstream, it widens, like a small lake. It's a sinkhole. Deep enough for a cloaked drop."

Crawler slammed his fists on his knees. "Shit! I *hate* cloaked drops!"

"Stick a rag in it, Sergeant."

Red squinted. "Sir, what's a cloaked drop?"

Crawler growled, "Oh, you're gonna love what you've been missing. They cram you into a big pipe and—"

Jim pointed to his satellite photo. "Get Red up to speed on cloaked drops later. We're dropping at twenty-foot intervals. Rendezvous at this point here. We'll swim downstream one mile to the warehouse dock."

He switched photos to a satellite image of the warehouse and surrounding yard. Marksman would set up on the corner of a flat roof of a different building fifty yards to the northeast, covering two sides of the warehouse. Crawler would be on the ground as Marksman's bodyguard. Two extraction teams would enter the building simultaneously, from the west and the south. The idea was to drive anyone trying to escape toward Marksman and Crawler. Lanyard would cut the electricity to the building and set up a CSS.

Red raised a finger. "What's 'CSS'?"

Jim hesitated a fraction of a second, frowning. "Communication Suppression System. Almost undetectable. It counters any radio transmission within a quarter mile. Doesn't scramble, just muffles. Like a gag."

"Do our comms work with it?"

"Of course."

Jim and Carter were command and control on top of a pile of boulders on the northwest corner of the lot. No comms were to be used until after the extraction teams entered the warehouse, and only on the lowest setting.

"Your primary ammo is four clips of subsonic tacs," Jim said.

He wasn't screwing around. So the four clips weren't regular subsonic ammo. Some doctor had weaponized the venom of the Inland Taipan snake over a decade ago. It was carried by a pressurized slug, like a flying syringe. Against Geneva conventions. Even a flesh wound would drop you in two seconds, kill you in six. Red smiled.

"You'll have eight clips of Det ammo," Jim said, "but do *not* use unless you have to. Our exfil depends upon a silent op."

He explained the exit plan and time line. Then everyone broke to review the photos and commit them to memory. Red and Lanyard went over the basics—hand signals, clearing orders, and protocols—for his own confidence as much as Lanyard's. Didn't seem to be anything new there. Then Jim broke the brief. Gerry tossed all the photos in the incinerator. With a *whooomp* they were ash.

Hot chow was waiting back in berthing. Red had something, but he couldn't say what. He only ate because he needed the energy. He sat on a bunk and rechecked weapons. Crawler waddled up, still chewing and looked down at him.

"Some of us has a wager goin', sir. Remember that drinking game we's had?"

An image of a shit-faced, shirtless Crawler sitting next to a dunk tank trying to reassemble his M4 shot through his mind. "Yeah. Guys, heavy drinking, weapons. Always a good combo."

"The drinks'll have to come after the op. The time to beat is fifty seconds. I've got money riding on you, major."

"Who bet against me?"

Crawler swallowed. "Ain't sayin'. Not yet."

This could go either way. If Red could break down and reassemble his main weapon in time, it'd be a boost of confidence to the team, and himself. Such a basic test wouldn't prove all his skills were up to par, but if he remembered how to do this, chances were better he'd remember the rest of them. But if he messed it up . . .

He sat on the floor, Indian–style. The concrete chilled his balls through the fabric of his trousers. He lifted his M4, fumbled for the clip release, and pulled back on the charging handle. He released the bolt, dry fired, and placed it in front of him. His hands shook, so he rubbed his palms on his thighs, as if trying to warm them. Crawler pulled an oily green square of parachute cloth from his pocket, twirled it into a tube, then tied it around Red's eyes. "On t'ree. One—"

"Hold up!" Dr. Ali said. "I'm timing him, too."

Red turned his head toward the voice. *"Et tu, Brute?"*

Everyone chuckled except for Crawler. "What the hell does 'et two, brutae' mean?"

"Go back to high school," Marksman grunted.

Crawler sneered, then finished the countdown.

Red snatched the rifle and pushed on the main retaining pins, breaking the weapon into two. Relief came as muscle memory seemed to take over. He removed the buffer assembly and spring, then went to work on the upper assembly. The bolt carrier and charging handle were on the floor in order, then the retaining pin, firing pin, cam pin, and bolt. He slapped his knees, reassembled everything in reverse order, replaced the retaining pins, charged the weapon and dry fired. He charged it again and tested the safety and bolt lock, then placed it back on the floor in front of him. *Like tying his shoes.* He rubbed his legs again, but his hands were steady now.

"Forty-four seconds!" Crawler said. "Doc's buying when we get back. And none of that piss water."

Red pushed up the blindfold in time to see Marksman's eyes roll. Crawler's idea of a premium brew had been Bud Light, and apparently the years hadn't refined him. He wasn't wearing any insignia—probably still failing his master sergeant exams. But he'd bet for Red and not against. The man couldn't be a complete idiot.

Jim stepped into the room. "Lights out."

Marksman took a step and swung into a top bunk. Crawler grunted as he eased himself beneath, the bedsprings *twanging* under his weight. Lanyard was silent. Unconvinced. Like the rest of the team. Everyone sacked out in uniform.

Sleep still wasn't an option for Red. Jim had said Ali couldn't give anyone pills to help them sleep in case Intel pulled the trigger early. So Red closed his eyes and tried to ignore Crawler's snoring, the wheezing broken only by an occasional gas leak.

He couldn't turn off his mind. Hell, he'd been under sedation for a day and a half. That would have to hold him. The round, white-faced clock ticked through the hours, like Gerry at the brief.

About 0200, he swung his legs down, stood, and walked out. The steroid-pumping squid barred his exit, but let him pass. "If you stay where I can see you."

Red glanced inside the Sikorskys twice as he paced around the hangar. Their familiarity reassured him. On his third round, he slid a palm over the starboard belly of the Pave Low. He smiled when he found them: two neatly patched 35 mm holes just forward of the gun mount. This was the same helo that had extracted them after the op in Brazil. She was ancient and quivered in flight, but he was grateful to the old bird. She'd flown a few feet above the trees through the thickest cloud cover he'd ever seen. He'd sensed it then, too: She was happy. She'd brought all her boys home.

Red paced, thinking about Lori, then tried to push it all out of his mind. No luck. His thoughts circled back endlessly to waking in the hallway with a gash in his head. And her gone. Forgot to warn the kids about Tom's knives on the counter . . . but Mom was good about that.

His family had been separated, spread out. All he could do now was wait. Wait for some Iranian traitor across the water to confirm some intel to his Mossad handler.

He stood next to a tan Humvee. His reflection was dim in the flat window, but clear enough to mirror watery, puffy eyes. It had been six years since he'd been active. Was it realistic to think he could jump back in like nothing had changed? He'd kept reasonably fit, but skills degrade. No wonder the team had doubts. And Lanyard . . . hell, it wasn't a good decision to partner a rookie with Red on his first op back. Jim's confidence was reassuring, but unwarranted.

Red rubbed fingers over the sleeve of his fatigues. He hadn't worn them for years, but their texture on his skin was as familiar as if he'd never taken them off. His boots echoed as he walked by the Pave Low once again. She'd been retired once. Patched up, like himself. He'd told Penny he'd get Lori back. How that was going to happen seemed a thick fog, but he'd bring her home.

He slunk back into his rack, then remembered Father Ingram's advice and said a prayer.

His eyes were closing when Jim stuck his head in. "Wake time! Wheels up in thirty!"

A glance to the white-faced clock. It was 0556.

Chapter 12
Tupolev

Breakfast was cold eggs and grits, prepped and refrigerated hours earlier. It could've been ice cubes for all Red cared. Jim insisted he eat something, so he grabbed a banana. Mossad had called with confirmation and the op was a go—nothing warmer than that. His fingers shook like he was on amphetamines.

He paced, pretending to check his gear while the rest of the team finished up. His palms tingled as he worked the action on his sidearm. He removed the slide and held the two pieces. He was looking down the fat barrel, trying to understand why it felt lighter than his old sidearm, when Jim called them to muster in the hangar. He slid the gun back together and they ran through their final check and inventory.

When a shrill whining came from outside, everyone lifted their gaze to the hangar doors. The sound swelled, deafening even inside, then wound down.

Jim pointed toward an EXIT sign. "Our ride's here. Strap it up and get on board,"

The pitch of the engines was different than anything Red could remember. Marksman beamed. The man always seemed most upbeat before an op. Jim led the column out the hanger door. Outside, Crawler flipped open a silver Zippo and lit his cigar. Tobacco smoke mingled with the scent of jet fuel. Not an acceptable combination, but Jim had always allowed the man a few pre-op puffs to satisfy Crawler's superstition. On the tarmac was a long, slender, white aircraft with canards and deeply swept delta wings. It looked like pictures of a Concorde Red had once seen.

Captain Richards pointed toward the plane. "What's that, the Aurora?"

Jim laughed. "Who the hell you think I am? Even I couldn't swing that."

Marksman turned to face him, walking backwards. The early morning sun reflected off his shiny dark bald head. "You weren't even born when this was built. It's a Tupolev, a 144 I think. Russian built, back in the early seventies, their competition to the Concorde. Economics are a bitch."

Richards frowned. "What you mean?"

"Costs too much to fly, like the Concorde. It was better, but still lost. Kinda like how Beta was better than VHS, but VHS won out."

"What the hell's VHS?"

Marksman turned back around. Jim shot a grin his direction.

"How'd we end up with it?" Richards asked.

Marksman rubbed fingers together as if counting money. "NASA bought one back in the nineties from the Russians. For tests, they claim. They gave it new avionics and slipped in new engines. Supposed to be out of duty."

"How you know so much?"

Marksman kept walking.

Crawler snuffed his cigar stub on the aluminum stair handrail. Two fuel trucks flanked the plane as they walked up thirty feet to the door. Its fuselage was slender, narrow, like a huge fighter but with four engines slung under its belly. For Red, it held the same emotion as racehorses in the starting gates. Tom had taken him to the tracks when he was only twelve, despite his mother's scolding. Even as a newbie he'd seen the excitement in their eyes, in the veins bulging on their necks. Those horses were made to run, bred to explode down the track, impatient in the gates as they anticipated the bell. Red put his hand on the plane's skin as he ducked into the doorway. It quivered. This contender was in the starting gate. A corner of his mouth drew up when he thought how Lori always teased when he told her how machines felt.

He couldn't see the pilots, hidden behind a bulkhead of instruments. One was talking with the tower. ". . . I told you *hold* runway 08. I only need four minutes. . . . We don't even get our nose up till two hundred twenty knots, *no* air wash. I don't care who the hell's trying to land, tell them to go 'round!" He clicked off and mumbled something.

The passenger area was empty, void, like a cargo plane. Except for a bank of old dials and scopes forward, the top liner was gone and panels only covered the bottom few feet of the sides, exposing the ribs of the fuselage. Red didn't know what he was expecting, but it was more than this. Narrow tubes and wires ran neatly along the centerline of the ceiling. In some places even the insulation between the ribs was removed, exposing the outer skin. The space was cold, naked, fragile.

About halfway down the aisle Jim turned around and their eyes met. "Been stripped of everything to make it lighter." He walked backwards and pointed to green webbed jump seats hanging from either side. "Red, Lanyard, Crawler, and Marksman, on the port. The rest on the starboard. Stow your gear and strap in."

A pilot marched down the aisle and stood, legs spread, hands on hips. His white hair was cut in a high and tight. Skin hung under his eyes, but they were alert. Broad shoulders, narrow waist, tall, and in charge. A dark blue patch over his heart displayed dark gold wings. Air Force. Subdued silver eagles perched on his shoulders.

"Okay, ladies. I'm your pilot for this gig. You're guests on my aircraft. Treat her with respect, understood?"

"Yes sir!" came from all.

He glanced at Sergeant Crawler. "You're sitting on thirty thousand gallons of JP-8, so get rid of all smokes, lit or otherwise."

Crawler yanked out his cigar butt and glanced around his seat, then threw it in his mouth and swallowed.

The pilot pointed toward the cockpit. "No getting up till we reach cruising altitude, at which time that light up there will turn green. Any Marines in here?"

Red sounded a "Hooah!" having cross-commissioned into the Corps directly out of college, one of the few allowed each year from the Air Force Academy. Lanyard echoed the same. He'd have to remember to ask the rookie what he did before he got assigned to the Det.

"At least Jim put the jarheads together." He slapped a finger on the crystal of a thick, black aviator's watch. "I realize we don't have Mickey to point things out, but don't move till that light turns green. Got it? Need me to repeat?" Marksman tensed, but a snort slipped through.

"Now, for your safety brief. If anything major goes wrong while in flight that light will turn red. At that point strap back in, put your head between your knees, and kiss your ass good-bye because at Mach two we're all dead. She's got the glide scope of a brick, so at least it'll be quick and painless. Welcome aboard and Godspeed."

He turned and jogged to the cockpit. Engines were winding up. Jim passed a bag of earplugs, throwing it across to Red. Through the few uncovered windows Red saw the fuel trucks backing away. The plane moved forward, pivoting on the landing gear as it pointed itself toward the east end of the runway. They taxied, turned west into the wind, and didn't stop as they hit the afterburners. The fuselage all around rattled and shook. Even with earplugs, the roar of the engines was loud.

"It'll be better at altitude," Marksman shouted. Red had to read his lips. They gained speed, then more, then kept going where they should have lifted off. The plane continued at full gallop, eating up runway until it finally nosed up. As soon as the rear wheels left the ground, the runway gave way to grassy field. They maintained a steep angle for several minutes and ran through turbulence that ended abruptly. He read Marksman's lips: *Sound barrier!*

Red gazed down the long, slender, naked tube in which they rode. It twisted in response to the air buffeting its skin like a boxer taking blows to his ribs. He put his hand on the undressed aluminum floor. The pilot had made the aircraft sound like a coffin, but it was happy now, sucking air and blowing it out white hot, finally out of the gate, hitting its stride.

The light turned green. Jim hopped up and pulled out his earplugs. "We only have two and a half hours to Ramstein and twenty minutes of it are gone. Let's get started."

Captain Richards glanced quizzically at Marksman. The old salt pointed back and said, "That's right, rookie! While you were sucking your mamma's titty my generation was stepping on the moon and flying across the world at twice the speed of sound. What's yours done? Internet, iPads, and terrorism!" The growl of the engines was the only remaining sound as the team stared back at him. Even the pilot peered over his shoulder.

"Feel better?" Jim asked.

Marksman leaned back and crossed his arms. "Sorry. It's all yours." The sun streamed through a window and Marksman closed one eye.

Jim ran them through the op plan again. They'd gotten their confirmation early that morning and the extraction had to be done under cover of night. That's why he called in a favor for the Tupolev. A prepositioned B-2 at Ramstein had been arranged at the same time. The schedule was imprinted at this point. Wheels up at Ramstein at 1500 zulu, drop at 2100, leave the rendezvous at 2115, showtime at 2145, exit no later than at 2215.

Jim released them, and Red leaned back in his seat, listing toward Lanyard. His head throbbed and he had to blink hard to water his eyes. "How long you been at the Det?"

"About two months now." Lanyard's voice betrayed edginess.

"Where'd you come from?"

"Same as you. Recon. Spec ops. Little this. Little that."

Red looked down at Lanyard's boots. The toes were gouged deeply. His fingers were rugged, too, calluses near the tips. "Do a lot of climbing on your last assignment?"

"Last four months in Afghanistan, mainly search and destroy. If I wasn't climbing, I was under the ground rootin' 'em out." His eyes looked toward the ceiling and followed the wires down the spine of the aircraft. "Never been to Vietnam, but the Taliban caves have got to be just as bad."

"You like doing that?"

Sergeant Lanyard scowled. "Hell no! My platoon was good, but no one *liked* it. Not even the hardcore ones."

Red covered his smile by scratching his beard. He had no patience for anyone that claimed to enjoy shitty duty. Some did, but those guys ended up in psych wards.

Lanyard rubbed his forehead with the palms of both hands. "You okay on this? I mean, your wife and all. What if—"

"What if we find her in pieces?" Red asked. "Then I'd want to be the one that did. Either way, I'm going to enjoy gutting the ragheads that did it." It was Red's turn to look at the ceiling now. How ironic that if someone cut the right wire it would bring down the entire team, the entire op.

"You heard the colonel. Grab the ones we can. Kill if we have to. Part of our deal with the Israelis. Something about VEVAK and the Iranian nuclear program."

Like hell. What could they do? Kick him out for killing the terrorists who'd kidnapped his wife? He'd already been out for six years and didn't like the idea of coming back full-time. A lesson from his past tugged at him. What was it? He couldn't remember.

His hand felt is if it was wrapped in Father Ingram's firm grip, shaking hands as he left his office. He couldn't face the priest if he ignored orders. But wasn't God in this? He was on a plane with seven other trained men for the purpose of reclaiming Lori. Surely that wasn't an accident. Not even Father Ingram could deny it. Allowing them to live wouldn't be right, would it?

Now I'm the religious fanatic.

He rubbed the back of his neck and closed his eyes. The image of Tom wielding his cane like a saber cut into his mind, his father plugging his fingers into Red's sternum. Yeah. Tom was right. The kidnappers had made it personal. It was on their own heads. What's that saying his father had taught him as a kid? *Kill 'em all. Let God sort 'em out.*

The webbed-nylon jump seats cut off Lanyard's circulation like the ones in the C-130s, in the Chinooks, and just about anything else in which he'd been carried. Seven miles a day kept his blood pressure low, so it didn't take much. He lifted one leg to let the blood run, then leaned back and stared at the major sitting there rubbing his neck. This guy was whacked. *I'd rather have some army puke leading me than this pussy. He's been gone six years. Why the hell did they stick me with him on my first op here? They think I'm expendable?*

Nothing like the colonel. Now, *he* was high speed. The only thing he'd seen a full bird do before was rest his fat ass behind a desk, only bothering to stand to chew someone out when things went south. This one, his hands got dirty. Even so, he didn't know how to put together a team. His A team leader's a psycho ex-operator who would probably pass out during the swim. Three officers on the same op? What the hell?

"So, you know everyone here yet?" the major asked.

Whatever. "First time I've seen Marksman. What the hell kind of name is that?"

"It's a nickname that stuck. He's got others. Never told us his real one. I know less now about the guy than on my first op." He looked off as if counting, then leaned back, close to his ear. "It's been six or so with him. He doesn't train with us. Just shows up when called and knows his stuff."

Lanyard pointed discreetly across the aisle at Carter. "Most teams like this? Patched together? Between Carter and Marksman, that's two we've never trained with. With you that's . . ." Lanyard held Red's gaze.

"Seems we always have at least one new face, depending on what skills we need for the op. Language, terrain, demolitions, engineering. Me? Hell, I've got enough doubts for the both of us. Carter? I gotta trust the colonel knows what he's doing. I don't like him here, either. But Marksman, you don't have to worry about him. Don't know his day job, but it's not domestic. I think he's Russian, Spetsnaz, probably Alpha Group by the way he handles himself. But he's old enough to have been KGB."

"How would that work?" Lanyard sneered.

"Don't know. Freelance maybe. Double agent. Doesn't matter, I trust him. He's saved my ass a couple times. That settles it. He's old, but the best shot I've ever seen. Put rounds through three heads at three hundred meters before the last one had time to duck. Like he didn't even aim, just point and shoot. Colonel says he knows Farsi. You like the captain?"

What the hell does it matter to you? "Good as most. One for sure, he can PT my ass into the ground. It's like he doesn't stop. Other than that, haven't been here long enough to say."

The major slapped his legs and stood.

Carter leaned forward, away from the side of the plane. The cold seemed to reach out from it. It had crept into his lower back and his muscles resisted the stretch. He glanced across the aisle at Red, standing. He made sense, now. His seeming evasiveness, the danger. Red hadn't known it was all there. Turbulence hit as Red stepped across the aisle, but his legs absorbed the bounce, his body floating for a split second before he spun and sat next to him.

"This your first?" Red asked. His white teeth shone against his blacked-out face. There was something else there now. What was it?

"Not my first op, but a first like this." In the few years he'd spent working counterterrorism at the Bureau, he'd put together several ops. However, all except one were stateside. Later working Chicago homicide, he'd organized his share of raids. But there had always been the realization if an officer went down, a fully staffed hospital was only a few miles away. He'd left that life, retired. But somehow it had stalked him down and sucked him back.

"Different than working for Sheriff Jenson?"

Carter forced a laugh.

"You've got a dark past if Jim has you on this one."

Carter didn't answer.

Red's smile receded and his eyes focused on the distance. There it was. The same look from the interrogation room after the Walmart incident. He wasn't schizophrenic, but couldn't be far off. "You have to take them alive," Carter said.

Red blinked hard.

"I know what you're thinking. But you heard the colonel. Israel is hungry for any VEVAK intel. We need some live ones."

Red exhaled slowly.

Carter glanced at the colonel. He had one ear plugged and the other to his sat phone. Carter grabbed Red's arm and pulled him close. "I don't care if you off every one of 'em. But this is bigger than you, bigger than Lori. This is for the U.S., the entire Middle East. If Iran gets to be a nuclear power, you know what they've threatened. We'll be at war with a crippled economy, trying to contain Iran backed by Russia. Everyone knows they're controlled by organized crime and KGB leftovers. I can see it on you. You're making this personal. You can't go there." He elbowed Red, trying to get some sort of reaction. "Plus, I'm married. A vendetta could get me killed. Understand?"

Red shut his eyes. The man had so little to lose right now. If Lori had been mistreated, he was not going to leave any of her abusers alive.

"Carter, I just want her back. For me, yes. But mostly for the kids. I won't be able to face them if I don't. Problem is, I'm not who I was a couple days ago, and I'm not who I was six years ago, either. I've still got stuff I can't remember, like black spots in my head. I half-lied to Genova to get on. I mean, I didn't make stuff up. I've got recall on most of what he asked me. But it's like there's more there that I can't get to. It's like he didn't dig deep enough, maybe on purpose. Big deal, I remember how to break down a weapon, but that's like driving. You don't forget it."

Red leaned back and pressed his fingertips to his temple. "I don't want to screw this up, but I'm the weak link. I've never been that before. Crawler still trusts in me, but he's got the IQ of a doorknob. I want to kill the guys who took her so bad I can taste it. I can't push it aside anymore. I'm gonna screw something up, maybe even lose her."

Carter scratched his stubbled face. His fingers slipped over oily skin. "You got no choice."

"What?"

"You heard me. They brought the fight. You finish it. No easy way out of this one, so quit trying."

"Sound like my father."

"Good. Then you know what you gotta do. Suck it up. Kill the ones you got to. Take the ones you don't. Figure the other shit out later. I believe in you, too, and pardon me if I don't think myself dumb as a doorknob."

Red's lip straightened. Consciousness seemed to creep back into his eyes. "Thanks. I'll keep my head clear."

Carter leaned back into the webbing again. The cold didn't sting so bitter now. The growl of the engines hung like white noise.

The colonel slapped his phone closed but it rang again. "Damn it! You'd think I'd get a break up here." He flipped it open.

"Hello!" His countenance softened as he listened. "Great to hear from you again, Sheriff, but I gotta go. How'd you get this—" A smile broke across his face. "That *is* good news. Thanks for running that down. I'll get him. He's right here."

Covering the mic, the colonel leaned into Carter. "Your boss sounds like a backwoods bootlegger, but he may have earned his pay today. Figure it out."

What the hell?

The colonel pushed the sat phone into his hands. "He's in D.C., at the Hoover Building." His lip curled in a cynical smile. "Says he's got intel on that bullet casing you gave him to keep him busy."

Chapter 13
Irish

Carter took the sat phone and covered the mic, musing how he'd handle Sheriff Jenson. He'd given him a bullet casing with a print just to stop him looking over his shoulder, calling every half hour and asking when he'd be back to work, trying to discover why he'd disappeared. The empty shell was the colonel's idea. "Let him help. Give him a hard one," he'd said. "One that'll keep him busy a while."

The phone was warm against his ear. The colonel had been on it for at least an hour. "How'd you end up in D.C., Sheriff?"

His North Carolina accent was even stronger when reflected off a satellite. "Where're you? Sounds like a locomotive goin' through a tunnel."

Carter leaned forward and glanced down the empty fuselage. Red caught his eye and winked. "You could say that."

"Know that FBI agent from last summer? The guy I ran into at the boat ramp when I—"

Carter spun his hand in a *hurry up* motion. "Yeah. You tore off his bumper, didn't you? You guys still friends?"

"Oh, yeah. He's a South Carolina boy. We patched that up a long time ago. He came up here two months back and I took him fishin' out to the rock, after striper. He got a—"

"Sheriff, please, I'm pressed for time on this end."

"You always is in a hurry. Remember that print you gave me? The one on the casing from your buddy's house?"

"I'm with you."

"I couldn't find nothing, but figured, what the hell? So I gave my FBI fishin' buddy a call. He'd invited me up to D.C. a while back and—"

"Had he been drinking?"

"Come again?"

"Sorry. Keep going."

"So I hopped in a cruiser this morning. He was surprised as hell, but here we are in his office havin'—"

Carter pushed back the cuff of his fatigue blouse and squinted at his watch. "You're in FBI headquarters, at seven in the morning?"

The sheriff's voice smoothed, almost losing the hillbilly drawl. "There *are* still some things this ol' man can teach you. Now, don't interrupt. I was halfway through my coffee when I slipped him the question. Asked if maybe he could help with somethin'. I passed him the print. He said it was a *thumb*print. Made sense, loadin' a clip and all. His secretary put it on some machine next to her desk. Next thing you know we're lookin' at that same print on his 'puter screen."

"And?" Carter rubbed the bridge of his nose.

"He picked up the phone and some kid, looked twelve, came through the door. He banged on a keyboard and after a minute said it was *typed*. Say, we gotta hire us one so's we can—"

"Sheriff, please."

"Okay, okay. My buddy checked their file drawers downstairs and nothing matched."

Then why the hell did you call? "Well, nice of you to let me know. Thanks for—"

"I ain't done yet! I made him a bet that if he could find a match, I'd take him back out to the rock next weekend. He called his buddy back at Langley, CIA. Somehow he got that fingerprint from his 'puter over to his friend while he was talkin' on the phone."

Carter pressed his fingertips onto his eyelids. *Does anyone know what I deal with?*

"His friend ran it through his files and in five minutes found something. Ain't much, but he said it may be from an Israeli."

Shit. A connection? This guy was CIA, so he's trolling the Israeli tidbit as bait. If they had a file on him, there was more than that.

Carter covered the mic and elbowed the colonel. "The print's Israeli. He got a match, at CIA."

"Our liaison didn't turn anything up. He's lost it." He grabbed the phone. "Sheriff, Jim again. You calling from a phone on your, uh, friend's desk?"

"Yep. Don't got no cell phone. They'll fry your—"

"I need to talk to him."

"Well sure! Name's Joe McRearden. Nice talking. Here you go."

McRearden had almost choked when the sheriff pulled a flask from his coat pocket and poured some cheer into his coffee. Sneaky hillbilly used a black plastic container so he didn't get pinged at the metal detector. McReardon had waved off his offer politely, then kept his eyes on his office door, hoping no one was walking by. As security manager for Cyber Division, he'd kept the clear doors in a spirit of transparency. Now he wished he had a wooden one.

Sheriff Jenson passed the phone over the desk. McReardon took it and punched the speaker button. "How can I help you?"

The voice said, "I'm not on a hardline. Switching to a secured channel using crypt code delta, tango, charlie, one, eight, three."

McReardon frowned as the speakerphone switched to scrambled, sounding an eclectic mix of static and fax signal. He looked up again to ensure his door was still shut, then shuffled papers. "Who in blue blazes did you call?"

The sheriff leaned back and sipped his mug. "My detective didn't answer, so I called a friend he's been helpin'. Gave me his number as a backup. Or maybe it was emergency. Hell, I can't remember."

McReardon's face was warming and he hit the intercom. "Marsha. Get me a printout of the crypt codes, ASAP!"

Marsha pushed open the door with a huff, stomped in, and opened a desk drawer, pulling out coffee-stained papers. She dropped them on the desk. "Here you go." She turned and started out.

McRearden forced a smile. "Thanks, dear. Don't know what I'd do without you."

He flipped through the pages, repeating the crypt code so as not to forget it. He found his reference and pounded several buttons on his phone. The static fell off. A red-lettered *Secured* lit up.

"Who the hell are you?"

"Colonel Jim Mayard, U.S. Air Force. Security ID is delta, bravo, oscar, niner. Verification is *St. Andrews*. I'll give you a second to look me up."

McRearden shook his head, fingers pounding on his keyboard.

He hit the mute button on the phone. "I swear, Sheriff, I will kill you if I lose my job over this." His fishing buddy smirked as if he knew what he'd done. McReardon found the security ID and clicked open the file. His eyes widened.

"Holy shit!" He looked up at his least-favorite friend. "You realize who you're dealing with? This guy—I can't tell you about him—but he's *not* a guy you want to work with. Or even call, for that matter."

He pursed his lips and took the phone off mute. "What do you need, Colonel?"

"The print was Israeli? I need to know everything. You've got ten minutes."

McRearden leaned back in his chair and rubbed his neck. "I didn't turn that up. That was my buddy over at Langley."

"I'll wait for you to conference him in."

McRearden pressed mute again. "If Frank doesn't kill me for dragging him into this, this colonel will." He hit the conference button and dialed Frank's number. They'd met at a technology symposium a few years back.

"Agent Workman."

"Frank? Doug."

"Why you calling on a secured line?"

"I've got someone holding. Already ran his security file. He checks out above both of our grades. A field operative with questions about that print. The Israeli."

McRearden held the earpiece away at the sound of Frank's nasal laugh. "He's calling sooner than I thought."

"I'll give you his security ID."

"Don't need it. He's not getting the file."

"What?"

"Look, you made the request to run the print and I did. A favor. But it's like all the others. I'll point him to the right department. He can go through them. No one's the wiser."

"Doug, you don't understand. Look up his ID."

"I don't care if he's the president. I'm not supposed to have this file! We don't have a central intelligence system. The only reason I got it is because I—because I work where I do. My balls would be in a sling if they knew. He's gotta go through channels."

"For the last time, please—"

"Oh, for Pete's sake! Give me the damn ID."

"Delta, bravo, oscar, niner. Verification is St. Andrews."

"That's only four digits. Need eight."

"It's an old one. Just look it up."

Frank huffed. Then, silence. Well, no one liked being put on the spot. Need to know is established at the proper levels, then information can flow freely. The colonel's access level simply read, "All." Beneath that, "Logging prohibited." So McRearden couldn't keep any documentation when he talked with him. The colonel was a ghost. Someone else held his reins. Only the director or someone higher could have agreed to it.

A *click* as Frank came back on the line. "Put him on."

He pushed the conference button and all three lines flashed active.

"Colonel?"

"Tell me about the Israeli."

"The print was matched with ninety-six-percent certainty to an unknown Israeli field operative. We know he's been involved with at least two ops—one in Russia, one in Iran."

"Iran?"

"Yes, sir. Both were a year ago. We believe he's with Mossad."

"Believe? Then ask them."

"They denied him. We don't believe it."

"So we don't know whose side he's on?"

"Based upon what little we've gathered, and the nature of the ops, it points to Israeli intel. His file's short. No name, so he's just I-29. There's more detail on the two ops than I-29 himself... or herself."

"Give that to me."

"The one in Russia was the killing of a Chinese oil tycoon. China was loading up on Russian oil to pressure Iran to drop prices. After the killing, China refused to fund Russia's development of a new field. Resulted in a twelve-month delay to their oil production schedule."

"And the one in Iran?"

"The assassination of Rahim Hafasi, an Artesh general. The Iranian Army."

"I know who the hell he is."

"Sorry. He was in charge of Artesh's nuclear program. This says I-29 is Mossad. Where'd you get the print?"

"In the U.S."

"Where?"

No reply.

"Listen, I may be able to help if I have the full story. Your call."

"Up the road from you in New Kent County. Couple days ago. Attempted kidnapping of one of my operators. They got his wife. We're using Mossad's intel for an op."

"You need to reconsider."

"No shit. Anything else in the file?"

"Nothing."

"Thanks, gentlemen. Out."

One of the lights on McRearden's phone dimmed as the colonel hung up. He thanked Frank, then placed the handset down in its cradle, as if trying not to wake it. He looked up and realized he hadn't sent the sheriff outside. Shit. "You know what you just got me into? You're like an inebriated bull in a china shop."

The sheriff lifted his coffee and smirked. "They do tell me I'm full of bull."

Doug took a gulp of his own brew, cold now, and shuddered. Bitter. Should've taken the sheriff up on his earlier offer of a spike. He leaned back and rubbed his neck again, then winked. "My wife'll come after you if I get shot because of this. I'm a computer nerd, not a damn operative."

Jim flipped his sat phone shut, gaze distant. When he brought it back, the entire team was staring at him. Eight men. His charge. Eight lives. With kids, some of them. Was this a game changer? Could he press forward, or should he reconsider as Frank had suggested?

Red asked, "What was that all about?"

"One of Lori's kidnappers has a link to Mossad, we think. His file's thin. Called him I-29."

"We're still going, then?"

The colonel walked toward the cockpit, several steps away from the rest. Red stood to follow, but Carter pulled him back down. Jim studied the scuffed aluminum floor, zigzagged with grip tape. He shouldn't have answered the phone. No way to know I-29's role in the kidnap, or even verify he was Israeli. Even then, he might be a double, or a mole, or who knows what. That's what reeked about working with spooks. You never knew who was on your damn team. It's why he'd always stayed on the operations side, where he had control.

He took a deep breath and held it. Any other information to change his decision about the op? No. There were always doubts, risks. You had to make the best decision with what was in hand. Then again, if intel was compromised, his team would be as good as dead.

Someone brushed against him. He glanced sideways. Ironic, a black man wearing blackout. "There're always loose ends," Marksman said. "You don't get to ignore whatever they said. May be a rogue player out there, but always are. This is a well-planned mission. Sometimes too much intel is just that, too much."

The colonel tried to read the man's dark brown eyes. He only called him for an op about once a year, but kept close connections the rest of the time.

"Out with it," the colonel said.

Marksman glanced toward the cockpit. "Sorry. I got nothing. You trust your liaison with Mossad?"

"No. But she's never been wrong."

"So why not trust her?"

"Easy for you." The colonel jerked a thumb over one shoulder. "You're not responsible for *them*."

"Shit, colonel. We all know the risks. Even if the team gets taken, you might get out alive. Maybe minus teeth, a few broken bones, but still. I get taken, inside Iran, they'll FedEx me back to Russia in ten different boxes. Yet, here I am. This is a good op, a good plan. I'm behind you, and so are they."

Everyone thought Jim knew Marksman's day job, but he didn't. The man had just showed up once after he'd sent a request up the chain for an operator who spoke Russian. Higher had said use him, but don't ask questions. But could he trust Marksman? His gut was confident, but caution flags were waving in his head.

He turned back to his team. "We're still a go." He met the gaze of each member in turn. Each gave a thumbs-up, even Carter. "Our intel sources have been confirmed. But keep your eyes open."

They all glanced up over his shoulder. He turned to see the pilot standing behind him.

"Okay, ladies. We're ten minutes out. It's been a pleasure. Transport for your next leg is warming up. Judging from the wings taking you, I'm glad I'm not going. Don't eat too much before loading. Godspeed." He looked back at the colonel and muttered, "We're even, shithead."

The colonel glowered and shot back, "Who's counting?"

A dismissive grunt. The pilot stepped back into his seat and the light glowed red again. The intercom squawked, "Pleasure being your pilot this morning. We know you have a choice in airline travel, so we want you to know we appreciate you choosing us. For the safety of those around you, please secure and recheck all weapons before landing. Your opinion is as important to us as crotch rot, so please fill out a customer survey and drop it in the shitter on your way out."

Jim peered through an oval glass pane at streets and white-topped buildings flashing by as the aircraft descended. Weather report had said six inches of fresh powder would welcome them at Ramstein Air Base, Germany. Piles of white and gray drifts lined the runway as they made a fast approach, apparently the only way this craft knew how to do it. The Tupolev touched, slowed, and turned off. The team stood and lined behind him at the forward door even before the plane stopped.

Jim ducked through the small opening and stopped on the threshold. An enormous gray hangar stood across the plowed tarmac, with the B-2 waiting out front. An airman leaned out the window of a stair truck, nudging the topmost tread in place below the colonel's feet.

The Tupolev's engines spun down. No other engine noise was apparent above the racket on the tarmac, but heat waves shimmered from the rear of the B-2. He started down the stairs, breathing the familiar scent of JP-8. It took him back to a kerosene heater warming the three-room boardinghouse in the Kentucky highlands where he'd grown up. He sniffed, almost expecting to smell wet grass and horse manure. As a child, he'd decided he'd make enough money to never have to live in a cold house again. He loved the country that had given him that chance and damned any son of a bitch who threatened her.

He jogged down the remaining stairs, then turned toward their new transport. Amid scrambling ground crews he spotted Top, standing in front of the B-2's nose gear, red-faced, earmuff-style comm set over his head, swinging a clipboard, yelling into his mic.

Chapter 14
Charged

Red had never seen a B-2 up close. Their geometric silhouettes had flown over him a few times, but on the ground they looked nothing like the aggressive, athletic shape of the Tupolev, an aircraft thirty years their elder. This B-2 was short, fat, and dumpy as a huge black boomerang. It had a snout only an engineer could love.

Beneath the wing, abreast the portside landing gear, stood at least fifteen crewmen beside what looked like eight torpedoes lying on waist-high stands. "Cloaks," Marksman said, pointing toward the black capsules.

Top snapped to attention, called the area up, and executed a perfect salute.

The colonel returned the show of respect. "At ease, first sergeant. We're at your disposal. Get us fit and loaded."

"Yes, sir!" The loadmaster's voice sent a chill across Red's shoulders, reminding him of an instructor for whom he held sincere disdain. It recalled his fiftieth push-up on a salt marsh after an early-morning ocean swim. The instructor was expounding on Red's questionable ancestry and insulting his hygiene in a thunderous voice, while delivering kicks to his midsection. The guy wasn't worried about conditioning. He was trying to wash him out.

"Yes, First Sergeant!" came a few automatic replies down the line, jerking him off the beach and dumping him back under the wing of the ugly B-2.

"Yep," drawled Marksman.

What had the first sergeant just said? Red needed to stay sharp. Must be the lack of sleep. Everyone was jogging toward the hangar, so he followed.

Inside was a mess line on white plastic tables. Crossing the threshold, Jim shouted, "Last hot chow for a while. You heard Top. Don't eat too much." An obvious glance at Crawler. "We load in ten minutes."

Experience said eat when you can, as fast as you can. Red downed a hot turkey sandwich in seconds, but only for the energy. Unexpected hunger like a bear's at spring thaw surged up. He grabbed a second, slurped the gravy from the plate, and shoved half the sandwich in his mouth as they jogged to the latrine. Last call before an op—eat, hit the head, gear check, go.

Sitting across from each other without privacy stalls, the team cracked coarse jokes. Their repertoire hadn't changed, which was strangely reassuring. Then it was back to the hangar, through yet another gear check and out onto the tarmac. The first sergeant directed each man to a specific cloak. One crewman stood at parade rest at the head of each. Red and Sergeant Lanyard were assigned an extra crewman since they'd never been dropped before.

Red ran his palms over the cloak's surface. The tell-tale carbon fiber ridges beneath a charcoal matte coating bristled against his flesh. It was like a fat torpedo, maybe ten feet long and two feet across. At what looked to be the tail it necked down, then bulged back out like a bubble. Against the narrow section were four neatly folded aerofoils, like knives in slots.

The first crewman pushed a small black circle on the top edge and it swung down. A handle. The cloak broke open along its length. The inside was empty. The skin was only a quarter-inch thick, maybe less. "You mean that's *all* that'll be between me and the outside?" Red asked.

"Yes, sir." The crewman smiled. "You guys are going in low, so these aren't pressurized." He held out a harness, like for a parachute, only minus the chute. Red slipped it on, maneuvering it around his gear, then lay flat in the cloak. The massive wing of the B-2 blocked the setting sun.

The crewman clipped the harness to a hard point above his head. "That'll hold you upright when you hit water."

Sergeant Crawler glanced up, sitting in the adjacent cloak adjusting his harness, then returned to the task at hand.

Marksman didn't let it go by, though. "Can you repeat that so I can hear? It's been a while. What happens when you hit the water?"

The crewman started to repeat his instructions. Crawler pointed and yelled, "Shut up or I'll unhook this death trap and shove it up your ass!"

The young airman first-class froze with his mouth open, staring.

Marksman pressed down on Velcro flaps, securing ammo clips inside chest pouches. "Give the kid a break, Crawler. Just a damn joke."

"And you!" Crawler wiggled his broad backside around to face Marksman. "You started it. If I wasn't strapped in this coffin I'd kick your ass, too, you little prick!"

Red opened his mouth, but Jim beat him to it. "Gentlemen!" His sharp tone made Top sound soft spoken. "Like herding cats with you idiots." Grins from the ground crew. "Grab-ass time's over. Marksman, quit poking your bodyguard. Sergeant Crawler, stop bragging about how you've got a pair. Grab those marbles, lay down, and shut the hell up!"

Jim could intimidate and motivate in the same breath. A natural, Red noted.

The crewman laid him flat, right arm down, left arm bent at the elbow, hand on chest. "That'll be most comfortable, sir. You can scratch and adjust most things." He fitted the cloak's earpiece and tucked the controller into Red's hand, then adjusted the harness so it didn't cut off circulation. "You'll be pulling ten G's hitting the water, for a couple seconds."

He reminded Red several times that his back and neck needed to be as straight as possible when the light in front of his face lit red. "That's when you're about to hit the water. You'll be coming in low on this one, so it'll come on almost immediately after you're dropped." Since the water wasn't deep, the drag chutes had been switched to a larger model. "Your terminal velocity will be around a hundred fifty miles per hour. That'll mean a softer landing, but a higher chance of being picked up on radar. The pilot will slow a little for the drop. Expect two opening shocks. The first when the drag chute deploys. The second when you hit the water."

Red frowned. "Won't they hear us hitting?"

The airman shook his head. "Been at some test drops. They're almost silent. The chutes are stealthy, the cloaks make a sound like doing a cannonball into a swimming pool. Unless some hadji's waiting for you, they won't know."

After they hit, the cloak would rise to about ten feet of the surface, break open, and he could swim away.

"What happens to the cloak after that?"

"Except for the skin, everything's off-the-shelf. It's like riding a GPS-guided bomb into the water. After you swim away, they'll fall to the bottom. There's a charge in the nose and tail, like a grenade. Large enough to do the job but small enough to only make bubbles at the surface. They self-destruct after a couple minutes."

His crewman glanced at the first sergeant, who was tapping his watch. The rest of the instructions were hasty, more like *Cloak Drops for Dummies*. After that both his crewmen stood next to the aerofoils and snapped to attention. Jim had said there'd be time to get him up to speed, but this would have to do.

Top scanned his crew and sounded off. "Arms check! No chambered rounds allowed on *my* aircraft. Once you're wet, charge your weapon to your bloody heart's content."

The crewmen instructed the team to remove clips and cycle bolts. The *tink* of ammo hitting tarmac came from everywhere, since Jim required every weapon to be charged once they deployed, going against everything Red had ever heard in a safety-minded military. "Long story," Jim would say, "but a kid in the Congo taught me the importance of always having a round chambered."

"Your sidearm," Crawler's crewman said. He growled, but cycled the slide and removed the chambered round. "Your other sidearm." Another snarl from Crawler. "Do you have any other weapons with chambered rounds?"

"Yeah, my dick's a flamethrower. You need me to—"

"Crawler!"

He glanced at Jim and pursed his lips, then lifted his leg, pulling a tiny 32 auto from inside the boot. He released the round from the chamber and handed it to his crewman.

Jim pointed at Top. "First sergeant, double-check his buoyancy vest. He's got fifty pounds of demo gear and already pushing reg weight."

All ammo and grenades were checked to ensure nothing could be dislodged during turbulence or opening shock. There'd be no bending down to pick up something that dropped. Crewmen fit the team with diving masks, clipped weapons to vests, and rechecked communications gear—all with the precision of a drill team, in under five minutes.

The first sergeant yelled, "Lockdown!" The world went dark as the door to Red's cloak hinged closed, like a coffin.

Red's eyes burned from lack of sleep. Or maybe it was the resinous stink coming off the cloak. He closed them tightly, attempting to make them water. He tried to rub them with his free hand, but only hit his diving mask.

It didn't take long for the air to grow thin and the walls to press in. He'd thought this might happen again. It had in SERE training last time, at the resistance phase, the "R" of the acronym. SERE prepared pilots and crew in case they were downed and captured. He'd been shoved into a crouch, head between his knees, then crammed into a crate and kept there for what seemed like hours. His spine had ached from the unfamiliar hunch. His legs had turned numb, a welcome relief from the throbbing. Once he'd been released, it took effort to stand, all the while taking blows from the guards.

Remembering the sheer misery of that crate helped the walls of the cloak recede. At least here he could move a little. A dim light glowed above his head as his eyes adjusted. It wasn't much, but helped.

The low purr of two munitions loaders reverberated outside, vibrations coming up through the cloak stand. Their tires scrubbed close, then pulled away. He'd be next.

His cloak jolted as the second loader picked it up and rolled underneath the bomb bay. Two men spoke nearby, only a mumble by the time the sound came through the cloak walls. More jolting and clacking, then a final *clunk* as the loader let go and he was suspended in place.

Here I am, inside a carbon egg, half paralyzed, suspended by a couple milspec pins in the belly of a strategic bomber.

He wriggled down a few inches to take the slack out of the harness. That might keep him from getting snatched unconscious when his cloak hit water. Nothing else left to do. He was done, for now. Everything since Lori had been taken was a blur. Recall, saying good-bye to the kids, op prep, the flight over. Even the sleepless night pacing the hangar was dreamlike. No, nightmarish. He was alone, but without any reassurance that he was getting closer to her recovery.

He wasn't getting out till he was underwater in Iran. It was like his first jump, kneeling in the door of the OV-10, one hand on the floor, the other on the jamb. That unnatural feeling of balancing on the threshold, looking past his nose down to blue-gray landscape from twelve thousand feet. The slipstream slapping his flight suit against his shin, the jump master slapping him on the ass, yelling *Go!* He had leaned into that terrible wind and arched hard. Then seen the shrinking prick waving back and had thought *I just screwed up*. Several hundred jumps later, he could almost sleep on the way down. It was okay. This was his first cloaked drop, and he hoped it would be his last.

Lori knows I'll be coming. Red couldn't disappoint her.

"*Comm check,*" came through the earpiece. Jim's voice. "*Carter is a go.*" Red pressed the button to confirm the same, along with several others. "*Crawler is a go,*" came through with a marked edge, followed by silence.

"*Marksman, you there?*" Jim asked. A comm clicked on, then the low buzz of snoring. Muffled laughter came through the resinous skin from all directions.

"*Comms are a go,*" Jim continued. "*We've got six hours till drop. I'll call fifteen minutes prior. Smoke 'em if you got 'em. Comm out.*" Jim's way of saying get sleep, if you can.

The engines wound higher, and the jet rolled with a lurch. Red sat up and smacked his head against a rib on the back of the cloak door. Resting back, he glanced down his nose and checked the time. They'd deplaned only thirty minutes prior. The carbon fibers in front of his nose made a frozen tapestry. The strands wove, interconnected to form a fabric stronger than any single material could be by itself. Jim knew how to build and hold a team together, each member coming at the same op from different directions, carrying divergent skills. That was his strength, but also the team's greatest weakness.

Am I a weakness? Will my shoulders ever be as broad as his?
Wheels up.

Chapter 15
Coffin

Red's cloak rocked and jolted inside the B-2. Instead of finding clear air, they were at low altitude, taking paths to avoid radar and hiding in the shadows of ground features. That was one of the ways the pilots hid the bomber. Even with its radar-absorbing skin and angular shapes, sophisticated equipment could still find it under the right circumstances.

Only the faintest whine from the engines came through the cloak shell. His crewman had said on the ground it only sounded like a distant airliner, even if flying a hundred feet off the deck. The low hum of something, maybe a hydraulic motor, was outside near his right thigh. From that same direction a high-pitched whine cut in with every move of the aircraft. Probably some sort of avionics controller.

"Won't they be able to see us, even with all your radar-absorbing crap?" Crawler had asked the pilot who'd been walking around the wing, doing his preflight.

"Nah," he'd said, expression masked by sunglasses.

"Don't they have mobile shit? I mean, someone told me you never know where their radar is gonna be."

"We'll see it. All of it. Where it goes. We'll stay low, in the shadows."

"What you mean you'll *see it*?"

A smile was his only explanation as the pilot had run his hand along the aileron, then turned his back and continued under the body.

Reacting to turbulence, the high-pitched whine of the controller was constant for a minute. Red had to adjust also. For the next few hours he had no control. It was strangely comforting, like being on a long bus ride, trusting the driver to get him there. The jostling of the cloak and whine from outside became rhythmical, then soothing. Like the rumba class he'd taken Lori to three anniversaries ago. He'd finally gotten it when he relaxed.

"Wakey-wakey," Jim barked through the comm. "Fifteen minutes to drop."

Red opened his eyes and looked down his nose. The face of his watch glowed 2043. When did he fall asleep? A nap was a good thing.

He tried to rub his eyes with his free hand, but hit his diving mask again. He pressed his comm button and said, "Red's a go." The rest of the team echoed in sequence, even Marksman.

"The navigator said we're on schedule for a drop at 2100Z, maybe a minute early. Rendezvous at 2115, kick in the doors at 2145, last train leaves the station at 2215."

Red had been reciting the time line in his sleep. He ran through the op plan again to ensure he was fully awake. "Two opening shocks," his crewman had said. "One when the drag chute opens and another when you hit water."

Jim cut in while Red was mentally kicking in the doors again. "The pilot just gave me our two-minute warning. Last call for alcohol. See you in the water. Comm out." Jim tried, but his humor always fell flat.

The next minute and a half stretched. A green LED he hadn't seen before glowed near Red's forehead. He grabbed the mouthpiece to a miniature scuba air supply and wrapped his lips around it. To maximize stealth they'd be released immediately once he heard the bay doors open—radar could reflect off all kinds of things inside the bomb bay. A small jolt, a couple of hydraulic pulsations, and the bay doors opened. Air pounded the outside of the cloak. A cool breeze came from a small vent above his head and chilled him down his spine. Several rapid clicks signaled the others being dropped.

Then he was weightless, released, following them down into blackness.

A loud *clack* sounded above his head as the drag chute released. The airfoils unfolded with the whine of electric servos directing him to his coordinates. No opening shock.

Shit! The drag chute should have deployed. Maybe a streamer? But that never happens to drag chutes. The green light changed to red, warning him he was about to hit water. He hoped it was sensory overload. Maybe he'd missed the opening shock.

He racked his chin into his chest, straightened his back, and braced for impact. He managed to cross himself, hitting his diving mask yet again. His crewman had said the cloak was designed to take it, even without a drag chute, but how deep was the sinkhole in the Pardis River?

Not very.

Red opened his eyes. Cold water splashing on the back of his neck snapped him conscious. His head hung and water was up to his belly. The dim light still glowed and his mouthpiece was dangling. Water was shooting in through the air vent above his head. That was normal, except his crewman had told him there'd only be a gallon or two in the cloak by the time it opened. He'd also said the cloak would be horizontal on the trip up, but now he was hanging in the harness at a steep downward angle.

His adrenaline came online as he remembered no opening shock. He checked his watch. 2105. They'd dropped a little early, so he'd been unconscious for six minutes. He put in his mouthpiece, trying to breathe slowly from the tiny air supply that was only supposed to be sufficient for a few breaths before surfacing. No opening shock meant he had hit at full speed. The high-velocity stream coming through the vent meant he was deep, lots of pressure, maybe stuck on the bottom. If it was soft, he could be completely buried. It didn't matter if he didn't get out soon—he'd drown or the cloak's self-destruction would bring everything to a merciful end.

No. He couldn't let Lori down. He couldn't leave the kids. He wasn't going to be the weak link.

He spat out the mouthpiece. The air in the cloak was low on oxygen, but he had to save the reserve. He inhaled staleness, grabbed his KA-BAR, and jabbed at what looked to be the opening catch above his head, close to where the crewman had pushed the handle to open the cloak. No one had mentioned a manual release. He'd be sure to put it in the suggestion box.

He pried, stabbed, and mauled the catch. It rewarded him with a loud *pop* as it released. He pressed against the door and the upper portion flexed away, shooting in more water. He let go and it resealed.

The rush of liquid brought it up to his shoulders and, with it, hope. The water was clear, meaning he may not have been completely buried in muck. There was either another catch holding the lower part of the door or he was stuck deep enough to prevent it from opening. He closed his eyes and reran the image of the interior from when the crewman first opened the cloak. There were two other catches, one in the middle around his waist and one below his feet.

He grabbed his sidearm from his vest and strained without success to contort himself to get his other hand up to where he could grab it. There wasn't enough room. One arm was up and the other down, just as the crewman had loaded him. The clearance in front of his belly was narrow, but should be enough to drop the weapon and catch it with the other hand. He snagged the rear sight on one of the cloak's interior ribs and pushed up, charging the weapon, then dropped it toward his other hand below. He must have missed completely, but then felt it brush his leg. He pinned it against the cloak with his knee and reached down, feeling the end of the silencer pointed at his gut. He turned it around and grasped the butt.

The water was up to his neck.

He took a breath and plunged his head under, searching for the second catch. His eyes adjusted and he saw it. Time to find out how good Gunny was. Would his sidearm work underwater? The barrels of some weapons exploded if fired while submerged, unable to force out the extra weight of the water. His might not since it was loaded with subsonic tacs, which were low power to keep their slugs slow and quiet. He aimed and squeezed. It fired and after the bubbles cleared the mangled catch was retracted like the first.

He tipped his head up, lips barely above water, and shoved in his mouthpiece. Fresh air filled his lungs. His body ached for more, but he held it and plunged his head underwater again. He strained to see around his feet but it was no use. The dim light didn't make it that far. He scraped the sight of the sidearm against the cloak's skin, trying to find another rib that could recharge it manually. Firing underwater meant it probably didn't cycle. After some frantic scraping, he moved his feet out of the way, pointed where he remembered seeing the lower catch, and squeezed the trigger. A pressure wave washed over him as the weapon fired again. He owed Gunny big-time.

The shot illuminated the catch like a camera flash, long enough to let him see he'd missed. He waited for bubbles to clear and squeezed again. His third round pierced his target. He didn't know if the shot retracted the catch but he didn't have time for a fourth.

The water was pressing hard, his ears almost imploding. With all the air bubbling out of the cloak, the water pressure inside was becoming the same as the pressure outside. He inhaled again to equalize, but it was only a half-breath. That was all that was left. The deeper you go, the faster your air is used up. He blew a snort though his nose and air squeezed into his ears, equalizing them.

He pressed hard against the door. The bottom held fast, but the top flexed out several inches—not enough. He used the extra clearance to maneuver his lower arm free and took aim at the upper hinge. Two shots shattered it. The dim light still glowed above him. Thank God for milspec lights. He emptied the rest of the clip across the midsection of the door, perforating it. He pushed again and it snapped in two, folding down against the bottom of the river, which was halfway up the length of the cloak.

He fought the haze in his mind and unclipped the harness. His body wanted to inhale anything, even water. Rushing to the surface would explode his lungs, even if they were only half full. He'd been trained on this, but had no depth gauge and no air. His body rose quickly because of the buoyancy vest. He exhaled, wrapped his lips around the vest's dump valve, and sucked a breath, welcoming the vinyl-tasting gas. He wanted more but held it, then blew through his nose. Gauging from the bubbles, he was still ascending too quickly. He stuck out his arms and legs and tried to tread water in reverse while extending his neck and exhaling what little air he had left to prevent an embolism.

He saw the light of the surface high above him, reminding him of the flickering orange glow of his parents' fireplace. Lori was holding Nathan on her lap in front of it. He was unwrapping that glow-in-the-dark sword, his favorite birthday present last year. Red had to spank him when he whacked Penny's shins with it. He looked over Lori's shoulder to the picture on the glossy walnut mantel of his grandfather and the B-17. *Am I going to make it?* "You've got no choice," came his father's voice.

He inhaled another quick breath from the vest, exhaling back into it. With each one the stale air was lower on oxygen. He stretched his neck again. The light of the surface seemed only an arm's reach now. The air escaping his windpipe was familiar from training, though his lungs burned like never before. He broke the surface and gulped. The deep blue of the starlit river rushed into view—he'd been seeing in black-and-white. After a couple more breaths, he dry-heaved till his stomach cramped.

He laid his head back against his buoyancy vest and blinked hard. Orion's club was directly overhead. One more breath, then his watch. 2112. He turned toward the rendezvous point. With his first stroke he realized he was still holding his sidearm. His knife must be with the cloak. He holstered the pistol, feeling his belly and finding the M4 was still clipped in.

That disdainful sergeant kicking his ribs was the same one that had his class practice underwater escapes and emergency surfacing until they were literally blue in the face. Maybe the bastard hadn't been trying to wash him out after all.

Chapter 16
Doors

Even with the drag chute malfunction, Red had hit on target. The rendezvous point was five hundred yards south. He needed to hump to make it in time. As he caught up, he glimpsed the rest of the team in the water near the base of large boulders against the bank. It was 2118Z, three minutes after they should have left. He swam next to Jim in the shallow water and wheezed. Ripples from his approach slapped the slimy rocks. Waving algae hair grew at water level, a blue-green mane in the moonlight.

Jim leaned to his ear, cupping his hand around it. "You okay?"

"Ran into some trouble," he gasped, trying to whisper. "But I'm a go."

"Carter saw you surface. We've got to make up the time. Strap it up. We're headed out."

Jim raised a hand and motioned as if pumping a shotgun. The team charged their weapons. Red reloaded his empty sidearm with a fresh clip of subsonic tacs. The operators followed at twenty-foot intervals. The current ran with them slowly but Jim set a fast pace.

The Pardis was scarcely wide enough for a large boat. Sandy banks rose twenty feet high on either side. Boulders perched on the river bends like sentries cast sharp moonlight shadows on the glassy surface. A few shacks silhouetted against the night sky interrupted the otherwise bare banks. No evidence of fishing boats in sight. Not even rotting carcasses of old vessels on the shoreline. Around a bend, barges heaped with sand angled against the dunes. The water smelled musty and stung his nose like sulfur. He pushed the distraction from his mind.

Only now did the cold press into his consciousness, robbing the heat from his chest and legs as he pushed to keep pace. Carter was ahead, behind Jim, but had started to lag. Soon the detective was abreast and breathing heavily. Red grabbed his hand and put it on his own load-bearing vest, then pressed ahead with powerful strokes, Carter in tow. Within a minute Sergeant Lanyard came from behind and the two shared the load. A few days ago Carter had been a detective working for the sheriff's office. Today he'd been dropped from a B-2 into a cold river under a cloud-spotted night sky, outside Tehran. He hadn't had time to condition. Roles had changed for all of them.

Jim checked his watch, then gave one last stroke, reaching to steady himself against a pole at the bottom of the warehouse pier. The water was up to his neck, but he kept his weapon high to protect it from stirred-up grit. He smelled the mucky bottom, rotting leaves, the scent kicked up by one of the team upstream. Mud molded around his feet as he turned and faced them coming in. The cold water energized him now, but he'd be shivering within a few minutes of taking up position, lying prone atop a pile of boulders.

Crawler drew in, looking winded but mean as ever. Marksman had his arms crossed over his buoyancy vest with his precious M14 resting atop. His grin was tight, hiding his teeth. He was the only other person beside the doctor who habitually smiled during an op. Everyone gave a thumbs-up.

Jim patted Carter's shoulder, and each pair helped the other stow water gear on their backs. No traces could be left. Dry goggles were fitted, then comm gear and night vision. It didn't matter if they got a little wet at this point.

The pier hovered above like a thunderhead. Jim scaled an algae-slick ladder to its deck, careful not to slip on the green slime. He peered over the edge, then waited, giving time for anyone who might be expecting them. Sometimes it was movement. Sometimes it was a careless cough. Moonlight peered through spotty clouds, enough not to need night vision, so he switched to thermal. After several minutes he mounted the pier and sprinted to the shore. He inched his head above the bank and waited again. *Still nothing.* He signaled to Carter, who climbed onto the pier and joined him. Carter provided cover while Jim moved to point Victor, the rock pile. He climbed the sharp edges of the boulders, his fingers gripping the half cylinder drill holes that remained after they'd been dynamited from the quarry.

At the top, Jim waited again. He scanned down a neighboring service road as far as he could. Twenty miles outside Tehran, nothing was moving this time of night. Orange gravel paved the lot outside the warehouse. It stretched for thirty clear and open yards. It was there his team would be most exposed. The wind was cold and shadows from high clouds flew across the land, flashing ambient light from darkness to dusk every few seconds.

All was as expected. Even the wooden pallets were in the same positions from the satellite photos, now a day old. The mucky fumes of the river wafted upwards, bringing an eerie warmth to his face. Still nothing. He gave Carter the all clear, which started the next chain of events, each step further outside his control. He clenched his jaw and looked back to the yard. The Pardis was calm, but from here on the op would be like navigating white water. Jim's control was slight. All he could do was react to the river. It set the tempo. Whether they capsized or not, they weren't getting off till the mission was complete.

Carter ran to the rock pile and clawed his way up. He topped it, but his breathing was too loud. Red sprinted across the lot to the warehouse's north side. At the corner of the warehouse he looked back. Jim scanned west one last time, then gave the all clear. Red moved around the corner and held, joined by Sergeant Lanyard.

Marksman made it to the warehouse then slid away to the far opposite corner. He peered around it, held up his hand, and made a sign like *hang ten*. *Obstruction*. A cloud blew in and cast a shadow, so Jim yanked down night-vision goggles from the mount on his helmet, positioning them over his eyes. Marksman glowed green, head low, peering around the corner. He turned toward Crawler and waved in a *come*, then sprinted to the neighboring building. Crawler galloped after him, running like a noseguard, slow and clunky, weighed down by gear. But his most valuable asset was his bodyguard's attitude. Crawler stood behind a row of wooden crates, leaned an elbow on top of one and aimed his weapon at the warehouse. Marksman scaled a service ladder and swung himself onto the flat roof without a sound. He unfolded his weapon's bipod and rested it atop a low wall.

Captain Richards and Dr. Ali were near Red on the opposite side of the building. All was a go. Jim pushed up his night vision. The clouds had passed. A bat fluttered across the yard and darted under a light pole, then out of its glow, into the darkness on the south side of the building. The one side no one had eyes on yet.

Red squatted in the dirty orange gravel. He shifted his weight and dust stirred over his boots. Water ran out the drain holes above the soles. He checked his watch. Seven minutes till showtime.

He stalked to the corner and peered around to the south side. An unpaved service road ran a hundred feet from it. It was smooth, well dressed, made from the same orange gravel. Dust stung his nose and he stifled a sneeze. *Better than the sulfur odor of the Pardis.* He squinted, looking down the road in each direction. Two ghostly images of the Israelis' white cargo vans—their exfil plan— were on the opposite side of the road, well outside the glow of the light pole that Lanyard was about to darken. He flipped down his night-vision optics and rescanned, then flipped the switch to thermal and did it again. All clear.

The road was silent. He squatted and leaned against the warehouse. He sensed Lori. Like a salmon scenting its stream, or a carrier pigeon homing in on its path, he was being drawn inside. *Yeah, she was there, somewhere.*

He glanced at Jim. The colonel held up a fist and pumped down. Move out.

Red pointed Lanyard to the light pole. He ran to its base, slung his weapon and reached down to his boots. He pulled what looked like a bootstrap and two slender spikes popped out from under the toes. Using the spikes and a wide belt, he shot up the pole like a lumberjack.

Lanyard had shown Red the Communications Suppression System (CSS) back on the Tupolev. Just a small black box with a six-foot wire dangling as an antenna, it weighed at least eight pounds, mostly from the lithium batteries. He'd said everything inside melted down when the batteries ran out in case they had to leave it behind.

Lanyard kept the transformer at a safe distance, reached behind him, and grabbed the CSS off his belt. He strapped it to a bracket and hung the antenna close to the pole, then signaled *OK*. The little green light was on. He leaned away from the high-voltage wire going into the transformer and placed wire cutters on the lower-voltage line running to the building. At 2144Z Red held up two fingers and snipped them together like scissors. Lanyard cut the power and was at the bottom of the pole in seconds.

Nothing happened. No backup generators came on and no noises sounded from inside. They'd been told power outages here were common. Maybe no one cared.

Red did a last check of the south side. He signaled *all clear* and Jim returned another fist pump. *Showtime.*

Red turned the corner and sprinted to the first door, a hundred feet away. Running was euphoric; he felt like a racehorse whose gate had finally flown open. He glanced back at Lanyard. *Kid better keep up.*

Lanyard heard gravel slip under the major's boots. He turned, but only a low cloud of dust floated where Major Harmon had been kneeling. *Shit.* He strained to catch up but Harmon was already at a full sprint, around the corner, thirty feet ahead. It was all he could do to keep the distance from widening.

This freak better not go off half-cocked.

The major stopped at their door, halfway down the long side of the warehouse. He raised his foot to it as if to breach the opening, but then dropped it and gripped the handle. It twisted. He stood to the far side, pushed the door open, and paused. Nothing.

Lanyard made it to the near side and pulled down his night vision over an eye. The major signaled a *follow me*, then stooped low and stepped inside, staying to the far edge of the opening. Nothing moved outside and no sounds came from within. Lanyard spun and followed the major inside, closing the door to preserve their night vision. The ceiling had six huge skylights, so he switched to thermal.

Two loud pops echoed. He pointed his weapon toward them. A third brought an infusion of light reflected off the ceiling. It lasted a few seconds and then swept away. The other door must have been locked.

The major nodded and both thumbed their comms. "E1's in. All clear." E2 confirmed the same along with Marksman and the colonel. The major explained the layout to the rest of the team. "It's split down the middle. West side is open storage. Crates and high shelving obscure most of the view. Stuff is everywhere, crates open, in the aisles. Lots of small arms. Ammo. Two troop transports in the middle. East side is walled off. Probably offices. It's got an open mezzanine above. Can't see anything up there. Requesting E1 and E2 clear west side of warehouse, then proceed through the offices."

"Affirmative," came the colonel's reply. "E1 and E2 clear west. Check in before entering east."

Marksman's voice was steady, but held an edge. "East yard is obscured by crates and all kinds of crap. Suggest any hostiles be herded out the north. I've got a clear line of fire there."

The major stooped and moved up the main corridor that divided the building. Lanyard followed, sweeping the aim of his weapon down the aisles as they passed and keeping an eye on the mezzanine. The high ground. Across from it were aisles of disorganized storage, spilling into the walkway. There were rocket boxes, mortars, and entire crates of ammo. Spare axles, tires, and brake sets took up an entire aisle.

Eyes up, the major signaled.

No shit. There were no skylights over the mezzanine, but thermal showed nothing.

All appeared a typical warehouse for a low-class military outfit. He'd seen worse in Afghanistan. Rockets, grenades, and anything else that could go *bang* should be in a special fire-protected portion of the building. Even better, a separate structure altogether, with blast walls to direct an explosion upward. Though disorganized, it was well funded, and certainly shouldn't have been unlocked. Too big of a mistake to be overlooked.

They did a quick sweep, only glancing down the aisles. The major hadn't said anything about clearing the mezzanine before going into the offices. Probably good because their footsteps above might give away their presence. All was quiet. Too quiet.

Lanyard walked backwards, keeping a watch on their six, but had to glance behind to ensure the major was still there. The only thing that gave him away was the water pumping out of his wet boots. Lanyard couldn't even hear him breathe, like a ghost. Harmon was a nutcase, but had skills. A soft mover. When they'd done their gear check, he had pieces of felt sewn in his vest between the ammo clips so they wouldn't rub. It was a brand-new vest, so he must've done it last night while everyone else had been asleep. At dinner, he'd wrapped his rifle sling clips with black tape to keep them from rattling.

Three minutes of careful moving and they reached the middle of the warehouse. Lanyard peered down the aisle. At the end was the rusted metal door where E2 had entered, two bullet holes above the handle looking like eyes on a smiley face. "South half clear," the major whispered into his comm.

"North half clear," came the captain's reply.

A shrill cry rang from the mezzanine, the sound echoing from the metal walls. Lanyard scanned it frantically. An AK-47 opened fire from the far side, pointed down at the other team. Muzzle blasts from a second shooter boomed, coming from above the doors they'd entered. Lanyard squeezed a three-shot burst in that direction when a strafing run blew across his belly. The projectiles hit the SAPI plates with a loud *tunk tunk*. Did they make it through? Lanyard tried to inhale but nothing would come, like the time that Army scum had kneed him in the balls at Fort Bragg. An old instructor's warning, *Shock can deceive you*, shot through his mind, but he forced it out. Duty first. He was going to bring the shooter down, even if it was with his last breath. He knelt behind a crate, took aim at the muzzle flashes pulsating in his thermal scope, and squeezed several more bursts. The fire kept coming.

The major returned shots behind him. Both their weapons' only sound came from the sliding bolt and spent brass hitting the floor.

He gulped for air and finally got some. "I'm hit," he squawked.

The major squeezed off a few more rounds, then spun and grabbed Lanyard's vest, yanking him down one of the aisles. He shoved him against a crate and thrust his hand under his Kevlar. "Didn't go through."

Lanyard gasped for air.

The major leaned to his ear. "Hit anywhere else?"

"No. Just the gut, I think," he wheezed.

"Your vest did its job. Maybe got a cracked rib. First time shot?"

"Yeah."

"Pissed off yet?"

"Gettin' there."

Harmon slapped him across the face with an open hand. It stung almost as bad as getting hit.

"What the hell was that for?"

"Tradition, first time shot." He slapped him again, this time harder, smiling.

Lanyard felt for his sidearm. "And that one?"

"You didn't look pissed. Now you'll be okay."

The major wasn't right in the head. Maybe he'd cracked under the fire. Before he could react, the major yanked Lanyard's KA-BAR, turned, and slashed across a pistol that suddenly protruded around the corner of the aisle. The hand dropped to the floor, finger still on the trigger. He pulled the screaming victim around the corner and knifed him through the throat, cranking the KA-BAR sideways to sever the spinal column. The knife was back in his sheath before the corpse hit the ground.

The major glanced back, eyes squinting. "Good edge on that. Just the closest thing I could grab. Mine's in my cloak. Now strap it up. Rearm with Det ammo and cover me."

Lanyard swallowed hard. *Gladly.*

He was in a different league now. He'd talked with a friend that was drafted in the fourth round by the Denver Broncos. He'd said pro ball was at an entirely different level than his Division 1 Hokies, like learning a whole new game. Like him, Lanyard was going to have to step up the pace.

He laid down fire using crates and shelving for cover. The pounding intensity of Det ammo muffled the gunfire coming from the enemy shooters. A roaring came from behind as Richards and Ali opened up as well. In his periphery, a ghostly figure ducked low behind a stack of tires. Neither team had clear shots. The major ran farther down the aisle. Where was he going? The only thing they could do from here was to keep the shooters' heads down. They needed to reposition.

Lanyard squeezed off another three-shot burst, the thunderous rhythm scattering pieces of cinderblock next to the tire stack.

The magazine release stuck. Red pushed till it dug into his thumb. It let go and he racked in a fresh one of Det ammo. With everyone's weapons clamoring away the silent loads were no longer needed. He peered around the corner of the aisle, trying to make out either shooter. Both were well covered. Thermal highlighted the arm of the one who'd hit Lanyard. The edge of his sleeve stuck out behind a milling machine. There was no way to lob a grenade that far, not accurately, and they didn't have launchers. It couldn't be long before others showed up on the mezzanine and routed them out, down the center of the aisle.

He commed in. *"Two shooters on the mezzanine. E1 is covered."* Captain Richards confirmed the same, between bursts.

Red looked down the center aisle but there was no way to get to the mezzanine stairs without exposing himself. Thermal showed the yellow glow of a rifle barrel coming up from behind the milling machine. He pulled back and shots ricocheted off the shelving above. He looked up to where they hit, then to the ceiling. Jim hadn't ordered them to pull out, not yet. Even though there were only two shooters waiting, the ambush would validate his fears about Mossad having a security leak. If so, they'd need any remaining time to exit before reinforcements showed up. Not much time.

Red closed his eyes for a split second. There it was again. He felt her close. *Lori was in the building.* The burnt aroma of spent gunpowder hung in the air like it had last Fourth of July when he'd held Penny on his shoulders underneath the fireworks show. A thin cloud of it floated atop an orange shelving unit twenty-five feet up. He slung his rifle, cinched it tight, then ran farther down the aisle and climbed up a metal post using the shelving as steps. At the top was a single flat bar running toward the mezzanine, but at the end was a twenty-foot aisle gap.

Lanyard's fire kept the shooters' heads down. The boisterous rhythm of Det ammo was a welcome contrast to the hushed *plinking* of the subsonics. In thermal, the white-hot rounds looked almost like tracers after they cut through the crates, blocks, and machinery the shooters were using for cover. A ricochet twanged, piercing the metal roof, smelling like a hot toaster oven.

"The op is off," Jim ordered through the comm. "Move to point Echo for pickup."

Red was atop the flat bar accelerating to a full sprint like a runner after the starting pistol. At the end of the bar he threw himself across the aisle toward the mezzanine, arms extended. Near the middle he grabbed a thick electrical conduit and, using it like a gymnast's high bar, swung his body forward. His trajectory took him on an awkward backflip, but he landed upright on the mezzanine, in an open line between the shooters. Pain shot through his ankles.

From a dark corner, a boy in olive green fatigues braced against his AK-47, firing down at E-2. His tight curly hair vibrated and his teeth shone white in a grin, or maybe pain. Red pulled his sidearm as he tucked his shoulder and rolled forward, stopping in a crouch. Bullets hit behind him. He'd counted on the shooters holding fire since they'd be facing each other. Instead, shots hit cinderblock in front of the boy. A little more luck and Red wouldn't have even had to kill him. The kid startled at the fire and turned. Red dropped him with a double tap, though only one was needed, hitting him square above the white grin.

He tucked his shoulder and rolled again, this time coming up to bear on the other. Three more shots whipped behind him. Moonlight glinted from the shooter's tall forehead as he swung his rifle and sprayed rounds haphazardly. Red double-tapped him through the brow and neck. The bullets continued undaunted on their course through the wall of the building, leaving twin rays of dust-refracted moonlight as the body dropped to the floor.

Red made his third roll, this time behind cover, anticipating fire from another shooter, but none came. He switched to night vision, then back to thermal. There were stacks of tires, a press brake, and other pieces of metalworking equipment, but everything looked cold.

It had been only a few seconds since Jim's order. Maybe Red could change his mind. He commed in, "Both hostiles down. Request permission to clear the mezzanine and proceed below."

"No activity here," came Marksman's voice.

"The op is off. I'm calling it in now. Move to point Echo."

Red shot to his feet and started clearing the mezzanine, checking behind the equipment and stacks of tires. Beyond everything he feared he might find Lori. She was in the bunker, he hoped, if there was a bunker after all. Maybe they'd only broken a few bones. She'd be walking again in a couple months. *God, let her be alive.* He came around a corner of a crate and put a three-shot burst into what ended up being a car seat with a parking brake sticking up next to it. He shook his head. *I've got to tighten up.*

The ground vibrated and he swung his rifle toward the stairs. Lanyard peered over the edge of the floor and Red waved him up.

His barrel glowed like a neon sign in thermal. Lanyard made a circling motion with his finger and pointed to the door where they'd come in.

Red shook his head.

Lanyard nodded, but turned toward the stairs. It was hard to tell someone's expression when only one eye was visible—the other was covered by night-vision gear. Lanyard was looking at the gaunt figure of the boy, lying sideways atop a white metal footlocker. He couldn't have been more than seventeen. "Good shooting," he mouthed, then lowered his rifle and looked away.

Chapter 17
Clearing

Jim made a quick scan down the frontage road in both directions from atop the rock pile. *Still empty.* The vans waiting to pick them up courtesy of Mossad were barely in view, tucked close to a wooden fence and partially hidden by a holly tree. The wind had picked up a bit, almost balmy against his face. He shouldn't be warm, not now, wet, in the breeze. The firefight had been muffled by the brick and metal walls, but not completely. The warehouse was relatively secluded, and the wind helped silence the shots.

The shooters had been waiting. Someone had been tipped off. But why only two? They must be trying to draw them in, setting an ambush. If his team was captured, it would be hell. If they were lucky, the Iranians would just kill them. Maybe they'd leak it to the press, maybe not. Maybe the team would be buried in a common grave and the entire thing denied. Where were the other soldiers, the main attack?

He pointed to Carter, then back across the road. Carter nodded. Jim turned and crouched with his sat phone to his ear, whispering. His orders had been clear, stopping short of the Spartan motto *With your shield or on it.* Higher was watching from a Predator drone circling three miles above, below the clouds, courtesy of the CIA and the Air Force. He didn't want to send out any radio waves, but needed to get their exit plan in motion.

A click in the speaker meant they picked up the line in the control center, this time at Langley. He pictured a bunch of suits drinking black coffee, watching good men risk their lives on flat screens, and his stomach soured. He didn't wait for a greeting. "We're pulling out. Have the—"

"Negative." Jim didn't recognize the voice, but English was the speaker's second language.

"I'm not asking permission. We're pulling out."

"Your orders are clear, colonel. All your men are still alive. You've got assets to recover."

"Rules of engagement. I call the shots in the field. I'm pulling out."

"We're not picking you up till it's done."

"Who the hell—"

"Jim, do it," came Admiral Javlek's stern voice. He was vice chair of the JCS, the one who had given a thumbs-up to the op and dozens prior, his only contact with Higher. "We'll explain later. Plug this security key into your locator: uniform, mike, niner, foxtrot, yankee. You'll get two extra tags. They're your target. If it was an ambush, they wouldn't be there."

Javlek spoke for another minute, then Jim slapped the phone shut. Carter turned toward the noise and Jim clenched his jaw, looking away toward Marksman's position. That was his first BTO, a *black tie override*. Something wasn't right. Javlek had never pulled one before. It was Mossad. They were worse than the Mafia. BTOs only came up when intel sources insisted. The excuse was in case the team was captured. *You can't leak what you don't know.*

If they ran into a heavy ambush that would confirm a leak, at which point he couldn't use Mossad's vans for their getaway. They might have to find a hole to hide in until he put together another exfil. The stench from the river blew across the rock pile. Jim grimaced, lifting his head. He pulled down his night vision and zoomed it out as far as it would go, scanning the service road. Still nothing was moving.

Red braced the stock of his M4 against his other shoulder, angling it around a bale of burlap bags. His boots had stopped squishing. He carefully placed his steps. A few empty cans were cemented in place by a petrified pool of blue paint on the floor. It was the last pile on the mezzanine he had to clear. No one other than the dead shooters had been waiting for them.

He turned and headed back toward the stairs, past a picnic table with a rusty engine block stacked on top. Thick dust covered everything except the narrow aisle between piles of junk. He stifled another sneeze. It was good he hadn't found Lori up here. He signaled Lanyard to head toward the stairs.

Jim commed in, "On your locator type security key uniform, mike, niner, foxtrot, yankee."

Red crouched behind a stack of tires and leaned over the small screen, fingering in the security key. Sweat dropped from his nose onto the display, or maybe it was still wetness from the Pardis. Lanyard kneeled beside him, but kept his head up. *I'll tell him how good he did later, keeping the shooters occupied while I was on the shelving.* The screen flashed and two extra tags appeared, but they weren't identified. They glowed green, so they were validated, meaning they weren't tag ghosts. Still, the locator didn't say who they were.

"These are our targets," Jim said. "We don't know their identity, but Lori is with them. Take them alive. We may be fighting our own kind. The building has no power and the CSS is making sure no radio gets out, so we're still covert as best we know. We've lost four minutes. Get moving."

When Red had joined the Det, the surgeon had showed him the tag before he put him under and implanted it deep into his right buttock. It had looked like a piece of aluminum foil, but more polished, half the size of a stamp. He'd asked their CIA liaison about it, and the only thing he'd said was that it didn't give out any signal. Something about reflecting a band of light that no one knew about. He hoped it didn't give him cancer. Only U.S. assets were supposed to have the technology.

The middle stair down from the mezzanine flexed when he stepped on it, as if it were going to give way. The enhanced auditory gear amplified the rubbing of Lanyard's ballistic vest behind him. It was how he heard the soldier whose hand he'd sliced off earlier before he came around the corner of the aisle. Yet it hadn't amplified the firefight.

"*Mezzanine clear,*" Red commed in.

"*Warehouse clear,*" came from Captain Richards.

Yeah, as clear as it could be in a hurried sweep. Hostiles could still be anywhere. Red's feet touched the warehouse floor and the cold came through the boot soles. At the far end of the aisle Captain Richards and Dr. Ali stood beside a door leading into the offices.

The foot of the dead boy stuck out from under the mezzanine handrail above their heads.

Red pointed to Richards and then to another door underneath the stairs, pumping a fist in a *breach* signal.

The offices were going to be dark, so he switched back to night vision, tapping the button so that Lanyard could see. Thermal was good to highlight warm bodies, but wasn't as good to see your way around. Lanyard had said they were getting new gear next month that combined the two somehow.

Clearing doors was like signing your name. It was learned by rote, but each time looked different. The occupants always had the upper hand. They could wait for the door to open and ambush. Lanyard stood on the side with the handle and Red to the other. Lanyard pushed it open a few inches and they waited to ensure no fire erupted. Red stooped low and led through with his weapon, sweeping the sides and down a long dark corridor. No movement.

The hall looked like it ran to the other end of the building, but it was difficult to see that far. Only the slightest green glow came from that end. Red kept his breathing slow, then started down. There were offices, storage, even a mailroom. They cleared each in turn. He paused in one that had a global map taped on the wall with colored dots pinned to it. The most heavily marked were England, Saudi Arabia, Iran, and the U.S. There was a separate map for Israel, but only a few dots on it. He made sure his video camera got it. All was clean, even lemon scented, but empty and with a light coat of dust. His soles squeaked on the waxed cement floor.

Halfway down the hall he could see it ran all the way to the end of the building. After they cleared the last room Lanyard was at point to clear around the corner. Footsteps came from the other end where they'd first entered and Red turned back. His night vision made out two figures. He switched to thermal and let out a long breath. It was Marksman and Ali.

He raised his free hand to his ear to comm in with an update when he smelled garlic and strong body odor. Red reached to grab Lanyard, but Lanyard had already committed, breaking the plane of the corner with his weapon. Huge arms came down and clamped on it, jerking it away like a dog shaking a squirrel. Lanyard released it, firing a three-shot burst in the process, then ducked as a pistol shot over his head. Lanyard pushed the pistol upward and several more rounds went into the ceiling. He spun and kicked, quick and light, like a boxer on a speed bag. A tall, muscular man with thick eyebrows and close-cropped beard wearing fatigues with a triangular patch on his shoulder fell to the floor, making no attempt to catch himself. His head smacked the concrete, eyes open. Maybe he was unconscious, but blood started to pool under his temple. Red glanced at Lanyard's boots. The climbing spikes were still protruding from his toes.

"Gotta get me some of those," Red whispered as he stepped over the body, angling his weapon around the corner. He held up a single finger. Why was this guy alone? Ahead was another long hallway with a faint light reflecting off the floor at the end. Red pressed the comm button on his earpiece. "South hallway clear."

"West hallway clear," said Captain Richards.

"Hurry up," Jim said. "No movement out here, but we can hear your fire."

Red's locator said they should be right on top of the tags. They had to be below because the mezzanine above was already clear. Probably in the bunker. Both teams headed north and Ali was the one who found the entrance. It was under the outside door that had Marksman's crosshairs fixed on it. The bottom few inches was rusted off and cast a glow of faint moonlight along the floor.

The stairs down to the bunker were steel, zigzagging back and forth in an open stairway like a hotel fire escape. He grasped the handrail and peered down, cutting himself on a rusty broken weld. He shook the blood to the floor. Even with his night vision the hole was dark, like trying to see into a tomb. He pointed to Captain Richards, then his eyes, then pointed down both ends of the hallway. Richards nodded.

Red started the descent, placing silent steps so as to maintain tactical advantage. If they got into trouble, Richards and Ali were upstairs while Crawler was outside the door. He reached up and turned the power on his comm up a notch, just in case the earth around him tried to silence it. The drying blood stuck his hand to the grip of his M4, as if it were a part of him. The deeper he went, the faster his descent, as if he was being pulled down by an unseen heaviness.

Three flights and he hit the bottom. It smelled with a clay dankness, same as the Pardis River. A half inch of water pooled on the floor. A sump pump stood silently in the corner. Electricity had been off for fifteen minutes now.

A steel blast door was inset into a thick concrete wall. Most bunkers were designed with only one entrance and an air ventilation system somewhere in the back that could double as an emergency escape. A rat scurried across Red's boot, unalarmed by the visitors.

This was the place.

Red's locator glowed dimly, highlighting two tags thirty feet away, somewhere behind the door. He moved forward, careful not to splash water, and tried the rusty handle. *Locked.* There could be one or even two more of them in series. He pointed to Lanyard, then the hinges. Lanyard handed his weapon to him and unclipped his tactical pack.

The door had to be removed all at once. If not, they'd just be creating a hole through which someone could drop a grenade. Lanyard padded a heat charge, a combination of thermite and plastic explosive, around the hinges and put another thick ribbon around the handle. The door was designed to withstand explosive pressures, but the hinges were exposed. A heat charge wouldn't make a big bang, but could melt through half-inch plate steel. He pushed in the detonators, grabbed his weapon back from Red, and the two stood against the concrete wall, one on either side. If he'd used straight C4 they'd have to remotely detonate, but with heat charges the concussion would be tolerable.

Red squatted in a fetal position with his back to the door, fingers in his ears, eyes shut, knees pressing hard against his goggles.

Lanyard commed, "Fire in the hole in five, four."

The pressure wave shoved Red forward and his head smacked the concrete wall. Heat flashed on the back of his neck. He spun around into a blue haze that clung to the ceiling, glowing orange from underneath. The door was upright with liquid-hot metal dripping where the hinges and handle used to be. He clutched a metal rib and pulled back. It crashed to the floor, thundering so loudly it rattled his chest. He was on top before it settled. A dab of liquid metal splashed onto his vest and the chemical scent of burning Kevlar jointed the pungent mixture of welding fumes and sulfur. Lanyard was right behind him. A cloud of opaque blue smoke filled the doorframe. Red charged through and stopped, terrified at what he saw.

Chapter 18
Carter

Beyond the first blast door was another, already open to the bunker. The blue smoke from the heat charge stung Red's nose like when he'd cut through the brake line of a '72 Plymouth Fury while learning to weld in shop class. The bunker was about thirty feet square, lined with black metal shelving. Two matching metal doors stood closed on the far end. Bare cement walls and ceiling were streaked with brown water stains. The room smelled like piss. A single fluorescent light, presumably on battery power, cast a dim glow.

Directly under it was Lori. Her hair was knotted and her pink pajamas hung stiffly, but she wasn't bruised or bloody. Her wrists lay handcuffed on her lap. *She was alive.* Her eyes were inset deeply, darkened in their sockets. She glanced at Red, smiled faintly, but then returned her stare to the floor.

A man in gray slacks and a white oxford shirt stood behind her with an automatic pistol to her head. He was Amin. Red had never heard other names, just Amin. He was the one who had tortured him six years ago and put an end to his career at the Det. With medium build, olive skin, and dark-brown eyes set close together, he had shiny black hair, neatly cut short; no beard or mustache. He was VEVAK, a spy, or maybe both.

Two Iranian infantrymen stood guard to the side, AK-47s trained on Red and Lanyard. A single star on the collar indicated one was a lieutenant. Several chevrons and rockers on the other meant a high-ranking noncommissioned officer, maybe master sergeant. The lieutenant jerked the aim of his weapon between Red and Lanyard, but the master sergeant held steady on Red. A purple scar crossed his cheek pointing upwards, as if smiling.

Who were the tags? Were they in the other rooms? They could go to hell. The red dot from his laser sight searched for Amin's head, but the torture master ducked behind Lori.

"Drop them or I'll shoot the girl!" he said with an accent from Massachusetts. "If you do anything other than what I say, I'll shoot the girl! If you move too quickly, I'll shoot her."

Red weighed his choices. If he shot Amin, the guards would get him, but Lori probably wouldn't make it. He could take out the guards and count on his vest to protect him, but Amin would shoot Lori. He dropped to a knee and placed his rifle gently onto the wet floor, then laid his sidearm next to it. Lanyard did the same.

Amin peered out from behind Lori. "I did not expect *you* to be here, Red. When I heard the shots I didn't get too excited, in case you were too cowardly to come. Do you remember me?"

"You still look like a camel's ass. That's one thing I haven't forgotten."

Red glanced sideways and noticed the two guards didn't react to the insult. They didn't speak English, so probably weren't tags.

"And you came anyway, knowing I would be waiting? Maybe I misjudged you. I heard you had some problems with your memory after I beat you senseless. I'm glad it's back. We've unfinished business."

"We've got an entire team upstairs. There's no way you're getting out. If you hurt Lori or any of us, it'll mean your death. If you lay down your weapon I'll—"

"You are not the one in charge here, infidel! You *and* your team will do exactly as I say or I will blow off parts of your wife, starting with her feet."

Red stood tall. "I'm ordered to take you alive. I'm extending the honor of—"

"You're as arrogant now as last time! You're blind. I've studied you many years. How ironic that I'm holding—"

Lori smashed her heel onto the top of Amin's foot, producing a muffled *crunch*. She ducked her head and his weapon fired, hitting one of the guards in the shoulder. She slipped her hand over Amin's and squeezed the trigger till the magazine was empty, before the other guard could bring his weapon to bear. As the enemies fell limp to the concrete, she looped Amin's neck with the cuff chain and pulled him onto her shoulders, suspended by his throat. He flailed until his eyes rolled back and his body fell limp. Where the hell did she learn to do that?

Red and Lanyard picked up their weapons and aimed them at the two closed doors. Lori dropped Amin to the concrete, catching his head with her foot and lowering it down. Then she wound up and gave him two kicks in the ribs. She leaned into his face. "First time in two days you've stopped talking, damn narcissist!"

Red kept his eyes on the doors and pulled a fragmentation grenade from his vest. "Don't kill him," he said.

"There's no one else down here. Those rooms are empty." She ran and threw her cuffed arms around his neck and gave him a bear hug along with a peck on the lips. "You're a sight! Haven't seen you in blackout for years!" She grimaced. "You smell like shit."

"I love you, too. The river doubles as a sewer."

"The kids?"

"With my parents."

"Oh, thank God! I thought they'd maybe gotten you or them or—" She put her hand to her mouth. A tear ran down her cheek. She pointed to a table in the corner. "The keys for the cuffs are there. He may not be out much longer. Get me out of these. You've got some serious problems with your exfil, whatever it is."

Red slipped the grenade back beneath an elastic strap on his vest, grabbed the keys from the table. Lanyard grabbed a spool of copper wire off a shelf and tied Amin in a wooden chair.

Red flipped on his comm and got Jim up to speed. Lori borrowed Lanyard's.

Jim's voice betrayed doubt. "Lori, you're a tag?"

She picked up Amin's pistol from the floor and rummaged through a wooden box on the shelf, pulling out a handful of 9mm ammo. "Jim, secrecy kept me alive for three days. I'm not gonna drop it now."

"Red?"

"Got a memory issue, sir. Surprise to me as well."

"Like hell."

Lori made a hatchet motion with her arms. "We need a new exfil. One of the drivers is a double. I'm not good at Farsi, but I overheard a little. The driver is pretending to be bought off by Mossad. I don't know anything else. There's no way you can call in an extraction here. The beltway doesn't have the balls for it. Who's your interrogator—or do I have to do this myself?"

"He's on his way in."

Gravel crunched in the distance and Carter turned toward it. The sound came from the road where they'd sent the Israelis to hole up one klick away. He pulled his optics back down and switched to thermal. His vantage atop the pile of rocks gave him a clear line of sight. A cat, or maybe a small dog, walked across the road with its young dangling by the scruff of its neck. Nothing else warm was moving.

Carter flipped the imager up and rubbed his eye. How the hell did this happen? He'd taken the cut in pay and put up with the sheriff to get away from stuff like this. Now he was in deeper than he'd ever been. His wife would kill him if she knew where he was.

He held up his hand and studied its calluses. Once a friend had believed in him, too, so it was only right that he was paying it forward. He leveled his eyes back on the road and flexed his biceps hard to keep from shivering. The wind came across the river and hit his wet fatigues, sending the chill deeper than he had felt in a long time. If he had to defend his position, he couldn't shoot true. The colonel sat one boulder above him and tapped his shoulder with his boot. "He's on his way in," he said, then pointed to the warehouse. *Go,* he mouthed.

Anything to get moving. Carter jumped down the pile of boulders and sprinted to the warehouse and down the stairs. The cool air in the bunker felt warm to his skin. He strode to a wooden table with a small bowl of half-eaten yellow rice and some green vegetable, placed his weapon next to it, and began shrugging off equipment. Pointing to Lanyard, he said, "Upstairs. You're with the colonel. Keep an eye to the west. I heard something earlier, on the road maybe."

Carter punched his comm, "Colonel, now is the best time to get info. What am I authorized to do?" The colonel wouldn't put any limits on him, but he needed the okay.

"Just don't kill him."

"Understood. What do you want to know?"

"Who and what. How is our exit compromised? We still need the good drivers for our escape, if there are any. You've got five minutes, unless someone shows up before then."

Carter grabbed Lori and Red and pulled them in. "I'm calling the shots on this. It's an act and you're a part of it. You do exactly as I say, no questions, no matter what."

A gurgle came from behind them. Amin's head was craned backwards and he was trying to raise it upright. Carter waited till Amin's eyes focused, then shoved Red toward him. "Hold his chair!" He pointed to Lori and yelled, "Get some water and throw it on him if he tries to pass out again!"

He came close to Amin and stooped. The man's pupils were normal size, expanding when Carter's head cast a shadow over them. A loop of Amin's *Misbaha*, prayer beads, stuck out of his chest pocket. His jugular swelled rhythmically, pulse only slightly elevated. This may not go their way. It was best to see some fear from the start.

Carter stepped to the table and unzipped a small black satchel, removed two syringes, and placed them on the table. "Hold him steady," he said. Amin tried to squirm away but Carter jabbed the first syringe into his arm, emptying its contents, then turned back toward the table.

"What was that?" Amin asked with a smirk. "Some kind of truth serum? It only makes me sleepy."

Carter whirled around and backhanded him. Amin's neck craned sideways and his incisor broke through his lip. Red's feet shuffled as the chair leaned with the blow. Carter grabbed Amin's head between his hands and screamed, "Listen, pig! I'm not new at this!" Then he bounced Amin's head off the chair's backrest.

He wound up and backhanded Amin from the other side. Pain shot all the way up to his elbow from a previously fractured knuckle. He wound up again, but paused when an image he'd tried to forget flashed into his mind. It was the bloodied face of an unconscious North Korean naval weapons officer, listing sideways in a metal chair. Carter had fractured his knuckle on the officer's jaw. He'd given them the information they needed, but it took three days. Carter dropped his hand and licked a corner of his mouth. He didn't have three days. He barely had three minutes.

"I just gave you a mixture I like. Midodrine and adrenaline. It makes sure you don't pass out from what I'm about to do to you. You won't get any relief, unless your heart explodes first. You'll feel it any second."

Carter took the second syringe and jabbed it into Amin's other arm. "This one is my own cocktail. Tumor necrosis factor and naloxone. Increases sensitivity to pain. Your nerves will fire uninhibited, and you won't pass out. Truth serum," he said with a laugh, "is for amateurs."

Carter's challenge was to leave no doubt Amin's answers were true, but with a short interrogation. He had to open strong. He grabbed his KA-BAR from his vest, bent down, and rammed it through the top of Amin's shoe till its point dug into the concrete floor. Amin's eyes bulged and watered as he tried to keep from screaming.

Carter pulled out a third syringe, put his boot between Amin's legs, then leaned into his face, putting all his weight onto the Iranian's crotch. Amin's jugular was bulging at a faster pace, but his pupils were still the same. Carter held up the syringe and pointed it at Amin's eye. "This one is a mild narcotic to take the edge off the pain. I'm *not* going to give this to you. Not unless you tell me exactly what I ask.

"You'll wish you could die, but I won't allow you to be a martyr. You'll live with your failures!" He pointed to the two bodies on the floor. "They died in the service of Allah. You couldn't even do that right. I'm an infidel, but even I know Allah is *not* pleased. You're a total failure, so he gave you to me."

Carter turned and let loose with his good fist across Amin's nose, offsetting it with a *crunch*. He pointed to Lori. "You were bettered by a woman! Allah even brought Red into your lair tonight and you failed again. Your commander will kill you when he learns of it! VEVAK will rape and kill your family. You know it's true. You've done it yourself!"

Carter stood upright and backhanded Amin repeatedly, alternating sides, spraying blood and drool across Lori's midsection. He stooped and grabbed the chair arms, his face so close that he could smell Amin's cigar breath. Spittle sprayed into Amin's eyes as he shouted, "You'll be treated in the afterlife like a pig, worse than an infidel! I've heard your imam. If I kill you now, you'll meet your family in hell and they'll curse you."

Amin squirmed upright, tilting his face away. Was that the start of what Carter was looking for? He struck again, the beatings flowing more naturally now. He couldn't lose control, but needed to get dangerously close. With each swing he was falling into his role. He turned his back and rubbed the snot from his nose onto his sleeve, hand quivering. His eyes were burning. Sweat ran down his face in the cold air.

He whirled back around. Amin groaned as he lifted him by the hair, craning his neck backwards, and put a finger into his eye. "Show yourself a man!"

Beads of sweat dripped from Amin's forehead. The pupil of the one eye he could see was dilated. It was a start. The seed of fear had taken root. Now was the time to show him an out.

"If you tell me what I ask, I'll let you live. You may even have time to seek Allah's forgiveness and make up for your failures."

Carter reached behind to the small of his back with both hands and pulled out two daggers. The blades were short but had gnarly, jagged edges clipped with wire cutters. He walked to the table, opened a small bottle, and poured alcohol over them.

"To increase pain," he said. He took a salt shaker from the table, shook it heavily on the blades. He turned back and put his foot into Amin's groin again and stretched out his arms with the daggers in firm grasp. Amin was a worthy subject. No cries for mercy. No shouts of anger. But fear glimmered on his face, from his swollen eyes. He could probably get honest answers from him now, but he needed to go a little further, to ensure he got the truth.

Carter whispered, "I am going to plunge these into your flesh and then you'll answer my questions, won't you?"

Amin stuttered a response. "But . . . but you haven't asked anything."

Carter smiled. "I haven't reached my fill. Not yet."

With machinelike precision, Carter pumped the daggers into Amin's thighs repeatedly. His screams were deafening. He paused only to refill his lungs. His olive face turned deep red. The veins in his neck and forehead stood out like poison ivy vines on the trunk of a tree. Blood flowed, but not in gushes. Carter stared into his eyes and laughed, barely audible during the pauses in Amin's screams.

Carter twisted the knives in Amin's thighs. Amin screamed for mercy, but Carter pulled out the daggers and plunged them in again, laughing hysterically.

"We have all night! No one knows we're here."

Amin begged for the question until Carter leaned in and shouted in his face, "Which of the drivers are traitors? Which are working for you?"

"Noam!" Amin cried, repeating it several times. He said he only knew the one name. Noam is what he'd told his handler. He'd never seen him before and didn't know what he looked like. Amin answered the rest of Carter's questions without hesitation. The warehouse was only a temporary holding site for Lori until VEVAK moved her the next day. They hadn't expected a rescue operation so quickly. They were keeping Lori away from military locations, hoping to lure in an American team. Then Noam would lead the rescuers into an ambush while on the way to the Afghan border. That way, no matter where or when the rescue came, the Iranians would take them all with the fewest casualties. Noam had called an hour earlier to warn that a rescue operation was in motion.

Carter smirked and the redness faded from his face. He stepped into the stairway. Red followed close behind. Lori rummaged through a battered cardboard box with a red cross on the side, resting on one of the bottom shelves. Carter grabbed the handrail and leaned on it as he commed in.

"You're four minutes late," said the colonel.

Carter's voice was monotone, as if reading a script. "Status is as follows. There's at least one traitor in the Israeli exfil team. They're planning on ambushing us on the way to the Afghan border. The traitor's name is Noam. Our prisoner doesn't know if there are any others besides him."

"He doesn't know or you couldn't get it out of him?"

Carter glanced back at Amin. Lori was pressing white gauze on one of his leg wounds. He was screaming for the shot he'd been promised. Red offered a wink and a thumbs-up.

"He told us everything he knew, but he might not know everything. I've got an idea I've used before that might confirm any other traitors. We can be ready to exit in five." Carter outlined his plan, but it only got them out of the warehouse and on the road.

"Marksman, you got anybody that can hide us?" the colonel asked.

"Maybe." Marksman commed.

"Can we trust them?"

"Hell no. But they all speak the same language. Money. As long as we can talk in those terms, I can get us a place."

"Carter, get us out of this damn warehouse. I'm calling the vans in four minutes. Marksman, once we're moving, you make it happen."

Carter dropped his head back and gazed at the ceiling, hands down at his sides. The stairwell above appeared as if he was looking up from the bottom of a well. He felt short of breath, as if someone had taken all the oxygen out of the air. He wanted to run up into the dim light at the top. His fingers shook and his refractured knuckle throbbed. He clenched his fists, then released. Walking back to Amin, he emptied the third syringe into his arm. "It'll take the edge off."

Captain Richards and Dr. Ali ran into the bunker. Dr. Ali looked at Amin's face, then at the KA-BAR sticking out of his foot, and back at Carter.

"Patch him upstairs, doc. No arteries. Only puncture wounds." The doctor glowered as he and Richards humped Amin up the stairs, still strapped to his chair.

Red studied Carter as he stood next to the wooden table, rubbing a swollen knuckle. In terms of tactical interrogations, the man had just performed heart surgery. So this was the reason Jim had put him on the op. Red put a hand on Carter's shoulder. "You okay?"

The detective smiled. "Yeah. I'm not proud of it, but I always get what I ask for."

"Looks like you took it easy on me that night after Walmart."

Carter laughed. "I thought about doing the dagger routine, but the sheriff shut me down."

Lori grabbed an AK-47 from the dead lieutenant's grasp. She rolled him over and stripped off his ammo belt. Who the hell was she? Where'd she learn her skills? The move on Amin's arm, shooting the guards, all that was close quarters combat. She'd been trained. But by who? Was he supposed to remember? Why hadn't she told him? Was she some sort of schizophrenic Jekyll and Hyde?

Lori held out Amin's pistol. "Recognize it?"

Red lifted it from her palm. "My old sidearm. That'll make Gunny happy, when I bring it back."

"Like hell you say." She snatched it from his grasp and shoved it behind the ammo belt around her waist. "Finders keepers."

Chapter 19
Exit

Both blue-painted doors on the far wall of the underground bunker stood shut. Lori had said they were empty, but Red knew he should clear them anyway, even if to only catch them on video from the tiny camera atop his helmet. He twisted a silver handle and scanned inside the first room. Inside was sparse, only a few empty metal coffee cans stacked in a corner, shiny red labels half-eaten by rust. He peered inside the other. It was empty, too, but a slanted crack in the concrete wall had a deep orange water stain running down from it. The same stain he'd seen in the background of the video in Jim's office.

He turned back. Lori was standing with her foot on the neck of a dead guard, the one with the scar. She checked the holes in the back of a clip, then shoved it into her ammo belt.

"You sure you're okay. Not hurt?" Red asked.

She smiled. "No. A couple bruises, and I smell worse than you. That's all."

He grabbed her arms and locked her gaze, to make sure it was the truth. "Anyone touch you?"

She pulled free and shoved a magazine into the bottom of the AK. "No. Well, almost. One tried, but a German guy put a stop to it."

"Who was he?"

"The trafficker. Then, while I was here, Amin never left me alone. He's gay."

Red grinned. "Why? Because he didn't come on to you?"

"Pretty much." She laughed. "Or it could be the way he looked at *this* guy." She kicked the shoulder of the dead guard.

"You gotta help me out. Why didn't I know you were a tag?

And where'd you learn those moves? Why haven't you told me any of this?"

She marched toward the stairs. "Later. Trust me for now. Gotta get moving."

He followed her up. The pink pajamas hung from her shoulders, brown stains running down her back. Her hips swayed as she adjusted the ammo belt at the first landing. "What about—" He stopped. She might not take a sexual innuendo very well right now, even if he was only trying to lighten the mood.

"What about what?" she asked, twisting the strap.

He looked past her, up the stairs. "What about you hurry up."

She smirked and shoved his chest. "Whatever. Don't think you got away with it." She ran upstairs.

Jim rallied the team near a door, then called for pickup. Marksman put a shoulder into Crawler's gut and scooped him up in a fireman's carry, staggering under the weight. Crawler hung limp. Jim and Carter stood next to Amin, still strapped in his chair with copper wire, strips of green fabric tied around his legs to stem the blood flow. His head hung low. The rest of the team lay down on the cement inside the door. The cold from the floor tensed Red's legs. They were supposed to be feigning death. Hard to do when you're shivering. What a lousy plan. But Carter claimed the ruse had worked before. Red hoped these drivers were stupid enough to fall for it.

The grind of worn brakes came from outside. Marksman heaved a deep breath and pushed through the door, wheeling like a top spinning down. The door closed behind him, scraping the floor as it went like the call of a seagull. Marksman yelled something indecipherable. The crunch of gravel under feet, the scrape of the door again, and Red squinted as four men in plainclothes came through.

Two had baseball caps, one bright red with a Coke logo. They ran to Ali, picked him up, and carried him toward the door. The other two stopped when they saw Amin, then took a step back.

"Noam?" Carter drew his sidearm.

They looked at each other, and ran back to the door. They flung it open and met the barrels of Crawler and Marksman trained at their chests. Red jumped up and blocked the aisle as they turned toward it. One of them, tall and wiry, almost pushed past Lanyard, but a blow to the groin had him sucking wind. Crawler handed Lanyard FlexiCuffs and bound the prisoner's wrists and ankles, then duct-taped their mouths.

Ali squirmed and the drivers with baseball caps dropped him. They yelled at each other.

"Marksman, get them to shut up. We need to get moving." Jim said.

Lori interpreted as Marksman spoke. The drivers thought they were being double-crossed. The one with the Coke cap wore pressed jeans and a shiny brown leather jacket. He jerked off his hat and shoved Marksman backwards. Crawler stepped closer, but Marksman continued to speak calmly. The other came near as well, talking loudly, one eye wandering as he spoke. The conversation grew louder and Marksman raised his hands, waving them in a *calm down* motion. The one with a lazy eye took a swing at him, but Crawler stepped in and punched him in the gut so hard he puked.

"Crawler!" Marksman yelled. "We need these guys on our side."

The one in the leather jacket spat in Crawler's face as the other retched on the floor.

Jim jumped in front and aimed Crawler toward the middle of the warehouse. "Over there. Keep an eye on the other doors."

Crawler looked down at Jim with pursed lips, wiping the spit from his eyebrow. "Yes, sir."

Red had asked Jim back in the hanger whether Crawler was still taking anger-management classes. Jim had said, "Nope. I pulled him. I like him better that way."

A few more minutes of heated back-and-forth, then voices calmed as Marksman pointed toward the other two drivers, bound and sitting on the floor. The one with the lazy eye stood holding his gut, yelling as he motioned toward the door.

"He's telling us to load up," Marksman said. "But he says they'll be looking for the vans now. We'll have to steal something along the way."

Crawler's New York accent echoed from across the warehouse, "Why not switch 'em out now?" Red glanced at Jim, then ran to where Crawler stood next to the two troop transports.

"These're in good shape," Crawler said. "I tapped the tanks and they're full up. I can hotwire 'em, then put a fifteen-minute detonator on these rocket boxes. This place will go up higher than a daisy cutter. They'll think they got hit with a tactical nuke. Won't be nothin' left to see their trucks are gone. Leave the vans outside, douse 'em with gas, and maybe the hadjis will think we went up in the blast. We can put a couple dead guys in the vans in our gear so's they find their burnt carcasses. May buy us a little time."

Marksman lifted an eyebrow. "Come up with that yourself? You're gonna blow an aneurism."

"Make it happen," Jim snapped.

Crawler slung his rifle and lifted the hood of the first truck. Marksman peered into the window of the other, opened the door, and got in. It turned over, fired up, and Marksman stuck his bald head out the door. "The keys are in the ignition, idiot, but you can still hotwire it if you want." He ducked back inside as a pair of pliers flew and struck the rearview mirror, spraying broken glass to the floor.

Jim grinned, punching his comm. "Crawler and Marksman, go downstairs and bring up those bodies. Marksman, get in one of their uniforms. Lori, you, too. You'll be riding up front with the drivers. Look Iranian. Cut your hair, smudge your face, whatever. Crawler, set detonators for thirty minutes. We need more distance before they come looking for us. Richards, get out to the rock pile, position Victor. You're lookout till we're rolling." He pointed to the far corner. "Ali, get those fuel tanks over there leaking. I want this floor coated by the time we leave. Red and Lanyard, get the two bodies from the mezzanine and strip 'em down." Jim kicked the head of the dead guard lying at the end of the aisle, the one missing a hand. "Lori, tell the drivers to strip these guys down and get into their uniforms."

Red ran up the mezzanine stairs, pausing at the top. He didn't want to get the kid, but couldn't make Lanyard do it, either. He reached down to grab the boy's shoulders but stopped, hands shaking, hovering above the glossy white box pooled with blood. The head was down, body slumped over it. One time at the Air Force Academy he'd fallen asleep on his footlocker while shining shoes. An upperclassman found him slumped over it like this kid, brush in hand. He and his roommate had paid for that in hazing for a week.

Lanyard grunted behind him and a rifle slapped the floor. Red glanced back. Lanyard had his guard over his shoulder, reaching down to grab his AK-47. Red inhaled, closed his eyes, grabbed the kid, and slung him over his shoulder as well. His arms hung limp against the backs of Red's thighs. Urine had soaked his pants, dampening the shoulder of Red's body armor. He breathed through his mouth, but the mixed scent of Kevlar, sweat, and urine made him want to retch. He swallowed it down as he descended the stairs. The bowed step cracked under his weight. He lurched forward, nearly falling down the rest.

Marksman and Crawler placed the other two bodies behind the second truck, breathing heavily from toting them up from the bunker. Someone had already pulled over the one-handed guard, leaving his lost limb back in the aisle. Red stooped and shrugged the kid off his shoulders, shuddering. There were five bodies now, lying like cordwood. He could see them all, except for the kid's face. He forced himself to look. It was the least he could do. The kid was still smiling.

Red looked up and breathed deeply. Diesel fumes mixed with gasoline from the draining tanks. Both drivers stepped onto the running boards and looked inside the cabs. The one with the lazy eye was half a foot taller. He jumped down, patted his own chest, and said something in Farsi to Marksman.

"This guy with the broken eyeball calls himself Salar," Marksman said. "Shorter one is Navid."

Salar walked to the front of the truck, then motioned for Jim to follow. Red came, too. Salar spoke rapidly, stroking a plate riveted onto the bumper, the outline of two green squares with a globe in the middle.

"Says the emblem on the bumper is a special unit," Marksman said. "I can't make out which one. He thinks it might get us through checkpoints. Says we should put this truck up front."

Jim cleared his throat. "Either that or he's setting us up. You know the language. Can we trust him?"

"With that eye jumping around like a one-legged grasshopper? All I want is to smack the back of his head, straighten it out."

Jim walked to the rear of the first truck, smiling. He commed in, "Fireball in thirty. Exit in five. Ali, make sure we can get the overhead doors open." He patted the liftgate on the back of the truck. "Everyone else, put a row of crates at the front and another at the back of the beds. It'll be empty in the middle. That's where we'll ride." He pointed to a pile of green canvas. "Pull one of those tarps over the whole thing for cover."

Red slapped Lanyard's shoulder and ran down one of the aisles, to some wooden crates the size of footlockers.

"What's wrong with these?" Lanyard asked, kicking the bottom of a stack of flat ones.

"Rockets of some sort, I think. When shooting breaks out, I don't want them getting hit."

At the end of the aisle Red grabbed one end of a small crate, light yellow and unsplintered, smelling of fresh sawdust. "This one looks like their MREs." They stacked two dozen of them in the beds and cinched them tight with wide ratchet tie-downs. The only way to get into the middle was by lowering the bed's side panel.

Red put the last tug on a strap and turned as Lori stepped out of the next aisle. Judging by the blood on her cuff, she was in the uniform of the one-handed guard. A beige beret was pulled over her hair. She'd chopped some off, but the fullness of the beret suggested she'd tucked most of it underneath. Brown camo paint was thinly smeared over her face and hands. He had to get her home. But who was she now?

There'd be plenty of time for that later. *Let your mind go and you'll get yourself killed,* he thought. The goal, the mission, getting her home. That was the only thing that was real now.

Lori slung an AK-47 over one shoulder and jogged over. The closer she got, the worse the picture.

"How do I look?" she asked.

He grimaced. "Like hell."

Lori glared. "Okay, this is the one time you get to say that."

"I'm not joking. You look like Shania Twain in camo and a bad haircut. I've seen Mexicans that look more Iranian. Plus, Artesh doesn't have women grunts. You can't ride up front."

She looked down at her chest, then pulled more of the blouse out of her ammo belt. "Jim wants someone to keep a close ear on the drivers. Marksman's taking the first one."

"But you said you don't know much Farsi."

"Still more than anyone else."

Red pulled hard on the ratchet handle, producing a *crack* from one of the crates. "You may be okay at night, but any hadji gets within twenty feet, I'm shooting the bastard. You do the same. Hear me?"

She tilted her chin. "I'll keep my eyes open."

"That goes for the driver, too. He's getting paid to betray his country." Red looked at Crawler lifting Amin into the back of the second truck. "This whole thing is out of control. We should leave Amin and the other drivers here. Take ours and head out."

"What did Jim say?"

"Can't. Mossad wants them, and we'll need Mossad before the day's out. At least if we left them here, it'd be a painless death. With Mossad, it'll be long and nasty."

Lori stepped onto the running board. "You think too much. Just be sure they don't make any noise back there." She caught Jim's eye, gave him a thumbs-up, then slid across into the passenger seat.

Red squeezed under the musty green tarp in back. He grabbed hold of one of the crates at the end of the bed and shook. It creaked, but the stack stood firm. He scooted toward the front and his feet hit Amin, lying on the floor, eyes closed. Red knelt and put a hand over the prisoner's nose and mouth. Nothing happened. Whatever Carter had given the guy must be stronger than he'd said. Amin wouldn't be making any noise.

Red thought of Father Ingram and what he'd said about killing, only when needed. He uncovered Amin's mouth and slapped his cheek till he inhaled, grimacing.

Jim gave the order and everyone squeezed into the trucks. The chassis shook as the driver released the clutch and drove outside. The overhead door screeched loudly as Richards rolled it closed. He lifted the tarp and passed Red his rifle, then slid into the truck bed, cursing when he tore his pants on a floor bolt. Red lifted the side panel and locked it in place. The air was close, stinking of sweat and sewer from the Pardis, mixed with mildew from the tarp. A cool draft blew by his calves when the truck turned onto the service road, toward Tehran.

The comm clicked and Jim's voice sounded in his ear. "Marksman, you're my eyes. If Salar does anything you don't like, shoot him. Same for you, Lori."

The brakes squealed as the truck jolted to a stop.

Marksman's comm clicked on. He spoke in Farsi.

Lori's voice came online. "Best I can tell, Salar doesn't like us heading west . . . Marksman's telling him they're waiting for us the other way. Something about a hiding place. In Tehran."

The engine raced and the truck lurched forward as the clutch grabbed. Ali braced himself against the crates, mumbling, "Even rather have Crawler driving than this one-eyed gypsy."

Red pinched at a splinter in his palm, trying to pull it out. "Wrong driver," he said. "The guy with the lazy eye's driving lead."

"We're straight," Marksman commed. "Salar says he'll take us. Seems this wasn't his first visit to the warehouse. Says he's taken pictures of it before and knows another way out, a trail that might get us past checkpoints. He's got my night vision so we're lights out."

The truck slowed. Red stooped, putting his knee next to Amin's head. He pulled up the canvas till it rose over the side of the bed and peered out. The first truck was turning off the road, between tall saltbushes. Branches scratched the side, then the front wheels dropped down a riverbank till the truck was almost high-centered. By the time the rear wheels were passing the bushes, it was pointed down sharply.

"Brace yourself." Red leaned toward the back of the truck. The branches scraping the sides tore a small hole in the canvas. The truck tilted forward even more steeply. But if Salar was driving them off a cliff, he'd be killed, too. Amin rolled, flopping against the front row of crates, frowning in his stupor. Red climbed on them, wishing he'd tightened the ratchets more since the ones in the back leaned hard toward him. It would not be a dignified way to die, crushed by crates of field rations.

The truck seemed to teeter, engine racing, tires spinning gravel against the wheel wells. Red pulled up the canvas and stuck his head out. Saltbush branches scratched his face. The front wheels hung low against the riverbank while the rear spun. Must be hung up on the undercarriage. "We're high-centered," Red commed. He dropped the side panel and rolled out.

"E2, guard the road," Jim commed. "Crawler, fix it."

Red grabbed a long branch from one of the bushes and backed down the short cliff, as if rappelling. He stopped next to the cab. Lori was braced with her feet against the dashboard. The driver looked like he was doing a push-up on the steering wheel, eyes large. The man opened his door and it slipped from his hand, dropping so hard it broke the limiting strap and bent the hinges, slamming against the fender.

Jim cursed at the sound.

Red pointed to the driver. "Lori, tell him to stay in. Once this thing breaks loose he's gonna need to steer."

"We've got something coming," Ali commed. "I can't hear it, but I see lights around the corner."

"Get us moving!" Jim said.

Crawler scrambled up the bank on all fours. It was loose and he slipped back with every step. He reached the bumper and did a chin-up to pull himself close, looking warily at the grille as it teetered up and down.

"That thing breaks loose, lay flat," Red said.

Crawler sneered. "This thing breaks loose and you're gonna see my white ass run." He flipped the release on the winch and un-wound the cable, cutting his palm on a barb, sucking at it and spitting the blood onto the sandy bank. He placed the hook onto the bumper of the lead truck, then had Red lock the spool again. "Marksman, tell the driver to ease her forward, slow. Keep her straight or we'll tip the other truck."

Ali commed, "Whoever was coming must've stopped. I still see a glow around the corner, but it's not moving."

If the warehouse blew it would silhouette them against the horizon and they'd be seen. How much time left? He twisted his wrist. Only a few more minutes, if Crawler set the fuses right. They had to get into the riverbed.

The cable drew taut as the lead truck moved, pulling the nose of the second forward like a horse bracing against a lead rope. It listed sideways, then the nose dropped fast. It shot down the riverbank, dragging locked wheels as the driver stood on the brakes.

Jim commed, "E1, hide our tracks."

A dust cloud kicked up by the truck's descent moved over the two vehicles below, now next to each other in the riverbed. The barrel of Marksman's M14 was sticking out one passenger window. He'd switched uniforms with a dead guard before putting the body in the van outside the warehouse and dousing it with gas. But he'd never leave his rifle.

Red hauled himself back up the riverbank. Lanyard was kneeling, eyes closed, listening. The two of them broke off branches from the far side of a bush and swept away the wheel tracks from the edge of the road all the way back down. They dove into the truck and signaled Ali and Richards to do the same. The engine raced again, but this time the launch was smooth.

The comm clicked in Red's ear. It was Marksman. "Salar says it'll be slow going for an hour. Then we'll be back on pavement after that, not far, till Tehran. Colonel, I need your sat phone."

Red leaned back on the crates again, feet against Amin's shoulder. Heat came through the wood slats, warming his legs, but his hands were cold where he braced against the jolting. Must be sitting over the exhaust pipe. He pulled up the tarp and dropped his night vision, in time to see Marksman lean out of the cab of the lead truck, long arms reaching back to grab the phone from Jim.

The truck squeaked as it rolled over the dry creek bed. Occasionally, the tires scrubbed the underside if pushed too far by rocks.

After a while, Marksman commed again. "We're set up. I need two hundred and fifty thousand. She gave me the number of a Swiss bank account."

"Dollars?" Jim asked.

"Euros. That's all she deals in. It's only half. Full price is five hundred thousand. Half now, half when we leave. Last time it was less, three years ago and only four of us. Deposited to her account in the next ten minutes or deal's off."

The jostle and screeching turned into slamming and pounding as the pace quickened, but at least they were still moving.

"Where we headed?" Crawler commed.

"A brothel. Downtown Tehran," Marksman said.

"Five hundred thousand? That's cheap for your ugly—" The comm clicked off. Crawler must not have been out of Jim's reach.

Not a perfect plan, but surely Tehran would be the last place the Iranians would expect them to run. They could hide out a few days, wait for security to relax again, then dash for the border.

Richards sat on the opposite side of the truck bed, leaning against the stack of crates, peering out into the blackness. "At least this way we don't have to rely on Mossad."

The eerie creaking and moaning of the crates tensed the back of Red's neck. A breeze whipped the tarp to life, making it slap against their heads, as if telling them to be quiet. A sharp pain stabbed Red's chest. He put his thumbs under his Kevlar vest and pushed it out. What was that? Had he been hit?

Dr. Ali frowned. "Pain?"

"Only when I breathe."

"Get shot back there?"

Red peered down over his Kevlar. "Don't think so. Probably coming down off the high. You know, adrenaline or something."

Ali hopped up and grabbed his vest, twisting him around, shining a dim light over it, shrouded by his hands.

A pressure wave swept over the truck. Everyone looked at Red. He pulled up the side of the tarp and gazed out. The sky was bright now. The long shadows of the trucks shortened as the fireball rose.

Lanyard was standing, pushing up the tarp to look over one of the crates, smiling. Was that joy in his eyes? "Crawler said she'd go up like a daisy cutter!"

Red imagined Crawler doing the same in the front truck. The guy was never happier than when blowing something up or running it over.

The fireball grew, dimmed, then disappeared into the blackness. Red sat, peering over the side of the truck bed again, at the brightness on the horizon that must be Tehran.

Pain filled his chest once more. He felt under his vest, then lifted his head again to the glowing skyline. No, he wasn't shot. He had a sense that Lori might have been safer where she was. That the hardest part of the mission was still ahead, under the smoldering lights.

Chapter 20
Jannat

After a half hour on the creek bed, a high-pitched whine of truck tires on asphalt came from ahead. Red put his eye to the hole in the canvas. A glow shone over a crest in the trail. At the top, a road came into view between tufted mounds of plains grass. The road was only a hundred meters to their side, the creek bank just high enough to hide them.

Lights from a passing vehicle swept above like a searchlight, illuminating a thin finger of ground fog bent overhead. If they were kicking up a dust trail, the fog would help hide it. Their truck stopped and the engine rattled as it shut off. Lights of another vehicle passed overhead with a *wump-wump-wump* from a flat spot on a tire, then silence. Their engine cranked over and the trucks raced up the bank onto the road, turning on their lights.

Red sat again and rested against the crates, legs straight out with his feet next to Amin's head. The prisoner's eyes were halfway open, only whites showing. Red placed his rifle on his leg, barrel angled toward Amin's neck. If they hit a bump hard enough, it would fire. He thumbed off the safety and moved his hand to the stock.

Red flipped down his night vision and gazed at Amin's eyes quivering under the lids. His cheek was swollen, maybe fractured. Red thought of being picked up six years ago. Jim had stretched his eyes open, then put his ear to his mouth. "Still breathing," he'd said. Red had passed in and out of consciousness during the exit. His wounds included three bullets, a cracked femur, a broken collarbone, burnt nipples, and crushed gonads. It was a miracle he and Lori had been able to have Jackson and Nick. Recall had its downside. Some memories should stay repressed.

He checked his watch. Penny was going to be worried. It would be days before he got back. Mom would be falling apart by the morning. But Tom ... Red leaned his head back till a nail poked his skull, jutting from the side of a crate. Tom was an emotional void. Yet he had strength. He'd keep them together till Red brought Lori home.

The nail smacked him as the truck bounced over a pothole. The rifle didn't fire. He grasped the pistol grip to help it along. How pleasant it would be to plug a bullet into the bastard's neck. They didn't need Mossad's help on their exit anymore. Mossad had screwed up. They lost their chance. Why was he waiting? Tom would say he was weak, that Amin deserved it, that it was the way of the world. Red pushed the safety back on.

I'm not Tom.

A stiff breeze came through the cracks between the floorboards. Red's fatigues had dried and he'd stopped shivering. He looked over at Ali blowing into his hands. Red slid over and patted the floor. "Sit here, doc. Exhaust pipe runs below. Warm up."

The road was wide, two full lanes in either direction. They didn't meet any checkpoints, though several white Mercedes with blue stripes whipped by, headed the other way, red lights flashing. No sirens, though. The buildings outside grew taller and the street lights more frequent till Red tapped Richards's shoulder, motioning for him to drop the canvas.

Marksman left his comm on when he spoke with Salar. Lori interpreted as best she could. They were headed to an intersection near something called *Park-e-Resvan*. She mentioned the Azadi tower and spouted a few directions, but Marksman was talking a lot more than she was.

The truck's springs screeched as it slammed over something. A sharp pain shot through Red's tailbone. The truck stopped and its engine went silent. Red tapped Lanyard on the shoulder. They pointed their weapons toward the side of the truck. He should have had everyone swap back to subsonics. Too late now.

"I see her," Marksman commed. His door sounded like sandpaper on metal when it opened. Footsteps, slow, and with dragging heels, came from down the street. Red reached toward the canvas, but Lanyard touched his elbow. The steps stopped behind their truck. He hadn't heard Marksman walking, but his voice came from outside.

"Followed, Rahim?" whispered a female voice.

"No," Marksman said.

"You are shot. Three times!"

"Not my uniform."

"*Alhamdulillah*! Whatever you did, I am not charging enough. All my customers left. But it will be easier to hide. Can everyone walk?"

"Three will be carried."

"Into that alley." The footsteps walked away, more briskly now, but still with dragging heels.

Red checked the local time on his watch. Two hours till sunrise. A tap came from the side of the truck as Marksman walked past. Red dropped the panel and rolled out. Ali carried Amin. Red and Lanyard covered while Richards checked the bed, then the cabs, ensuring nothing was left.

Red trailed, scanning behind, following the team. A small cloud of steam rose from under the hood of their truck. It plumed, then dissipated, like the warehouse fireball. Their footsteps in the frost looked like a migrating herd of Cape buffalo had run into the side street. He hoped no one came by till fresh frost built up.

The alley was not wide enough for the trucks. Red stretched his neck, squinting to make out their guide. A dark *chādor* covered her head and body. She walked with a stooped posture, hobbling, maybe even using a cane. Had it been Halloween in the States, she'd make a great grim reaper. Crawler carried one of the traitors over his shoulder. Drugged by Dr. Ali back at the warehouse, the man was limp, arms flapping. The sound of so many boots, bodies, and equipment echoed off the hard walls of houses, like a duck call heard from across the water. Why didn't the capital city have any background noise?

Their guide took up a brisk pace, pausing at each crossway. Maybe she didn't care if they were spotted. A few houses ahead a dog barked, followed by a hollow ringing, as if it had upset its water bowl. A minute later came shouting and a yelp. Funny. Red had been briefed Iran was cracking down on owning dogs. Maybe it was a stray.

Red switched to thermal and kept his eyes on the alley behind them. The only thing that glowed was a rat as it disappeared under a wooden privacy fence.

"Moving," Marksman commed. Jim had him at the front of the column, on point. Everyone emerged from the shadows and continued the trek. They mazed through alleys, taking ways that provided the most darkness, keeping to shadows created by the moonlight. Red walked backwards mostly, senses alert.

After ten minutes, Red heard Ali's breathing, deep and hard, as he carried the other traitor. Red was about to signal Lanyard to relieve him when they came into a small courtyard, paved in river stones, like the cobblestoned streets of downtown Charleston where Lori's parents lived once. Light shone through a cracked door of a three-story house across the yard. Their guide opened it, motioning them to enter. Marksman whispered something to her as he ducked in.

Red followed, taking one last look behind. The guide closed the door, then waved for him to follow the rest. The dim light suggested a young face under her hood. He trailed through a kitchen with orange countertops into a large room with several couches around the walls. The middle was left open with a blue-and-red oriental rug, now host to a dozen pairs of boots. Their hostess would be insulted by that, Red thought, if she was Muslim. The room was warm and smelled of kerosene heat. Wall sconces cast an orange light upward onto cheap tapestries.

Marksman walked back to their guide, still covered in her *chādor*. "Customers?"

"None now. They left. I sent my girls away after that." She walked to a hutch along the wall and pulled out a box of plastic trash bags, then handed them to Marksman. "Upstairs. Take off everything. Anything that can burn goes in these. They'll go in the furnace downstairs. I have uniforms, enough for all of you."

Jim frowned.

"Many of my customers are soldiers," she said, pulling back her hood a little, lifting her chin. "High-ranking ones. And politicians." She looked at Marksman's arms, following his form down to his waist. "Sometimes they lose clothes, forget things."

"English?" Jim asked.

"The language of business." She raised herself upright and pulled the hood back from her head, releasing a button beneath her chin. Marksman helped the cape off her shoulders. She stood much taller now. As it came down, a mellow scent of flowered perfume warmed the frigid mood of the room. Her forearms were bare and the flesh of her face was dark, smooth, inviting. Jet black hair covered her shoulders. No dot on her forehead. Late thirties, in a red linen dress falling gracefully from narrow hips down to her ankles. Her pedicured feet were in leather sandals adorned with small gold chains, matching ones around her neck.

Something hit Red on the back of the head. He turned to see Lori in green fatigues, crossing her arms.

"Quit drooling," she said.

Their guide smiled. "I am Jannat," she said, then raised her arm toward a hallway with a dark-stained wooden staircase at one end. "Go upstairs one floor, to the right. There are two rooms." She placed her hand on Marksman's forearm. "The same as last time. You will fit, but it will be tight."

"What about customers?" Jim asked. "You closing your doors till we're gone?"

"No. Too suspicious. They stay in the front rooms. But keep your doors locked. No moving, no noise. We are empty at day, busy at night. There's a bathroom between your rooms." She squeezed her nose. "Please use it. I'll give you an hour."

She pulled Marksman to her side, her voice calming. "You will stay three days. They bore easily and will not be looking so much after that. I have transport." She waved her hands. "Enough! Too long here. Upstairs. One hour."

Salar said something in Farsi to Jannat, then to Marksman. "He thinks they're done," Marksman said, "Needs to be at work in a few hours or they'll look suspicious."

"Tell him he's staying till we're gone," Jim said. "If they try to leave, we'll kill 'em. Be sure to smile when you say it." He walked toward the stairs, stopping next to Jannat. "Don't worry. If we do, we won't make noise. I'm sure you've used that furnace to get rid of things other than uniforms."

Jannat maintained her empty smile, keeping her gaze on Marksman.

Jim aimed two fingers at Red, then swept them toward the stairs. Red thumbed off his safety and took point, Lanyard behind. Red remembered that Jim never trusted safe houses, wherever they were. "An oxymoron," he'd say. None were safe very long.

Red angled his M4 up the stairs, each tread announcing his presence. The air warmed his cheek as he ascended. He was moving across the first landing when Lori said, "Thank you," walking past Jannat. Her voice sounded emphatic, even sincere. She'd always been a quick judge of character. Red had learned to trust her discernment through their years of marriage. He was too apt to trust anyone. He blinked as a drop of sweat ran into his eye. *Trust no one.* That's what Tom would say.

Chapter 21
Jamileh

Jim knelt outside the first room and reached to steady himself against the door's trim. White paint flecked off the rough woodwork, catching on the hair on his wrist like a fly in a spiderweb. Red gave him a thumbs-up from inside. Jim stepped to the next door. The floor creaked under his foot, vibrating through the shank of his boot. Safe houses weren't supposed to squeak. He placed his hand on the knob. Carter, squatting low across from him, looked like he might know what he was doing. He hoped the interrogator could clear a room better than he could swim.

Jim pushed the door open and Carter led through. All clear. Glass broke in the bathroom and Jim's finger tightened on the trigger, then relaxed when Red stepped into the doorframe.

Red dropped his eyes. "Sorry," he whispered, brushing shards of a broken drinking cup to the side with his boot.

Jim split the team the same way as in the trucks, keeping two-man groups together. The rooms were about the size of his storage shed back home. Each had a bunk bed, a dresser, and a single window. The floors were unfinished plank, worn down to a pale shade near the doors. Crawler grunted as he knelt and dropped one of the drivers in the corner.

Jim pointed his chin toward the door. "Crawler, keep your eye down the hallway." He pushed the curtain aside with one finger. The window overlooked the courtyard where they'd come in. He switched to thermal, but only the neighbor's chimney glowed yellow. The curtains were thick and the only light came through the cracked door. He took a wool blanket from the bed and threw it to Richards, who draped it over a lamp and switched it on. It cast enough light to see without night vision.

The river had been rough tonight. It had its own plans, taking them far outside Jim's control. How the hell had they ended up here? Jannat would sell them out first chance she got. It was one thing that she'd hidden Marksman and a few others before. But he'd just kidnapped a VEVAK operative, one who supposedly had inside knowledge of Iran's nuclear program. He'd also stolen back their only bargaining chip, killed five guards, and blown up a VEVAK warehouse. Jannat could name whatever price she wanted. Only asking five hundred thousand euros could be an unwitting tip of her hand. He'd have felt better if she'd demanded more.

Something touched his arm and he spun away. "It's me!" came Carter's voice. Jim was in the middle of the room with Carter's arm pinned high against his back. He released him, then stepped away. Jim needed another plan. No, first he had to secure the area. But he and his team were like the deer he had used to hunt with dogs back in high school. Everyone on the Elkton Blue Jays baseball team had them. Some were bloodhounds that could follow a scent even if it was days old. Others were mutts picked up from the side of the road. They'd trained the dogs together all summer, to run their prey into Bailey's Gulch. With nowhere for the deer to escape, everyone would hunt his season's limit in a single day.

A knock came. He swung his M4 toward the door as five safeties snapped. Crawler waved them off, stepped back, allowing Marksman to slip in.

"Where you's been?" Crawler asked in a whisper. Marksman leaned back, resting against the wall.

"Status?" Jim asked.

"Too early to tell. She's got transport, like she says. She won't call till it's time to go. Less chance they'll sell us out." He put his hand on the doorknob. "She's insisting I stay down there."

"Down where?"

Marksman tilted his head. "Down the hallway, with her."

"She is, or you are?"

Marksman's temples tightened. "She is. Part of her deal. Always is."

Crawler looked like he was sucking on a SweeTART. "She ain't getting paid enough for your nastiness."

This wasn't good. The team would be too spread out. Or maybe he could use it to his advantage. "You did well. Stay close. Be my ears. Keep her busy. Don't let her have time to think about what she'd make by selling us out."

Crawler slapped Marksman's chest. "Why can't I get dem orders? 'Crawler, go keep a whore busy for a couple days. We're payin'. See the doc for meds if you get tired."

"We move tomorrow night," Jim said.

Marksman's eyes narrowed. "Barely twelve hours. Why?"

"I'm arranging another safe house, outside the city. Need time to put it together. Keep your comm close."

"One hideout is as good as another," Marksman said. "At least here we're with someone that's done it before." He patted his chest. "Plus, we've got eyes watching Jannat."

Jim's comm clicked in his ear. Red's voice. "She's coming."

Steps with dragging heels came down the hall. He'd almost made Jannat take off the sandals back in the alley because of the noise. But now, it was a nice way to distinguish the sound of her steps from others. She knocked twice, then pushed the door open. Sweet perfume filled the small room.

"You've got to be more quiet," Jim said.

"No one is here. I locked. I told you, I am giving you one hour."

She carried a tray of flat bread and cheese. Over her arm lay what looked like sheets in drab prints. The door closed and she smiled when it revealed Marksman behind it. Crawler grabbed the tray and she held up one of the sheets. "Once you get dressed, put these *chādors* over. Keep them on always, in case someone sees you. Many women wear them inside when it is cold like this. You can hide anything under it."

"Where are the uniforms?" Jim asked.

"I need two of you to bring them up."

"Marksman, you and Crawler. Go."

Marksman held up a *chādor* and pulled it over his head. It was dark gray, patterned with geometric shapes, in a design that looked like Turkish pottery. Jannat helped with the veils so that only their eyes were visible.

"All my girls wear them outside their rooms," she said. "Veils, too. Part of our job." She cracked open the door and put her eye to it. "I'll check the house again," she whispered, "then come for you."

She took off her sandals and slipped out. With her long legs she could have been a dancer for the Iranian National Ballet, if the revolution had never happened. And if she could learn to walk without dragging her feet. Instead, she was a high-end whore.

Jim commed, "Everyone, rearm with subsonics. Red, you and Lanyard are first watch. I want one set of eyes on the hallway, the other on the yard behind us."

Jim unbuttoned his cargo pocket and searched it with his middle finger. He felt the sticky rubber armor of his sat phone. Time to call the fusion cell. *Screw higher. Screw Mossad.* They could sit in their little control center at Langley and feel like they were running the show. Hell, the leak might be with CIA instead of Mossad.

He flipped the phone open, then slapped it shut. "Ali, your Toughbook. Can you get something to our fusion cell that the control center can't see?"

"They'll be able to see it, but I can make it so it'll take a day or two to decode. What you need?"

"DEA liaison. Get her to—"

A click came in Jim's earpiece, then Red's voice. "She's back."

Jim lifted his eyes toward Crawler. "Get going." Crawler slipped out. Marksman had just left when a door slammed somewhere else. He stepped back in and swung the door till it was almost shut, eyeball close to the crack. A male voice, in Farsi, sounded from down the hallway. Marksman grabbed the fabric on his head and yanked it off in one motion. His pistol was drawn, barrel at the door gap.

"She sold us out," Jim whispered, raising his weapon.

Marksman kept one eye on the crack. He covered his mouth with his hand, pushing the mic close, and whispered, "Jannat and an Artesh soldier are near the stairs. He hasn't seen Crawler yet. Take down?"

Jim held up his hand, palm facing Marksman. If she'd sold them out, she wouldn't be there. If they took the soldier down, she could get hit and they wouldn't have transport. They couldn't risk getting back in their trucks in daytime.

"Shit," Marksman said. "He saw Crawler. Take down?"

Jim kept his hand up. Crawler could handle it if he needed to.

Footsteps trod closer. The male voice carried through the walls. Jannat's was low, serene, seductive. A minute, then Marksman lowered his pistol. Heavy paces walked away, then fell silent.

Marksman opened the door and Crawler stepped in, followed by

Jannat. Jim drew his KA-BAR and grabbed her arm, pinning her against the wall.

"It's not what you think, sir," Crawler said.

Jim raised the knife to her chest. "We're moving. You're coming."

Crawler stood next to her. "She kept him from touching me. I was gonna gut 'im. He kept reaching out, but she pulled him back."

"He is Kia," Jannat said, trying to yank her arm away. "He is arrogant, a bad lover, but our best customer. He protects my business, like a partner. I told him your man was a new girl and wasn't ready yet."

Marksman holstered his pistol. "That's truth. I heard it."

Jannat thrust her shoulder's back. "I offered myself, but Kia wants the new girl. He always gets the girl he wants."

Jim furrowed his brow. "Crawler looks like the Hunchback of Notre Dame wearing that thing. Expect me to believe that?"

"He is like a girl that Kia enjoys. Kia has . . . other tastes."

"Men?"

"Not Kia." Jannat glanced at Crawler, then dropped her chin to her chest. "Fat women. He likes them big."

"You saying this guy wants Crawler instead of you?"

Jannat nodded.

Jim let go and sheathed his knife. "I should let him have Crawler. Where'd he go?"

"In front. He has his own room. He is waiting for her."

Marksman slapped Crawler on the chest. "Got your wish, lover boy. Keep him busy. Like you said, see the doc if you get too tired and need meds."

Crawler gripped Marksman's throat and pinned him to the wall.

"Cool it," Jim said, barely a whisper. "You're going to take him down."

Dr. Ali was standing in the bathroom door. "We don't have to. I've got Ketamine. It'll put him out a couple hours."

"Then what?" Jannat asked.

Crawler let go of Marksman. "If I off him, we could cut him up, drop him in the furnace."

"Kia is an important man," Jannat said. "His guard knows how much time he spends here. They will look here first. Plus, he is important to my business."

Steps thudded from the hall. Jim reached for Jannat but she slipped out the door, closing it behind her. Kia's voice was clear, just outside.

Marksman put his ear to the wall, giving a smile and a thumbs-up. A door slammed in the distance.

Marksman turned the black iron doorknob. Jannat was alone outside. "Lucky break," he said. "Terrorists were seen headed into Tehran. He's been called up." Marksman smirked at Crawler. "He told Jannat to tell the new girl not to be disappointed, he'd be back. Seems your Iranian name is Jamileh."

Jim walked to the window and pushed the curtain aside. He drew back and kicked the leg of one of the drivers huddled in the corner. "They're gonna lock down the city if they think we're here. We're better off on the move, outside the capital. Ali, get the DEA liaison. We need the coordinates of their safe house."

Jim stood in front of Jannat. Her slate-blue eyes were set deep. The skin wrinkled gently at the corners. Her job must be aging her faster than her years. "Where's the uniforms?"

"In the basement."

"Call for transport. You're taking us to the pickup point. Make a wrong move, we'll kill you. I'll tell your transport where we're going once we're loaded."

"What about the prisoners?" Red asked. "We gonna take 'em or burn 'em?"

Jim's hand edged back toward his KA-BAR. Jannat stepped forward and held her arms out straight as if she still carried the tray. They were shivering. "I have baskets. Big ones. The bread merchants use them. You can knock them out—or I have heroin. We can shove them inside, carry them between us, walk through the market to where the transport will pick you up. It's not far. You'll wear the *chādors*. No one will know."

The creases next to her eyes were crisp now, no longer soft and inviting. What was her angle? Why did she care about their prisoners? Wouldn't she want them dead? Fewer witnesses. Could a whore have a conscience? No, it had to be fear for her life.

"Go make sure the general left," he said. A nod to Lieutenant Richards sent him following her. Jim grabbed Salar's shoulder. He looked at one eye, then the other, trying to figure out which he was supposed to focus on. "I was told one of our drivers is a pilot. Who? One of them?" he asked pointing toward the corner.

Salar winced and looked at Marksman standing with his hand

still on the doorknob. Marksman spoke in Farsi and Salar pointed at Navid.

"What can he fly?"

Salar spoke with Navid, motioning with his hands like an Italian newscaster on speed. Navid glowered.

"He can fly most anything up to twin engine jets," Marksman said. "Mehrabad International is down the street. Says he could smuggle us in, then we could steal a plane. We'd be at the Gulf in thirty minutes."

"Ali getting us a safe house outside the city is plan one. If not, that's our backup."

Navid walked to the window, driving his thumbs into his hips, gaze searching the room. "He's worried about his cover," Marksman said. "If he flies us out, it's not like he can go back. He'll have to come with us."

"We could beat him," Carter said. He was standing next to the bathroom, rubbing his knuckles as if trying to hide them. "Not that I want to, but there's an airport right on the Strait of Hormuz. We could bloody him up to look like a hijacking, maybe break a rib, then leave him behind. We can call in a sub, a SEAL team for pickup."

"Good luck with that," Jim said. "Plus, we're almost at daybreak. We'd have to wait till night."

Marksman leaned toward Jim. "They'll kill his family. The only way we get out and his family stays alive is Carter's idea. Even then, there's a chance VEVAK won't buy it and still kill him."

Jim rested his hand atop his holster. "It's our backup. Hope we don't need it. If we do, we won't need to fake anything. He'll be flying with my barrel in his ear." Jim licked his bottom lip. It was salty and chapped. "Ali, get that message to the fusion cell. I need coordinates. We'll knock 'em out downstairs. Everyone else, to the basement with Jannat. We leave in thirty."

Chapter 22
Obstacles

The stairs to the basement were rough-hewn slate, cold and dusty. Sharp brown and orange rocks were mortared into the walls. Red followed Lori down, ducking the AK-47 slung over her shoulder. Its barrel waved across his face each time she took a step.

The basement was large with a hotel-sized washing machine. It smelled of moist earth and something else that clung to the back of Red's throat, like a hint of pepper spray. The furnace sat in a sunken area that resembled a seventies-era conversation pit. No windows. A single bare wood door, looking like an oversized Williamsburg window shutter, was on the far wall, padlocked. Jannat slipped a key from her pocket and opened it.

Inside were several racks of uniforms in various colors. It was like a military thrift store, though much better organized. Similar uniforms were grouped together and civilian clothes separated. Chevrons and insignias were piled on a white plastic table.

"How'd you get all this?" Red asked.

"My girls steal it. I pay them extra. I tell them I sell it on the black market."

Jim walked by a section of naval uniforms. "Stick with Artesh. Marksman and Lori, get a clean blouse."

The team stripped down and pulled on drab green fatigues. As Red pulled off his boots, the last remnants of the Pardis dropped onto the dirt floor. Lori was unbuttoning her blouse in the far corner. He picked up one end of a clothes rack and pulled it over, making a changing room.

Marksman tossed Crawler insignia with three diamond-tipped chevrons and a rocker at the bottom. "Thanks," Crawler said. He looked at them in his open hand, then closed his fist so tightly that the tendons stretched. He threw them back, hitting Marksman's chest. "Prick," he said.

Must still be failing his master sergeant exams.

Red pulled on a too-tight boot. All the larger ones were taken, and he certainly didn't have the largest feet of the group. He patted his chest pockets, feeling naked without body armor. Lanyard pulled up his T-shirt. Two bruises discolored his belly, one large and gruesomely purple. "That must be the one you felt."

"I felt all three," he said, twisting around as if trying to find another.

They carried only weapons and ammo. Jannat didn't have any small arms, so they'd have to carry their M4s and pray they didn't need to take off the *chādors*. Jannat's hands shook as she attached a veil over Red's face. The veins on her hands stood out. They looked paper-thin, old. The dim light reflected from her oily skin, which smelled sweet, like honey. Her upper lip lifted on one side, as if she were trying to smile. Her breath stunk of garlic as she spoke. "Veils are not often worn. But some tribes do. Don't walk close to each other. Try not to look like a group."

Jim had Ali save his Ketamine and took Jannat up on her offer of heroin. Crawler and Jim held the prisoners while Ali shot them up, then stuffed them into the market baskets, sideways in the fetal position.

Jannat pulled out a frayed paper map and placed it on the earthen floor under one of the lights. Everyone stood around her as she squatted over the map, the bottom of her red dress fringed with yellow dust. She pointed to the location of the house and the pickup point for their transport. "One truck, a refrigerated one with a picture of fish on the side. That's what they use. Go through the market, here. We'll not be noticeable among all the people."

Jim's thick index finger followed a different route over the map, then punched down. "The trucks from last night. They here?"

"Yes." Jannat tapped the same spot.

"If we get split or the transport goes bad, that's where we rally."

A click sounded in Red's ear. Covered in a *chādor*, he'd forgotten he had it.

"Comm check," Jim muttered.

Thumbs-up from everyone.

Jim put Jannat in the lead. He and Carter tailed her, carrying a basket with one of the prisoners between them. "Red, you and Lanyard follow after the drivers. If they run, shoot 'em. Marksman, make sure they understand."

Red walked up the stairs, glancing back at Lori. He wished she could walk in front so he could watch her. At the top, through a window, he saw an orange glow behind the Tehran skyline, reminding him of the dark silhouettes of the trees during his cold morning runs. Their skeletal lines, though bare in winter, had always given him a sense of energy, just before the sun peeked out and warmed his face. The hard edges of these buildings were cold, unforgiving. Yet, both shared the same backdrop. What was it that drove humanity to such misunderstanding and violence? Was he part of the problem? He pushed the thought from his mind. Now the only thing to do was get Lori home safely. Get everyone home safely.

The cold air from the street pricked his skin. He walked through occasional warmer pockets, the timid heat rising from the heavy stones underfoot. He looked over his shoulder. Lori was still there, but too far back. Crawler looked like an elephant under a black sheet waddling before him. The group was entirely too large. They should have left the traitorous drivers to burn back at the warehouse. Now they were just dead weight, slowing them down.

Jannat kept a brisk pace, welcome in the cold. Jim had given her a comm since she was in point. At least with comms they could communicate if they lost visual.

The rope handle dug into Red's hand. The basket creaked as they walked. He tried to get out of step, to look more like two normal women carrying produce to the market, but Lanyard kept synchronizing his strides.

The market wasn't crowded yet, but vendors were raising umbrellas and sweet pastry smells filled the air. All the alleyways they passed had several people headed in their direction.

"Four soldiers," came Jannat's voice through the comm. Red stretched his neck to look. She'd already passed the men in uniform. Their rifles were over their shoulders, but they looked more interested in the stand of steaming pastries.

"Keep moving," Jim said.

Red kept his nose down, but his eyes looked ahead. Jim and Carter passed the soldiers without a glance. Red held his M4 straight down his belly, leaning over to ensure it didn't poke out of the *chā-dor*. He was careful not to make eye contact. Jannat had said that would be improper. One of the soldiers was smiling as he looked at a pastry with honey-brown glaze. His boots were highly polished. Could be a desk jockey pulled from his paperwork to look for them. Red strained to keep from glancing back, but had to turn his head. Lori was still there.

Crawler had just passed the pastry stand when his foot slammed against a stone. He stumbled, but continued. The noise from his boot made two of the soldiers turn their heads, but only one did a double take. He turned toward Crawler and looked at him as he walked away. Taking a couple steps in halfhearted pursuit, the soldier shouted something.

"Keep going," Marksman commed. "He's telling you to stop."

The soldier shouted again.

"Ignore him," Jim said.

More shouting. Crawler kept up his pace but the soldier quickened, too. Now the other three were following.

"He's looking at your feet," Red commed. "He sees your boots."

"These ain't old-lady-sized," Crawler said.

"He's not giving up. Take down?" Marksman asked.

"Nothing unless he stops you," Jim said.

The soldier jogged to catch up with Crawler. One of his buddies put a cell phone to his ear. Red slipped his free hand forward and rested a finger on the trigger guard. There was no good way this was going to play out.

The soldier stopped and reached out to grab Crawler's shoulder, then fell to his knees as a 9mm hole puffed silently out through Marksman's *chādor*. A second later, the man fell forward onto the river stone pavement.

"One down," Marksman said. Red hadn't even seen him reach for his sidearm.

A woman was raising a faded red umbrella over a stand of oranges and grapefruit. She turned toward the clatter of metal hitting stone as the body fell atop its weapon. The other soldier kept the phone to his ear, backing up till he stumbled over a basket of bread. A white-haired woman with furrowed skin yelled at him, while the other two ran toward their fallen comrade.

"Heyvoon! Gom sho!" the woman shouted, picking up the trampled wares.

The soldier with the phone looked at the crowd, ignoring the vocal woman. His gaze met Red's. He dropped the device and reached for his AK, shuddering and falling atop powder-coated pastries as Red placed a three-shot burst into his chest. Brass tinkled to the ground. *Shit, I wasn't as discreet as Marksman.*

Red picked the basket back up and kept walking. Loud footsteps from dress shoes on stone ran away behind him. "Two down, but he was on a phone," Red commed.

In a few more seconds panic would break out. They could make their escape in the chaos. He pushed the basket toward Lanyard, aiming them to the next alley. A woman in a gray wool peacoat and black hijab over her head trotted into the market, a cell phone pressed to her ear. She passed a squat man with a unibrow thick enough to use as a comb-over. He stared down at a video camera, panning across a box of yellow chicks.

The two last soldiers reached their fallen comrade lying in the middle of the market, looked down and said something to him, laughing. One tilted his head, then dropped to a knee and rolled the dead soldier over. His eyes widened and they shouted at each other, looking around. They pointed folded-stock AKs toward Crawler and yelled.

Crawler spun and from under his *chādor* came a deafening stream of muzzle blasts. His covering blew into shreds, revealing an extra-large brassiere stuffed with a blue towel over green fatigues. His square frame braced against the recoil of the weapon. His veil blew out, exposing an unshaven face with a cigar butt clenched between smiling teeth.

"Break off!" the colonel commed. "Rally at secondary. Meet at our trucks. Red, keep track of the drivers."

Red crawled atop a display of apples. Their sharp, green scent reminded him of helping Tom make hard cider last fall. Over the displays he saw Salar and Navid sprint into the next alley as many in the crowd dropped to the ground. He and Lanyard grabbed the basket and ran. At the end of the block, he turned to head them off. One ran across the opening ahead. As the other came into view, two red plumes sprayed from the driver's chest, followed by the reports of small arms fire.

Red ducked behind a dusty green hedge at the corner and signaled Lanyard to fall in behind him. He strained to hear footsteps over the screams and shouts coming from the market. A balding gray-haired man with a little potbelly trotted across the alley, carrying a 9mm. When he stopped at Salar's body, Red dropped him with a double tap, then glanced around the corner. A crowd from the market that had been running toward them stopped when the man went down. None of these were in uniform, but then neither was the man who'd shot Salar and Navid.

Red ran to Salar. Lanyard took position at the corner of the hedge, covering their tail. Red pushed the potbellied man off him— the guy was heavier than he looked—then rolled Salar onto his back. Blood was seeping from his chest. His eye wasn't wandering now. His pupils constricted as he faced the sky. Red searched his pockets and found the truck keys. He put a finger to Navid's neck. The pilot had no pulse.

"Got the keys," he said, lifting the basket.

Lanyard jerked his head at Salar. "One still looks alive."

"He'll be dead soon." Only a few more blocks lay between them and the trucks.

Red commed as they ran, "Salar and Navid are dead. We've got keys. Be there in two."

"Hurry up," Jim said. "We're all waiting."

They turned another corner and saw the first vehicle at the end of the alley. They yanked off their *chādors* and shoved them behind a moldy stack of cardboard boxes. Several other *chādors* from the team were already there. The only other person in view was a street down and walking away, a man in brown slacks, apparently unaware of the chaos a few blocks over.

The side of the first truck dropped and Crawler and Marksman rolled out. Red threw one set of keys to Crawler, hoping it was the right one.

"Marksman, get us to the airport," Jim snapped. "Red, drive the second."

Red opened the door and slid across the seat, snagging one cargo pocket on the stick shift. Only a few hours ago he'd seen the plume of steam rising from the vehicle's hood. He hoped the engine was still warm enough to make a fast start. He punched the clutch and turned the key, then tilted his head back and said, "Thank you, God," as the engine fired. He raced the motor but it sputtered off, the truck shuddering. He turned the key again. This time the engine cranked for several seconds before it came to life.

Crawler was pulling away. Red eased the gas this time and the engine revved slowly, but kept running. "Shit," he muttered. Were gear patterns universal? He moved the stick to where he thought first would be. The shift box resisted with a crunching sound.

"Like the farm," he whispered. "Grind 'em till you find 'em."

"What?" Lori's voice.

Red snapped his head around. She was climbing into the seat beside him. "Where'd you come from? Get in the back!"

"What if we hit a checkpoint?"

"I'll run 'em over. You don't look Iranian, and I can't protect you up here."

She waved the barrel of her AK-47 toward the windshield. "Stick a rag in it and drive the damn truck."

Ahead, Crawler was almost at the end of the block. Red popped the clutch, snapping her neck backwards. "Why do you have to be so stubborn?"

"I'm not the one who went ape-shit at Walmart and blew your cover."

Red's face warmed despite the cold draft coming from the door. What was she hiding? "Maybe if I had a wife who'd told me I had a cover . . . maybe then—"

Her voice softened. "Red, we decided it was best."

I'm the husband! Shouldn't *we* include me? "Who the hell are you talking about? You're a control freak. Or wait—" He frowned. "Did *we* include whoever you're carrying a tag for?"

She shook her head. "Red, you know why I've got a tag."

"No, I don't!"

Lori frowned. "But—"

He jabbed two fingers at his head. "Didn't get the memo. Had a memory issue for a while. No damn clue why my wife's a national asset. It sure as hell isn't your cooking."

The comm clicked in his ear. "Plug it," Jim's voice crackled. "I can hear you two bitching all the way back here."

Would he ever know Lori? Could he? Why was he trying to rescue someone who'd helped hide his past? Who was behind all of it? But she was the mother of their kids. That much he remembered, with fondness. He'd promised them he'd get her back. He could do that. The rest would have to wait.

"I'll get us to the airport, but we've got no pilot," Marksman commed.

"We'll take one hostage," Jim said.

Red smiled and jabbed his comm. "Sir, we've got a pilot."

Lori palmed her mic and snatched the comm out of her ear. "You better not be talking about me!"

Red yanked his out as well. He whispered, "Stick a rag in it and drive the damn plane, *dear*."

"You're such an ass!" she hissed. "That was before I even met you. In my twenties!"

"You said you flew twins."

"Ten hours of cockpit time, Red. Turpboprops, not jets. I never even qualified."

"You had your license before that. Singles. Might be a turboprop at the airport. You can get us off the ground."

"Shit, Crawler could get us off the ground. It's landing that's a bitch."

Crawler's truck slowed at an intersection and turned onto a busier road. Red stopped at the corner, then gunned it to keep up. Lori was looking out the window, the corner of one eye shimmering, hands clasped, fidgeting as if playing thumb-war with herself.

Red patted her knee. "Sorry. But for real, we need you. It'll come back, just like things did for me. With enough clear runway, you'll do great." Red slipped the comm back into his ear.

Jim was calling his name. "What happened?"

Red looked at Lori. "Um, communication issue, sir."

"What did you mean, we've got a pilot?"

"Lori used to have her license. Got some twin engine time. She's rusty, but if we can't hijack a turboprop, she'll fly us out."

Chapter 23
Takeoff

Crawler shoved the shift lever forward to where third gear should be. The handle wobbled. Was it even in a gear? He released the clutch and the truck jerked like it'd been hit from behind. What a piece of crap. Not that American trucks didn't have loose linkage, especially the older, well-worn models. But give him a good ol' AM General Duece-and-a-Half any day over this Iranian shit-box.

Marksman pointed to a green sign, scrawled in something like Egyptian hieroglyphics. "Take a right on Saeedi Highway."

Crawler squinted at the signpost. It looked like one of his ink blot tests from Dr. Genova. "Where the hell's that?"

"Just go right."

"Give 'em to me like that," Crawler said. "None of that other crap."

He rolled down his window and adjusted the side view. Red was keeping up, though Crawler noticed he had trouble at intersections, lurching his starts. The engine knocked. He hadn't heard it last night, sitting in the back. Sounded like a bad exhaust gasket. Vapors coming from the firewall confirmed it.

A white Mercedes with a blue stripe passed going the other way. A block down, it made a U-turn.

Crawler glanced at the mirror next to Marksman. "Sorry to interrupt your fun."

Marksman slid down in his seat, planting both feet flat on the floor. "It's not what you think. Jannat and I are business partners."

Crawler ignored the distant white-and-blue car. Probably headed to the market where he'd just saved everyone's ass. "Yeah. Right."

Marksman put an arm across the back of the seat, the wrist as thick as an axle tube. For an old guy, he looked like he could still hold his own in a fight.

"Make it whatever you want." Marksman swept a hand across a dusty green dashboard. "But I've been married thirty years. Like hell I'm going to throw that away on some whore. She's pitiful. You imagine being the pet of that general?"

"I almost was," Crawler said, thinking how the arrogant prick had tried to grab his ass. Yet Jannat had somehow stopped him. She was discreet. The general had never suspected a thing.

Marksman tilted his head to both sides, cracking his neck. "Then, like all whores, she has to pretend like she enjoys it."

Crawler blew through tight lips. Right. She'd said it in the way she looked at Marksman from the start. He wasn't stupid, though he supposed the team thought he was. She enjoyed it. She loved it. How could she not? He mustered the most condescending tone he could. "How sweet."

Marksman drummed his fingers on the roof. "Ain't worth my breath. Take the next right."

At the end of the road stretched an open grass field, then a runway. If the street didn't turn, it would lead onto the overrun strip. "That it?"

Marksman gave a whoop. "Mehrabad." He raised a long finger and pointed. "Looks like the small aircraft terminal's at two o'clock. That's where we go. Take another right, around to the other side."

Crawler peered in the side view, then accelerated. He pressed his comm while searching vainly for a safety belt. "Get ready. We're goin' Dukes of Hazzard."

"We're doing what?"

Crawler gritted his teeth. "Hold on."

"Go around!" Marksman yelled, gripping the dashboard.

Crawler kept his nose straight at the end of the runway. The street merged ahead with another that circled the airport. If he could jump the drainage ditch, all he'd have to deal with was a chain-link security fence.

Something was going on in the seat next to him. Marksman was yelling, one arm clamped to the underside of the seat, the other braced against the roof. Crawler couldn't hear him over the roar of the engine and the knocking, coming louder and more rapid. What was Marksman's problem?

Crawler checked his speed. What the hell? Ninety? He wasn't going that fast. Speedo's broke. Going to have to wing it. Drainage ditch didn't look that wide. He shot across the opposite side of the road, timing himself between oncoming vehicles. There was a culvert with a small upward angle to it, like a ramp. He floored the accelerator when he hit it, remembering how his cousin had taught him to keep his nose up when jumping dirt bikes. Couldn't be much different. They lifted somewhat, the engine red-lining when the rear wheels left the ground. The landing was smoother than Crawler had anticipated, the front axle slamming against the bump stops on the frame, but no grinding gears. No snap of mutilated shafts.

"The fence!" Marksman yelled, ducking below the dashboard. *He must not have found a seatbelt, either.* Crawler kept the accelerator down and leaned sideways till his nose touched the shift knob. The security fence ripped over them, taking the side-view mirrors and the top of the windshield frame with it.

He sat back up and gazed at Marksman huddled on the floorboard. The tagline from a motivational poster he'd seen hanging in an office came to mind. Maybe he could teach Marksman something. "That's the difference between you and me," Crawler said. "You see an obstacle as something in your way, but I never sees 'em cause I gots my eyes on the goal."

"Idiot!"

Crawler stuck his head out the shattered window and looked back. Red was still there, but his front bumper was gone and dirt was caked in the grille. The driver side wheel was wobbling, trying to rip itself from the lugs.

"We had company," Crawler said. "A police car."

Red's wheel grabbed a rut and his truck steered sideways enough for Crawler to see behind him. The police car was angled toward the culvert. It launched well, but didn't have enough speed. The nose plowed into the ditch bank and flipped an endo till it stopped upside down, leaning against a broken patch of chain link.

The truck slowed in a soft spot and Crawler downshifted. "The major did okay," he said, "but the police didn't commit. Probably better. We'd have to kill 'em if they made it." Crawler leaned back, crunching against broken glass. At least Red had learned something. Everyone should know how to handle a truck. Marksman was back on the seat, gripping the dash with both hands. He always had a big head, thinking he was so much smarter. Would he ever listen?

Red scanned the runway. Not a single plane on it, or the taxi-way. "Must've locked down the airport," he commed. "All the planes are at the terminal." Glancing to Lori, he said, "I don't see any props out here." A small white dual-engine prop plane rested on the far side of the runway with several single-engine ones, but it wasn't nearly large enough for everyone.

"Go for the light blue one in the middle," Lori said. "The one with the fuel truck next to her. Gulfstream. I think it's got a built-in auxiliary power unit so we can get her started."

Crawler cut in front of him as he pointed his truck to it. Red turned the wheel, its spokes shaking so hard he had to keep a loose grip on the rim. "Gulfstream," he said. "We can squeeze into it. Only a couple hundred miles to the coast. We should try for Al-Asad. No, Balad's closer."

"Jim's working on it," Lori said. "Right now I just want off the ground. Any chance of getting a pilot?"

"I don't even see baggage handlers. If they've locked down, we won't find any pilots."

Crawler slammed the brakes and skidded to a stop, broadside to the aircraft. Red did the same near the tail.

Jim rolled out the back, yelling as he came. "Richards, cover the far side. Lanyard, clear the aircraft. Everyone else, defensive positions."

The sides of the trucks dropped and the teams rolled out as in a Chinese fire drill. Lanyard drew his sidearm and ran up the stairs. "All clear except a steward in the bathroom," he called after a quick check.

"Keep him there," Lori said, running into the plane. "I may need him."

Red stood next to the front wheel of his truck. The rim was bent inward so badly the tire should have blown. He scanned the perimeter fence. Open ground and runway stretched for at least a half mile to it. Two green jeeps and a few trucks stopped close to where they'd busted through. He ducked and looked under the plane. On that side were other small aircraft and the airport. The best place for the Iranians to attack would be from there, using the terminal and planes as cover.

Lori was yelling something in Farsi inside the aircraft. Then it sounded like French. She ran down the ladder, pointing to the near wing. Her jugular bulged blue from her neck, contrasting with the chalky paleness of her face, making her eyes dark and sinister. "Only one tank's full. We have to balance, and the steward's useless. It'd be faster to fill the other tank."

Crawler slung his weapon and ran to the wing. As he dropped to his knees, his momentum carried him below it, leaning backwards like he was doing the limbo. He slapped the underside like he was swatting flies until a panel dropped. With a grunt and a firm twist he connected the fuel hose.

"How long?" Jim asked.

"Five minutes, maybe, once I figure out how to turn this thing on," he said.

Jim pointed above his head and made whirlybird swirls. "We need a perimeter for five minutes. They'll try to block the runway. At this point I don't give a shit who they are. Police, military, civilian. Shoot anything that gets in the way. Use the trucks to clear the runway if we have to."

Red scanned the airport perimeter again. "Marksman, what we got?"

Marksman was standing behind the front of Crawler's truck, M14 resting atop the hood, aimed toward the breach in the fence. His head was forward, peering through the scope. "Three jeeps and three ten-wheelers. Same ones we got. Ambulance just got here and someone's coming out of the wreck." He lifted his head, squinting. "The mashed car is in the way. Can't come across the ditch like we did."

A flicker of light glimmered from Red's periphery. Seconds later the distant clatter of rifle fire sounded across the open field. He ducked, though any shot from a half mile away would be luck, unless they already had a sniper on scene.

"Marksman, keep their fire down," Jim said.

Marksman hugged his stock and spread his legs. Red lifted his gaze, exposing his head over the hood, squinting at the distance. A few stick figures near the road stood between two jeeps. Marksman's rifle boomed, two beats of a heart passed, and one of the sticks dropped flat backwards. The other men dove behind the jeeps without trying to help him. Seconds later, the rifle's echo roared back across the expanse like far-off thunder, bouncing off gray-brown office buildings.

"That was a lucky shot," Marksman said. "This ain't my 50 cal."

"Keep them behind cover," Jim said. "They should know we've got hostages. Won't make any moves till it's too late. Disable the trucks if you can."

This place will go to hell when the plane starts rolling, Red thought.

A white sedan with flashing yellow lights screeched around the corner of a Boeing 777 at the next terminal over. Crawler followed it and shot twice. Blue smoke billowed from underneath as the engine self-destructed, metal grinding and snapping in low grumbles. A small piece of it punched through the hood before it died. The sedan slowed and ran off the jetway. The driver threw open his door and dove into the grass. A flame came through the hole in the hood and thick smoke streamed from the wheel wells. The driver stood and sprinted away from their position. Crawler took aim.

"Let him go," Marksman said. "He'll be gone by the time we get rolling."

Something moved near the fence. Red squinted. The larger trucks were pulling away, moving along the perimeter road. Lori leaned out the door of the aircraft. "We're at a quarter full," she yelled.

Marksman nuzzled his stock. "There's an old Jeep Wagoneer, their command car. Looks like—" He lifted his head and squinted, then stared through the scope again. "Your boyfriend got here, Crawler. He's squatted behind the Wagoneer."

"How you know it's him?" Crawler asked.

"I stared at his ugly face through the crack in the door."

Crawler's day-old whiskers darkened in the creases of his skin as he smiled. "Bet you can't hit him."

Dust blew from the hood as Marksman's rifle boomed.

Red flinched. "You get him?"

"No . . . But he'll change his pants before going back to Jannat's."

Jannat. Where was she? She'd never have sold them out, Red thought. If she did, VEVAK would kill her anyway. She'd been doing this too long. He glanced at Jim. His gaze was hard, unyielding.

Red drew a line with his arm. "The trucks stopped a half mile down the road."

"What's over there?" Jim asked.

"Can't tell," Marksman said. "There's a gate, so there's a way across."

"They're going to rush us," Jim said. "Pull the trucks closer together. Protect this broadside." He stooped and called under the plane, "Richards, this could be a diversion. Keep your eyes on the terminal. Red, you and Lanyard stay here but back up Richards if he calls for it." He turned and yelled in the direction of the cockpit, "How we doing?"

"Almost half," came Lori's voice from inside.

Red backed his truck closer, parking it in front of the jet's engine. There was no way the Iranians could have organized a diversion and an assault in such a short time. The enemy knew they'd be taking off soon. If the Iranians were going to do something, it would be now and it would be desperate.

Chapter 24
No Man's Land

Red stood behind the front wheel and alternated his attention between the fence and the cockpit. The ambulance was pulling away from the overturned police car. Something moved down the road. The trucks again? He squinted, then dread pitted his stomach.

"Lori! We need to get moving *now*!" He ran to the end of the truck and pointed down the road. A tall-tracked armored personnel carrier was running toward the trucks waiting outside the gate. "Looks like an M113. We've got nothing against that."

"Crawler!" Jim shouted. "Unhook the fuel truck. Lori, get us airborne."

"Two-thirds full," came her reply from the cockpit. A low growling came from under the engine cowling. "I need a few minutes to get wound up."

"Crawler, grab the steward and get him in front where they can see him," Jim said.

Red turned his ear toward the engine. Starting a jet wasn't like a piston aircraft, was it? Were the controls even written in English? Maybe she needed Marksman to read something. The Iranians wouldn't care about hostages. In two minutes, they'd be overrun. They had to get in the air.

"Marksman, I've got an idea that could buy us a couple minutes," Red said. "Next to the gate. What is it?"

Marksman adjusted his rifle a few degrees. "A fuel station. Little planes over that side. Props."

"That a fuel truck?"

"Yeah."

"Can you set it off?"

"Jet fuel don't work like that," Crawler said, shoving the barrel of his 9mm into the side of the steward's neck. "It's like diesel. You can throw a match into a can and it won't burn."

Red pointed to the fuel truck. "We're not at a military base. You said those are props over there. The truck could have some avgas in it."

Marksman's clip clattered onto the hood of the truck. He pulled another from a satchel near the small of his back.

"Incendiaries?" Red asked.

Marksman's stock pushed up against his cheek. "I wish. Armor piercing. All I've got. Maybe it'll spark on the way through."

The large green trucks lumbered behind the APC like tired trail horses. Marksman got off a shot. Nothing. Marksman lifted his rifle a little higher. Red wondered, could he even see the truck through the scope at that angle? A large tanker, but at this distance it would still take luck to hit it. The APC pivoted on its tracks, turning off the road, heading to the gate. Marksman's rifle rang: two, three, four times. The gate blew open and slapped against the fence as the APC hit it center on.

Maybe Red could cripple it if he rammed it with the truck. He was groping in his pocket for the key when a flash of heat hit his face. An orange balloon rose silently, several stories high where the fuel truck used to be. It faded to yellow, supported by a column of black soot. A section of piping shot out from it, flipping like a leaf blown by a passing car. A second explosion, maybe from a divided tank, shot yellow-blue sideways and low, soaking the gate and several small planes in flame.

A crack, then a guttural rumble shook their truck, like hearing distant thunderstorms over the Chesapeake. The blaze stuck to the ground, burning hot like napalm. The APC emerged from the fireball covered in flames. It slowed and three tiki torches stumbled from the back, dancing a short time, silhouetted against the backdrop of black soot, then fell and burned out.

Red's smile faded as he remembered one of Father Ingram's sermons on hell. "Separate from God. No one to hear your scream, or even care." He imagined being one of the tikis, skin scorching, running around with his only consolation being it would be over soon. Or would it? A howl from Crawler shook him from his stupor.

"Beautiful." Jim slapped Marksman's shoulder. "Get ready for the rest!" He squatted and yelled under the plane. "Richards, anything on your side?"

"Negative."

The engines whined and everyone looked at Jim. The ten-wheelers and several jeeps skidded around the edge of the flames, running in the open grass, moving fast.

"Hold your positions," Jim ordered. He walked to the nose of Red's truck and pressed his comm. *"Can't have any alive."*

Even a lucky shot from a sidearm could take down a jet. It was good the trucks were coming now instead of when they started down the runway. If Artesh had any sense, they'd wait till the plane was moving, most vulnerable. This might still work out for the better.

Next to Jim, Red laid several clips on the hood. Lanyard knelt at the bumper. Crawler shoved the steward toward the terminal and the guy ran off, hands skyward. Artesh wouldn't be stopping for hostages. The trucks spread out when they crossed the runway. One of the jeeps smashed a raised red landing light on a yellow pedestal in its grille.

Marksman shot first, well outside everyone else's range. Red leaned into his weapon, eyeing the lead jeep. It slowed as its fractured engine block self-destructed. Marksman fired again and the second jeep turned away. The edge of its wheel caught the pavement and the truck rolled onto its side, sparks flying from the grooved runway. At around three hundred meters everyone fired. *Get enough bullets flying, someone's got to get hit.* Red took aim at the drivers, or at least where he thought they'd be hunched below the windshields. Men leapt from the stalled trucks and followed their comrades on foot.

At a hundred meters, Crawler got off a well-placed shot with his grenade launcher. The front wheel of the lead truck dug in. Soft earth dragged it to a stop like a plowshare in a field. The driver shifted to a lower gear and it struggled forward, then stopped when Marksman punched a hole below the windshield frame.

The last truck sped forward, accelerating toward the plane. All rifles followed its progress. *Driver must be dead*, thought Red. The guy's head was slumped onto the huge steering wheel. It kept coming toward Red's position as the Gulfstream's engines wound up behind him. Everyone backed away as the dead driver crashed into

Red's truck, careening off, and just missing the tail of the Gulf-stream, resting once it collided with a Jetway.

The plane rolled forward a few inches.

Red ran back to the nose of his truck. Oil was leaking from under the engine, a tinge of carbon adding to the acrid stink of gunpowder. He rested his rifle on the warm, crumpled hood. Soldiers were out in the open field, sprinting from truck to truck as cover, though Marksman still brought several to a halt with rapid, accurate fire. After that they stayed put, occasionally exposing themselves to fire, but scampering back before being hit.

Jim pointed to no-man's-land. "*E1, E2, finish them off. No prisoners. Crawler, protect our backside. Everyone else, cover.*"

Red sprinted around him to the open field. As he passed, Jim knocked his legs out from under him, driving Red into the patch of warm oil under the truck. Jim opened fire. The crack of an AK-47 came from behind, bursting the bent tire in front of Red's face, loud as a grenade. Crawler knelt by the far side landing gear, firing at something hidden behind the Gulfstream.

At last, the AKs stopped. Jim's boots staggered next to the bumper. Red rolled out and caught him as he fell back.

"Doc!" Red shouted, dragging Jim to the burst wheel, leaning him against the rim. From a small hole in the chest of his blouse, blood dyed the green of his fatigues brown. Red laid him flat and pressed a palm over the wound, stopping the bleeding.

Jim stared up into the sky. When Ali leaned over and opened a green attaché, Jim wrapped one hairy fist around his collar as if grabbing a dog by the scruff of the neck. He pulled him close. "Don't let me die in this damn uniform," Jim said.

Eyes still on Jim, Red felt the team's gaze burn into his back. He looked up, still applying pressure to Jim's chest. The men were different now, their eyes clouded with doubt. Fringed like the dust on Jannat's dress, in the basement, when she stooped over the map. They'd all stooped too low. Doubt was an infection that needed to be cut out. It rattled a cage inside his belly.

Ali pulled Red's hand off Jim's chest. "I need to get at the wound, sir."

Sir? The entire op it'd been *Red*, or maybe *Major*. Something awoke now, inside that cage, as bullets clattered against the engine and gearbox. Thick sulfuric gear lubricant fell, mixing into the oil pool like cream in coffee. Jim was right. No-man's-land had to be cleared. Red looked at Lieutenant Richards. No, Richards shouldn't go in case Red got killed. "Lanyard, Crawler, Carter, follow me. Everyone else, cover."

Red ran past the mangled front grille of his truck, accelerating to a sprint, Lanyard right behind him. Footfalls from the others running to keep up followed close. A hundred meters lay between them and the first dead truck. A soldier in a maroon beret stepped out beside the wheel mired deep into the earth. Red dropped to his knees, sliding in the muck, bringing his rifle to bear. His finger wasn't yet on the trigger when half the soldier's skull exploded, spraying tannish brain matter across the heads of uncut grass. That would be the last time Marksman beat him to the shot, Red resolved.

Red hid behind the grille of the truck. Crawler scurried up, breathing hard. Red held up two fingers, then a fist, and pointed to the rear of the truck. Crawler smiled and pulled two grenades. He tossed them below the rear axle. The grenades boomed, one after the other, the second blast muffling a scream. Red circled around. A soldier wearing the same epaulets as Crawler was sprawled on his back in the grass, clawing away from the truck, digging in with his elbows, knees too mangled to rise. Red looked away and squeezed the trigger.

AKs clattered from the direction of the next truck only the width of a football field away. Red flattened himself behind the body of the soldier he'd shot and Lanyard dove behind the truck. He couldn't see any shooters, only muzzle flashes from behind the tires.

He stayed flat, shots passing overhead, the pressure waves slapping his back, deceptively gentle. The *crack-crack-crack* rang in his ears.

Marksman's rifle sounded again. *Thank God.* Red brought up his M4 in time to see a helmet roll out from under one of the other truck's wheels. A second soldier stood and ran away, keeping the truck between himself and Marksman. Red put his iron sights two feet ahead of the guy and squeezed the trigger, dropping him chest-first.

He held up a fist and pointed to the truck. Crawler took aim and launched a grenade behind it. Several soldiers abandoned cover and ran into the open field. Shooting them in the back as they're running away only *seems* cowardly, Red told himself, squeezing the trigger again and again, raising his sights higher for the faster ones headed to the edge of the runway. He couldn't risk even one getting a lucky shot at the Gulfstream. After that, soldiers abandoned the other vehicles like rats fleeing a warehouse fire. His team got all they could, but the smart ones would still be out there, hiding in the grass, waiting for them to move to the runway.

The pitch of the engines rose. Red ran back to the plane, Marksman's rifle punctuating the end of any Artesh soldier stupid enough to break cover. Fire came from the perimeter fence, but only a few bullets slapped the concrete. *Time to get in the air, before someone shows up with a heavy MG.*

Ali had the colonel's shirt off and a mound of bandage strapped to his chest, crimson blooming in its center. Red was glad not to see any evidence of an exit wound as he helped Ali lift Jim in a fireman's carry, staggering under the weight.

The plane rolled forward. Lori yelled something from the cockpit, her words indecipherable above the whine of the jets.

Crawler stood beside Marksman, eyeing the field as everyone scrambled up the ladder, throwing the baskets that carried their prisoners onto the floor, like thoughtless baggage handlers. Red kicked them down the aisle; Richards pulled them the rest of the way. Red envied their heroin-induced oblivion.

He leaned outside the open door and called, "Crawler, Marksman." A bullet smacked next to his skull, and burned itself into the plastic bulkhead. It was turned sideways, keyholed, having lost ballistic stability during its long flight.

Crawler cut the tie-down straps that held the crates in the back of his truck. He pushed the stack out onto the tarmac and heaved one of the larger ones onto his back. A flat box.

Marksman had one foot on the ladder, running with the other like a skateboarder shoving off as the plane rolled forward.

"Leave it!" Red yelled, scowling. Crawler held it tightly, trotting toward the ladder.

"Son of a bitch!" Marksman said as he jumped off and pitched his M14 up to Red. He grabbed the other end of the crate and helped run it to the plane. Red jumped out of the way. The crate landed at his feet, gouging a long rip in the carpet. He was about to shove it back out but Crawler and Marksman jumped through the door and hefted it to the back of the plane.

Jim was on the floor, legs elevated on an Italian leather chair. The prisoners were still in the baskets, now atop the cracked wooden crate in front of the bathroom. Everyone else was gaping out the windows.

"Shoot through them if you see anything!" Red yelled.

Ali reached into Jim's cargo pocket and tossed the sat phone to him. He needed to get in touch with their Navy liaison. Maybe get an escort. Probably wouldn't work without notification. He hit speed dial for the Det. Judging by the echo on the other end, they had him on speakerphone in the fusion cell's command center. He gave their status, then said, "Give them our position. Make sure the trigger-happy squids know we're flying toward the Gulf, low altitude, not squawking shit."

Cold wind swept through the door as the plane lurched forward. They weren't even on the runway yet. Red pointed Richards to the door, then ducked into the cockpit. Lori's fingers were stretched across the throttles as she pushed them forward. In front three security cars were headed onto the far end of the runway.

Crawler yelled from the back, "Jeeps are swarming the runway behind us."

Red leaned over to Lori. "Maybe there's a cross runway."

"Taxiway's empty. Should have enough to get us in the air." She worked the rudder, weaving the plane back and forth like a drunk. Ahead was a break in the pavement, a thirty-foot grass strip.

"Stop there and make a run-up in the other direction," he said. "More distance that way."

Lori pushed a lever down and the flap gauge pinned out at forty. She shoved the throttles forward all the way. Red jumped into the other seat and punched his comm. *"Brace!"* She was going to try to make it across.

As they approached the grass strip, she pulled back on the wheel and the nose angled up. When the rear wheels reached the opening, Red was pressed forward in the harness as the earth clawed at the tires of the heavy plane. Metal utensils tinkled in the pantry. Wood snapped near the back as the crate crashed into Crawler's seat. The nose slammed back down, but the plane was already on the other side of the strip and they were accelerating again.

At one hundred ten knots Lori mumbled, "Close enough." She pulled back on the wheel once more.

The rumbling of the taxiway fell silent. The plane lifted off. Lori held it on a shallow angle till the airport fence, then pulled into a steep climb, banking away.

The plane shuddered. "Look for a lever with a little wheel on the end," she said. "Put the gear up!"

Red flipped the control and the vibrations stopped. The plane fell silent. Tension seemed to vaporize into the thinning atmosphere through the craft's metal skin.

Red reached across the console and kneaded Lori's shoulder. "You did good," he said, smiling. Her traps were tight under his fingers, then softened as she relaxed her neck and breathed a sigh. Her cheeks bloomed pink and the paleness of her knuckles on the wheel disappeared.

They'd be out of Iran in less than an hour. All they had to do was land the plane.

Hope pressed Red's consciousness, asking to be let in. But they weren't out of danger yet. "Get distracted, and get killed," Tom always said.

Red twisted as far as he could to look down the aisle. It was a private transport with plush lavender carpet and fuchsia paneling. Ten steel-blue seats and room for more. He unhooked himself and walked back. Marksman had his rifle across his lap, reloading, still smelling like the Pardis. Crawler pushed the crate back and righted the three market baskets, then lit a fresh cigar. Richards and Carter kept watch out the windows. Jim was still on the floor, one eye cracked open.

Red pointed at Crawler, about to tell him to put out his cigar, but noticed he was still holding the sat phone. Its clock said it had been on for four minutes.

He put it to his ear. Bitching Betty droned "*Altitude, altitude.*" He looked toward the cockpit. It wasn't coming from there. Must be from the phone.

Then a young female voice came through the mic, drowning out Betty's warning. "*Repeat, two bogies. Time to intercept, five minutes. Look like MIG 29s.*"

Chapter 25
Improvise

The wheel went slack in Lori's hands. The port wing dropped and slammed down, as if there was a pothole in the air. "Turbulence," she said, remembering a rough landing once following a turbo-prop, not allowing enough time for the air to settle.

"How long?" Red yelled into the phone. His eyes were sharp and anxious. This couldn't be good. He stretched a leg over the throttles and jumped back into the copilot seat, fumbling with the straps. "We've got MIG 29s headed our way," he said.

Pain cut through Lori's head, like a rod twisting from spine to temple. *MIGs?* There wasn't anything she could do about intercep-tors. They'd blow the Gulfstream out of the sky without even get-ting a visual. Or gun them down with one pass. How'd they get airborne so quickly? "Maybe we can tail a civilian plane. They won't be able to tell us apart."

"The Iranians won't care," Marksman said, wiping his nose with the back of his hand.

Lori flinched. She hadn't heard him slip up and kneel in the aisle behind them.

Red held up a finger, ear pressed to the phone.

"Can we put that on the radio?" she asked. "I need to hear."

Red shook his head, finger still up.

"We could," Marksman said. "But it wouldn't be secure."

Red put the phone on speaker and held it between them. "This is the Navy. A Hawkeye, headed our way from the Gulf. She's track-ing us and the MIGs."

"I have escort from a Growler," came a high-pitched female voice, full of static. *"I've sent him ahead. He'll jam the MIGs."*

"What the hell's a Growler?" Lori asked. "Can't it take out the MIGs?"

"Maybe. Shorter range," Marksman said, voice low. "But Ali never had the chance to get out a message, back at Jannat's. Navy probably doesn't know what to make of us. Treat us like a threat till they know different. Won't be splashing any MIGs over Iran."

"Can't *you* shoot them down?" Red asked into the phone.

"Negative. But if they threaten the fleet I'll send an SM up their ass. Same goes for you."

Great. So all Lori could do—again—was wait. She had the wheel of the plane in her hand, yet nothing had changed. *Still stuck in a damn cell.* Maybe this Growler thing could jam them long enough to get out.

Her vertical velocity indicator was blurry. She rubbed her eyes with a cold, chapped knuckle. *Damn it. Never been farsighted before.* After a minute the gauge came into focus. It was angled so low she felt light in her seat. *Been yo-yoing up and down ever since takeoff. Where the hell's the trim tabs?* She eyed the multi-display in the center. Its green background glowed evenly, as if nothing was wrong. Two hundred more miles till the border. Then she had to get someone to talk her down into Balad. How the hell was that going to happen? How was she even going to know where it was? She never asked for this. Everyone would be killed if she augered the landing. What about the kids? Who were the godparents in the will? Was it the in-laws?

Red laid a hand on her knee. "You'll do fine. Keep the throttles down and the nose west. We'll get this other stuff straight."

The voice on the phone squawked, "Growler will be close enough to jam in two minutes."

"So they won't be able to shoot us down?" Red asked.

"Maybe," said the voice. "Growler will jam radar. Fry their nuts like popcorn. Infrared's less reliable. If they've got heat seekers, they might be able to get you. Most of their stuff is old. Jamming should work."

"But they could still ram us?" Lori asked.

Marksman switched his weight to his other knee. "Won't go kamikaze, but they've still got guns. Hell, they could make a supersonic pass and blow our plane apart with the shock wave. Even if the Growler jams everything, it's only buying time."

Lori thought back to the summer her family had lived in Spain, when she was in seventh grade. Their hacienda had a swimming pool bordered in shiny blue and red mosaics. She'd played Marco Polo with her brothers and friends from school at her twelfth birth-day party. Then opened presents, all wrapped in bright orange tis-sue paper. Maybe this could be like their pool game. The MIGs blind. If they hadn't gotten a visual, she might be able to sneak out.

She turned toward the Gulf.

"What're you doing?" Red asked.

"Headed to the carrier group. Calling Polo."

"The Navy will blow us out of the sky."

"I'm gonna break off when they start jamming. Maybe the MIGs will think that's where we're headed. With any luck, they'll do something stupid. Then the Navy can deal with them."

A minute later, the phone shouted again. "Growler reports jam-ming in operation."

Lori dropped the nose and banked right. The ground came up faster than expected. She was pressed back hard into her seat, pulling level, just off the deck. She licked salty perspiration from above her lip, then leaned forward and looked out the window, searching for the planes. Tehran stretched across the far horizon. Visibility was good, but a brownish haze capped the distant sky-line, like what you'd see over Denver. Out the other window rose the Zagros Mountains, jutting rugged from the tan plains. Red's eyes were pinned forward. "Still don't like my driving?"

He mumbled something about the Pennsylvania turnpike.

"Ha. Wasn't too long ago you called *me* a control freak." His face went blurry, like the gauges. Outside, tan earth streaked with orange veins gave way to an ice-blue lake.

"Keep us out of the drink," he said.

"They didn't follow," bubbled from the phone in tones of girlish excitement.

Red covered the mic with his thumb. "Won't be long till they figure out what's going on. Stay low. Keep the throttles open."

Lori looked at the multi-display again. Its green glow was blank. She tapped it, then grabbed the wheel like she was going to lose balance. "See if you can get that thing fixed."

Marksman pounded on the gauge. "It's jammed. Have to wait to see if it comes back. Don't worry, the Hawkeye won't let us get lost."

On cue, the phone voice said, *"We've got approval for armed response. Launching soon. We'll vector to intercept. Escort you out."*

"Thank God. How long?"

"Seventeen minutes."

The rod twisted and the console blurred again.

"We'll be dead by then!" Red shouted, realizing too late his voice carried beyond the cockpit. How'd the Navy get the approval for armed response anyway? The Det's Navy liaison? No, not that fast. Maybe someone in the command center. But with the rush and the firefight, he hadn't put in any request. So, how'd they know? *Oh, the tags.*

He leaned into the aisle. "Now that they know we've picked up their assets, we're politically safe again."

Lori had dropped even lower once they were over the lake. Seemed to him the mast of a sailboat would slap their belly. He remembered his uncle Art telling how once he'd run into a SAM nest in Vietnam. He'd turned and burned, dropping his Phantom low and punching the throttle. Followed his wingman out through a valley and over a lake, their shock waves exploding the grass huts along the shore.

Red forced his mind back into the cockpit. Airspeed was four hundred fifty. He struggled to do the math in his head. "Fifty minutes," he said. "That should get us to Balad."

"MIGs are changing course," the sat phone announced. Her voice was too calm for the situation, like a doctor saying, *It's cancer.* Red stared at the rubber-coated demon in his hand. Its battery warmed his palm as the words vibrated down his forearm, distorted from the speaker's volume. He wanted to crush the girlish voice inside, tell it to go to hell, to get some balls next time it opened its mouth.

Lori glanced at him, a quick shot, but long enough to see the fear in her widened eyes.

"How far away are they?" he asked into the phone.

"About seventy miles," came the voice.

Relief. He leaned back into the seat. "No way they'll find us. Needle in a haystack."

"Then why are they turning toward us?" Lori asked, voice tight.

"Probably figure we're headed for Iraq. By the time they find us, we'll have an F-18 escort."

"Unless they've got eyes on the ground," Marksman said. "We were headed to the Gulf when they started jamming. If they were trying to get a visual on us, that's the direction they'd fly. Someone's tracking us. We're not out of this yet."

From the phone came *"MIGs on course to intercept."* Now the device felt like a chunk of ice in his palm.

"Can you jam their guns?" Red asked it.

The radar operator's voice was professionally eager, as if she was taking an order for a hamburger. "Parts of them. The laser range finder and the radar tracking. But we can't keep them from gunning you down freestyle."

Would you like to supersize that?

A heavy New York accent called from the rear of the cabin. "Lookee what I found!"

Smoke circled Crawler's head. He sat on an opened crate like a guy on the john. A fat green tube lay across his lap. He rose and strutted to the front of the plane, petting it like a *Price Is Right* model showing off the next prize. He butted Marksman in the chest with one end. "You owe me an apology for bustin' me while I hefted these on the plane, man."

Marksman's smile was gratuitous.

"My parents *were* married," Crawler said.

"We don't have time for this shit," Red yelled. "What the hell's that?"

Crawler ground the hot ashes of his cigar into the stainless-steel sink. "Russian issue, heat seeker. A shoulder-launched SAM."

But it wouldn't work air to air, would it? "You know how to use it?"

"You kiddin'? Russian grunts are dumber than shit. Damn thing doesn't even have a safety. You point this end at an airplane and squeeze this trigger. Last time I did that, a helicopter blew up."

Red had been on that op, in South Africa. Crawler'd shot an old Huey out of the sky, but the missile had locked onto the wrong helo, leaving the gunship to deal with.

"You are *not* lighting that torch in my aircraft!" Lori shouted.

"You can't just bust out a window and squeeze the trigger. That thing's an open tube. All the exhaust goes out the back and will blow the plane apart!"

"Can't we slow down and open the door?" Red asked.

"Even if you shoot out a few windows so the air escapes, you'll set us on fire," Lori said, scowling.

Marksman waved a hand. "Lori's right. He'd still be dumping liquid hot exhaust into the plane."

Crawler looked at the door, then across from it at a coffeemaker built into the side wall. He ripped it off and tapped the aluminium behind it with a knuckle. "We pressurized?"

"No," she said. "Why?"

"Where the wires run? The controls. Through the walls?"

"Don't know."

Marksman tapped a boot on the floor. "Below the deck."

Crawler swung his M4 and pointed it where the coffeemaker used to be.

Marksman grabbed his arm. "Hey."

Red lifted his thumb from the phone mic. "MIGs still on a course to intercept?"

"They'll pass a couple miles behind you," the high voice advised.

He covered the mic again. "Let him go."

Pressure waves smacked Red's chest as Crawler auto-stitched a semicircle, like an upside-down smiley. He loaded a fresh clip and finished the loop. It reminded Red of the old carnival booth game where he used to try to shoot out the star from a piece of paper with a BB gun. Crawler pried at the middle with his knife, bending it inward and leaving a hole the size of a small melon. Wind howled through, launching paper napkins into the air like oversized confetti. Crawler stuck the butt-end of the SAM into the hole, pushing hard until it went through. The gale stopped then, replaced by a hum like a vuvuzela's, turning the SAM into a huge musical pipe. Crawler hugged the tube between cheek and shoulder, pointing the business end toward the door. He peered over at Red and flipped up a thumb.

Red ducked back into the cockpit. "Slow us down as much as you can," he told Lori.

She frowned. "But they'll catch up faster."

"Our escort's still fifteen minutes away. The MIGs are almost on us. Go slow now so we can drop the door. If they see us, I'll give the word and you turn broadside to them. Got it?"

The whine of the engines lowered. The nose pointed up and leveled. The flap actuators under the grass-length lavender carpet droned like an electric mole trying to eat its way through.

"Thirty seconds to intercept," advised the radar operator.

Will that be all for you today?

Red held the phone to his mouth. "Turn off jamming, on my mark."

"Jamming off, on your mark," she agreed, girlishness gone now. "Call out their position."

"Four o'clock and twenty seconds out. They'll cross two miles behind and high. They're at your five o'clock . . . six . . . seven . . ."

"I see them!" shouted Marksman, peering through the small window on the door. "They're headed away."

The rest of the team moved to the port side of the aircraft and pressed their cheeks to the windows. The planes were like two tiny arrowheads above the horizon, flying like racehorses with ears pinned back. They kept going till almost out of sight. A flash of reflected sunlight came from both.

From the phone: "They're banking toward you. Vectored to intercept."

Lori brought the plane about. Red held on to Marksman's belt and braced as he dropped the door. Barren earth flashed by, the plane's shadow bouncing up and down over ravines like a swallow fluttering in the dusk. The wind blasted him as Marksman dropped to his knees, pushing the door the rest of the way down. It seemed to vibrate in the fury, but the hinges held. If the door tore off, it'd run down the fuselage right into the engine. Freezing air whipped down Red's back and filled his blouse, sucking the breath from his lungs.

The horizon came down as Lori leveled off. Red yanked Marksman back from the edge. The MIGs were only dots now, an arc of gray mist marking their trails. He put the phone to his ear and shouted, "Jamming off!" Then tapped Crawler on the head.

"They're homing!" said the Hawkeye, with a vibrato of adolescent fear. "They've got—"

Red bounced against the bulkhead as the SAM leapt from the

tube, the hiss of motor exhaust breathing heat into his chest. The rocket left the door and disappeared aft. Had it tumbled in the slipstream? Or even had a chance to acquire its target in the turbulence?

The MIGs banked sideways away from each other, ejecting white-hot flares like drops of liquid sun. Red held the bulkhead and inched toward the door. The SAM came back into view, arcing upwards toward one of the planes, closing so quickly the MIGs now looked slow. The SAM appeared as if it would pass behind the MIG's tail, but took a sharp turn at the last second and hit the centerline of the fuselage. The MIG rolled forward, broke in the middle, and dropped out of sight behind them, falling in two burning chunks of metal.

"Splash one!" Red shouted, slapping Sergeant Crawler on the back. He stumbled over something in the aisle. The empty tube. Crawler already had a second SAM ready. "Start jamming again!" Red shouted into the phone. The rushing air was so loud he couldn't hear, even with the speaker pressed against into his frozen ear. He ducked into the cockpit, slamming the flimsy privacy door behind him. "Where's the other MIG?" he asked.

"Headed home," the radar operator said.

Red dropped onto one knee. "You sure?"

"I'm reading his damn logbook. I'll tell you if he comes around. Good job."

Thank you. Please come again.

Something slapped the wall. Marksman was on the floor, Lanyard and Crawler each holding onto one of his boots. He hung halfway out the plane, pulling up the door. It closed and he cranked the handle hard, sealing it. The cabin was quiet again except for the hum of Crawler's vuvuzela. A paper napkin floated down in front of Red's face like a toy parachute. He snatched and crumpled it. He hadn't seen the pilot eject. The distance was so short, maybe the poor bastard didn't have time. Or maybe lax maintenance and no replacement parts kept the seat from working.

He stretched a boot over the throttles and dropped back into the copilot's chair, setting the phone on the console in front of them.

"Come to two-six-five. I'll talk you into Balad," the radio operator said.

Lori blurted, "We're headed to the carrier."

"Negative. Come to two-six-five."

"What're you doing?" Red asked. Her face was flushed. Sweat dripped from her chin. She kept blinking, shaking her head.

"One tank's bingo fuel," she muttered. "Must've taken ground fire. Only got a third left on the one Crawler filled. The carrier group's closer. Jim's almost dead. Who knows what Balad's got. I'm putting us down on the carrier."

"Lori, that's crazy. Even if you could, they'll blow us out of the sky if we even fly close."

The veins in her neck bulged again, like back at the airport. She probably hadn't slept for days. When was the last time she'd eaten? They'd probably pumped her full of drugs. No way she was thinking straight now.

"It's on the carrier, or in the water next to it," she said. "Even if they have to fish us out, we get Jim to someone that can help. And we're on American soil."

Red tried his calmest tone. "Lori. You can't do that."

She turned toward him and flapped a hand. "What you gonna do, Tony? Got anyone else that can fly this thing? Now tell that bitch what we're doing. Then they blow us out of the sky or we land on the carrier. Their call."

"But you'll kill us."

She twisted her grip on the wheel. "Conversation's over."

"Red," Ali called, an arm extended, waving him back. He took Jim's T-shirt and pressed it to the scarlet mound of bandage atop his friend's chest.

Jim pointed a bent finger at the phone. "Give it to me." Jim took it in his hand and shut it like a billfold.

What the hell? "Sir, we need—"

"You need to listen," Jim wheezed. One eye was open, moving as if trying to focus, to find Red. "They won't shoot us down. But she can't land on a damn carrier."

"I know. She's not thinking straight. She looks like hell. Doc should take a look. She's . . . broke."

One side of Jim's mouth rolled up in a smile. "Then you've got no choice. Sounds like we're landing on the carrier." He pushed the phone into Red's chest. "Don't ever let them think they've got the power. Higher, I mean. Or whoever's in the control center. Once they pull the trigger on an op, you're the one in charge. The rest can go to hell."

Red went back to the copilot seat. His boots fell like stones as he walked. Lori was sweating even more profusely. He passed her a canteen, got a tense nod. Hit redial and the Hawkeye gave him the radio channels. Jamming was off, so they could use it now. He placed headphones over Lori's head. They pushed her hair down, exposing darker roots.

An F-18 escort pulled next to them. The pilot waved and the radio crackled in Red's ear.

"Guido here, on your starboard."

Red waved.

"Can I talk you out of this?"

"You may not have to," Lori said. "We're low on fuel. But I'm not putting down in the water."

"Whatever. You'll probably miss the carrier. Don't undershoot. Ramp strike's a bitch. Follow me. The strong headwind will help. The ship's steaming away, full power. Since your normal landing speed is around one-ten knots—"

"You know that?" Lori asked.

"Not for sure. But that'll give you a deck speed around sixty knots. We'll arrest you with nets. It'll be sudden."

Lori frowned. "How sudden?"

"You're gonna crash...twice. Once on the deck and again in the net. The headwind's your friend." Guido gave more instructions. She couldn't aim for the tail of the carrier. Aim past it. "We set you up, you fly it into the deck. Just hit the damn thing. I'll yell to go around if you're going to undershoot. Once you hit, throttles back, controls forward. No touch-and-go's with a net. Carrier's ten minutes out. Follow next to me."

The late morning sun was still low in the east. At least it would be to their backs. The carrier was a fleck of copper atop a sea of molten lead. As they got closer, the ocean turned frothy. White water churned from the ship's stern.

Guido helped Lori line up and drop the flaps. "Go in gear up. The deck's foamed," he said.

Red had everyone strap in. The small plane didn't have enough seats for the prisoners in the baskets, so Crawler shoved them into the head, one atop the other, still tied in the fetal position at the bottom of their woven grass wombs. *Soon to be tombs?* Richards and Ali doubled up in one seat. Jim was upright now. Ali tied his blouse around his chest and chair, like a safety harness. Amin was strapped in, forehead wrinkling as if trying to open his eyes, moving the bloody foot across the lavender carpet, brushing it with highlights of crimson. Crawler tucked the busted crate behind the last row of seats.

Red sat back in the copilot chair and crossed himself.

"Do that for me, too," Lori said, a pale pinkness flushing her cheek. The F-18 bobbed up and down outside the window.

"Why's Guido moving like that?" Red asked.

"He's not." Her lips stretched thin. "We are. I'm trying to follow him in."

"Listen, if you miss, put us in the water. I'll—"

"Shut up."

It would be over soon enough. No way they'd all survive this. If she was able to hit the deck, maybe a few of the team would live. Probably the ones near the wings, where the fuselage was strongest. If they ditched, they'd hit the water at over a hundred knots, so it might as well be cement. With the wind turning up the waves they'd be under in minutes. If the plane broke apart, seconds.

It was his fault, letting the pilot get killed. Penny, Jackson, and Nick would be raised by his parents. At least Tom had mellowed in his old age. Maybe he wouldn't screw them up too badly.

"You know I've seen this before," Lori whispered under her breath. "Remember?"

"What?"

"I was in your seat. The real copilot was puking his guts out. But then the captain was Navy, and our plane had a tail hook, so it wasn't the same."

The story felt familiar, as if Red had heard the joke before but couldn't remember the punch line. He closed his eyes and tried, but the memory was like a butterfly that landed all too briefly, then flew away. He tried to picture Lori in the copilot seat, but all he could see was her determined eyes as she emptied the 9mm into the guards at the warehouse. How smoothly she had caught Amin's neck with her handcuff chain. "Who are you?"

"Sorry if I let you down," she said.

That's not what he'd asked. "Father Ingram said he'd be praying. He's an old Navy guy. Maybe God will listen to him."

The fuel gauge had a sliver of space between the bottom pin. Lori said, "I'm gambling we'll have enough to do a trial run."

The carrier was huge and flat-topped. A superstructure rose from one side reaching seven stories into the air. The island, the Navy called it. It was topped with antennas and whirling radar dishes. The flight deck was divided into two main runways, one near the front pointed straight ahead with twin catapults sunk into it for launching aircraft. The separate landing runway, the one at which Lori steered the plane, angled nine degrees to one side in case of an accident upon approach. The damaged plane would be less likely to endanger other aircraft on the deck. A likely scenario, currently. And the Navy, in their forethought, had provided the courtesy of spraying a thick white layer of fire retardant foam in anticipation of their arrival.

But no other aircraft were on deck. It was like a ghost ship. Except for two white uniforms on an observation platform, nothing was moving. Having lined up her approach and flared close to the deck, Lori pressed the throttles forward and performed a go-round. Not bad, a little far to port, trying to stay clear of the island.

"Pretend it's not there," Guido said. "Up close, all you'll see is the butt of the flight deck. Pretend there's a big red dot there. Run right into it."

Red cinched Lori's harness, then his. Final approach, if they had enough fuel to make it. The wheel in front of his face travelled in and out, twisting, mirroring Lori's movements. Sometimes when it moved, the aircraft didn't, as if she was feeling the wind, listening to its thoughts, reacting before it changed. It was a battle between will and fate, woman and nature, skill and doubt.

The morning sun shot pink on the contrails of two airliners crossing high above. On the water it paved a golden highway over windswept sea, like a sandbar emerging after ebb tide. The red dot grew, rose, then fell. She flared.

The tail hit with a crack as loud as Marksman's rifle. A flash of light shot through the fuselage as the back of it ripped off behind the bathroom. The plane pitched forward, dropping the cockpit hard, digging Red's harness into his shoulders till the belly smacked the deck, driving him back into his seat. Pain shot up his spine to the crown of his head. Screeching, crumpling metal was under his feet. Foam sprayed ahead like a hundred fire hoses. A thick glob of it splashed on the steel net, approaching fast, not slowing, right where his window hit.

The sun warmed Red's cheek. Cold air blew down his neck. Pain shot through his arm. He opened his eyes. He was in the copilot seat, but his shoulder was twisted. Someone was going to have to put it back in its socket. *Where is Lori?*

Boots holding a smallish man in blue fatigues were standing on the console between them. How was he doing that? The sun glinted off the multi-display, cracked. Damn, the roof was gone. Red leaned back and hit something hard and hot against his scalp. A cable from the net. Behind were the crumpled remains of the canopy, the orange morning sun burning his eyes. *Lori?*

He leaned around the boots on the console. Yellow-clad arms were lifting her out over the nose of the plane on a stretcher. Red unhitched the harness with his good hand. A drop of blood fell from his nose onto the catch.

The boots turned around. "Whoa. Hold on theyah, sport," said a corpsman with a deep southern drawl.

Red brushed his hands away.

"Hey, sit down or I'm gonna have to—"

Red crawled over the controls toward the nose of the plane. A shard of glass sliced his palm. "Lori!" he called, blood running over his lips. His reflection in the multi-display showed his nose had been flattened sideways. *Not again.*

The corpsman jumped in his way. "She's okay," he said, grabbing Red's shoulders. "A slice on the forehead. A dozen stitches and she'll be shiny. Now, you need to sit down or—"

Red stood in the seat and waved him off. "Touch me again and you'll be eating your hand."

"Reicherd!" the corpsman shouted. "Need some help on this one!" He pressed Red back into his seat. "Please, sir."

Red grabbed the corpsman's hand and twisted till it was scratching the back of the guy's neck. He screamed. Red stepped into the aisle and let go, stumbling back into the cabin. Crawler was hopping on one foot, moving the remains of the crate so he could open the door to the head. Jim and Ali were gone. Carter lay outside on a stretcher, in a neck brace. Lanyard jumped across the threshold, which was canted, the door lying on the deck. He swung an arm around Red.

"You need to sit down, sir." He pulled Red in to lean on his shoulder.

"Status?" Red asked, highly nasal, nose clogged, spraying blood with the question.

"We're alive. Took a few minutes to get my wind back. Damn, and I thought getting shot hurt."

Red pushed away and stepped through the doorway onto gray steel deck plate mounded with foam. He had to get to Lori. Why did everyone seem to be leaning? The wings were cut jagged where the plane had slid sideways and hit the net. The air smelled of JP-8. White streaks from the belly of the craft painted the deck where hoses were washing the foam off. The turbine in one of the engines whined, spinning down. The former ghost ship was crawling with life. Skittles everywhere, yellow and red and green jerseys, lugging fire hose, running lift trucks, and pushing the tail section into the sea. White jerseys carried stretchers. Amin was attached to one, arms strapped down as in an asylum. *Good riddance*, thought Red.

A man in a khaki uniform stepped around the nose of the plane. "You Major Harmon?" he shouted over the wind.

Wait. There were two khaki uniforms now. Red blinked hard, then again. Nope, still two. "Yeah."

The guy grabbed his hand and shook it hard, slapping his shoulder. Red winced.

"Your corpsman told me you're in charge."

"Where's Lori?"

"Who's she? The pilot? Don't know. I'll take you there. You need a corpsman yourself."

"The colonel, he okay?"

The officer scowled. "Y'all got no insignia. He the guy shot? Lost a lot of blood. Looks like shit. You got him here alive. We'll try to keep him that way."

Red tried to focus but the officer kept moving, both of him. Damn. He was a captain. Red offered a salute.

"Steady. Ship's nurse'll get you to sick bay." Red refused a stretcher. Lanyard came back over to walk him upright. An MP followed—didn't look old enough to shave yet.

"Hope you don't mind," the captain said with an eat-shit grin, "but your team will be escorted till you're off my ship."

The MP drew a pistol, aiming at the door of the plane. Crawler stepped out with a SAM slung across his back.

"Shit, Crawler," Red shouted. "You're on a carrier. Don't be a dumbass here, too."

Crawler paused, frowned, then set the SAM behind him, back on the floor of the plane.

White jerseys laid the prisoners on stretchers, handcuffed them down, and carried them toward the island. A guy in a bright blue jersey ran to the captain and leaned to his ear.

The captain shouted over a gust of wind, leaning into it. "Anything else you need off your plane?" he asked Red.

"What plane?"

The man in blue smiled, turned back toward the Gulfstream, raised a finger and swung it in a tight circle. Then tractor drivers pushed the aircraft into the sea, followed by a brigade of street sweepers pushing foam and jagged metal and glass in front of them, off the deck.

Chapter 26
Today

Carter jerked the cuffs of his Brooks Brothers pinpoint oxford down over his wrists, maintaining a neat half-inch reveal from under a crisp blue Armani suit coat. Better to go cheap on the shirt instead of the jacket. The hard soles of his Gucci lace-ups clacked down the tiled hallway in the basement of El Maruot, a vending concessions depot off of Nassir Fawzi, outside Cairo, Egypt. The corridor smelled of bleach, the chemical scent a welcome change from the stench of the Pardis River that had taken days to scrub off.

The busy distribution center above buzzed with hundreds of workers and salesmen scampering around the maze of a warehouse, a perfect cover for any screams that might escape from the basement. Fifteen inches of concrete and steel separated the two floors.

He turned a heavy handle and pushed through a thick metal door into a dim room the size of a single-car garage. Seats in two rows faced a huge flat-screen television, like a movie theater. Carter slipped back into a padded folding chair beside two Israelis, one a black-haired woman in her mid-thirties with long frizzy locks and the other an older man with bright white eyes rimmed in red at the bottom like hardboiled eggs floating in blood. He'd met the man, Mr. Levine, a Mossad spy, early this morning, and his eyes had appeared the same then.

The screen displayed an interrogation room, the interior of an ocean shipping crate with deeply corrugated walls. The view of the high-definition camera came from one corner of the ceiling, behind the interrogator, who was sitting with legs crossed and with his hands knit together, resting on a clipboard on his lap. The subject, Amin, sat on a wooden stool, arms and legs shackled by dull steel chains to an eyebolt in the floor. Black stubble grew across his face into a short beard, thin down his neck, flecked in white. Greasy olive skin glowed in a pale shade of yellow, as if jaundiced, wrinkled across his nose like creased wax paper. Puffy close-set eyes were flush in pink exhaustion. A small wooden table separated the interrogator from him. The layout was similar to Carter's debrief room stateside, next to the sheriff's office. Except this space had a plywood floor, stained various shades of brown in overlapping splatters like dried petals of a huge flower. *Blood*, Carter thought.

He leaned toward Mr. Levine. "Anything happen since I stepped out?"

The bags under Levine's bright eyes vibrated as he spoke. "Nothing." The man slapped his thigh. "We will get it. We have ways. Wut not here." His B's sounded like W's.

Of course they had ways. But Mossad would put its best foot forward at this stage, trying to maintain a civil appearance while among unfamiliar company. They couldn't act in a politically incorrect manner when CIA was present, since you never know when that organization might bust at a seam and spew leaked intelligence to the world. Lately it seemed to happen once a year. Ever heard of Mossad having a leak? No, these guys plugged them with dead bodies. "I'm not CIA."

Levine's chin rumpled as he stuck out a lip. "None of you ever are. If it makes you feel wetter, I'm a sales executive for Filo Caldo, an Italian manufacturer of wire products."

Carter pushed up a cuff and glanced at the black blades beneath the watch crystal. The interrogation was wearing into its fourth hour. Mind-numbing. Mossad's tactics thus far had not proven to be worthy of their reputation. Carter had gotten more out of the man in five minutes than they'd produced in two days. Might as well call it an interview. But at least he'd be able to slip home tomorrow. Mossad had requested Carter to be present for only the first three days after Amin was turned over. Two down, almost. One to go.

The interrogator's voice through the speaker was a monotone hum. All day yesterday. And four long hours today. Hell, Carter was about to confess to the crime. Anything to get moving. Except there had been no wrongdoing, according to Amin.

"Tell me about the hidden centrifuges," the interrogator droned.

He slid a photo across the table. Amin reached for it, but his cuffs stopped his arms short. "How many are running now?"

Amin stared at the picture. "I've never seen those things."

"We have photos of you next to them."

"Show me."

"It would compromise those who gave them to us. We can't."

And on and on it went. A dog chasing its tail.

The interrogator held up two fingers toward the camera. *Finally!* An odd gesture, but clear to Carter. The detective stood, brushed his suit straight, recinched his green silk Ferragamo tie, and stepped outside the door. Slipping through a wide opening covered by ribbons of thick clear sheet vinyl, he strode down an elongated white room past three green shipping containers, stopping at the third. His breath frosted in refrigerated air; outside the building it was a balmy fifty degrees. A loudspeaker gushed waves lapping against a bulkhead, accented with an occasional laughing seagull and clanging buoy. All a play, an act, for Amin. As far as the prisoner was aware, he was inside an insulated ocean container on a dock outside an abandoned salmon processing plant somewhere in Alaska.

One of the crate's end doors stood ajar. Carter slipped through it into a cramped space, a foyer he'd call it, had it not been the entrance to an interrogation chamber. One last tug on his jacket, a lift of his chin, a final turn of a handle, and he pressed through the last door.

Carter stepped onto the plywood floor. The room was just as sparse as revealed by the video feed to the joint CIA/Mossad observation room he'd just left. He entered behind the interrogator and stood. It had been a week since Carter had questioned Amin in the basement bunker, and the slice in Amin's cheek where his teeth had broken through was healing nicely, held together by knotted black threads sewn by a corpsman trained to be expedient in battle, not to minimize scarring. Eye sockets were still sunken in purple. Orange prison clothes hung loosely from his body. His lips were purple, not quite blue, and he shivered.

Amin's eyes widened as he lifted his gaze from the photos on the table. He backed away from the detective as if he were radioactive waste, slipping off his stool, but was caught by his shackles with a jerk.

Carter twisted his neck to one side, popping a vertebra that had become particularly noisy since Lori's crash landing. He slipped onto a matching stool in a corner, below the video camera, rested one foot on a rung, and leaned toward Amin.

The interrogator didn't miss a beat. He tapped the picture on the table and rubbed an eyebrow. His English was flat, without any noticeable accent, as if from Maryland or Virginia. "The Americans who brought you here, they did not want to give you up. But we persuaded them. It appears you made a personal attack on the family of a high-ranking politician. The U.S. has lobbied for your possession." The interrogator looked up now, a weak smile hanging on thin lips. "We acknowledge their significant investment in obtaining you, and since you appear to not have any information of value to us, I am inclined to allow them to have you."

Carter stood.

Amin shuddered. He brushed his thin pants as if sweeping off ants. "This man is not American! You can't turn me over to him."

The interrogator covered his mouth as he yawned. Good move. Carter was going to have to remember that one. "The Americans will treat you well."

"This man will kill me. He's the one who stabbed me in my legs. He put a blade through my foot!"

The interrogator straightened in his chair, arched his back, and rubbed his kidneys. "This man saved your life. He pulled you from a burning plane after it crash-landed. Your own air force shot it down. I've shown you the news clip from your own state-run news agency. The fact you came out of it with only a few dozen stiches shows how much the Americans care for your well-being."

Well played. Carter held out a hand. "I'll take him now."

Amin jerked his arms away. A crimson dot spread on the thigh of his orange cotton pants. All the jostling he'd just performed may have opened a stitch. "Those news clips are a lie! We didn't—"

The interrogator squared to Amin, placing both feet on the plywood. "But it is a state news agency. You mean we can't believe what your government says?"

Amin stuttered. "N-no. I mean, yes. You're putting words in my mouth."

"If we can't trust what they broadcast to the world, we can't believe their denials of secret weapons-grade-uranium-enrichment facilities." The interrogator tapped the photo.

Amin glanced at the picture again, leaning over it. "I—I may have been here before." He smiled, uncovering a chipped front tooth. "Yes. I believe it was a petroleum laboratory. That is why I didn't recognize it at first. Yes, just a few months ago." He sat down on his stool, gazed locked with the interrogator. "I stay in Israeli custody. You move me from this site to a secure location, within Israeli borders, with white-collar criminals. You do this, and I will tell you all I know about this photo."

The interrogator was a genius. He'd just moved the conversation from Amin denying any knowledge of Iran's underground nuclear facilities to full disclosure. And in the process Amin had unwittingly sealed his own fate. This droning monotone man had just pulled a rabbit out of a hat.

Carter sat back down. He pushed aside a pang of guilt, knowing Mossad wouldn't let Amin live but a few more weeks. You don't make deals with the enemy. What a joke. They don't speak that language. But Amin deserved what he was going to get.

And the Middle East would be that much more stable. Carter mused how restful his flight home tomorrow would be. CIA would spring for first-class tickets, with plush seats and complementary champagne. His cheeks drew tight as he smiled, realizing he'd soon be back to his semiretired state, a detective in New Kent County.

Where he'd never have to be dropped from an aircraft or carry an automatic weapon again.

The old gray Sikorsky MH-53J Pave Low shuddered as it lifted from the huge concrete apron behind the Det, where the Tupolev had picked up the team a week earlier. The huge cargo bay was lined down each side with drum-tight nylon seats that could double as stretchers, useful for both infil and exfil. Red had patted the two patched 35mm holes before climbing in. It was becoming a bit of a superstition, maybe like Crawler's pre-op puffs on his cigar. But today the team was in blue jeans and sweat shirts. A winter heat wave had rolled through the Mid-Atlantic states, and sixty degrees felt like summer. Most of those who had participated in last week's op sat inside the helo. The venerable craft could carry up to fifty-five troops, so plenty of room remained beside Dr. Ali, Capt. Richards, Marksman, Crawler, and Lanyard.

Marksman stood and strode to the front of the craft. He gripped the twin handles of the port-side minigun, then pulled the trigger and the six-barreled column spun, but didn't fire. The weapon was empty for the joyride. He pivoted and squeezed at imaginary targets as the helicopter gained altitude. "You know they make a fifty-cal minigun now, a GAU-19. Ought to get one of those."

Across the aisle, Red stared at a blue and white bumper sticker stuck to the ship's olive drab aluminum skin, above Lanyard's head. *I Love Jet Noise*, it stated, with a silhouette of an F-18 Hornet. Red wondered which Navy squid had snuck into the hangar and stuck that one up there. He opened his mouth to tell Lanyard to rip it down, then decided against it. The Det was a purple-suit organization if there ever was one. Inside were members of every military branch, plus liaisons from most departments of the U.S. government and several foreign ones. RECON, SEALs, FBI, CIA, even a rep from British SAS and another from Russia's Spetsnaz. Like someone had opened a knife drawer and tossed in every blade they could find, then shaken it up till the daggers were strewn haphazardly. How had Jim kept them so neat and in order, lined in their little slots and not sliding around and dinging other blades?

Jim. Red hadn't allowed himself time to think of his commander's death. Jim had hung on for three hours after the landing on the aircraft carrier, but one of the bullets he'd taken in the chest had plunged close to his heart, so Red had been told. Jim had saved Red's life, throwing him under the truck, taking shots that had been aimed at him. Sick bay hadn't allowed Red to see the body, and within eight hours a hasty evacuation in a blacked-out Grumman C-2 had taken the team and prisoners off the carrier.

Jim's absence had left a huge hole at the Det. A hole Red had been assigned by Higher to fill. He had to seal that void, to honor the man Jim had been. He pushed it from his mind once again. He'd allow time to process those thoughts later.

Because today was a happy day, a celebration of an op well done.

The helo climbed into a shallow bank, and afternoon sun gleamed into the open rear cargo door, highlighting a Browning fifty cal, mounted there and casting its shadow across the ramp, moving in an arc like a sun dial as the chopper turned.

Red gently squeezed plastic ribs taped across his nose. Still sore.

Dr. Ali had said it'd be another few days till he could remove the splint. At least now he didn't have cotton gauze shoved into his sinuses. He drew a deep breath though his nose, just because he could. The aroma of jet fuel greeted his senses. One of the many scents of freedom. He leaned forward and placed a palm on the floor. The old gray girl felt joyous, like a mother released from prison, reunited with her family.

"How we going to get to the beach?" Lanyard shouted above the whir of dual General Electric turboshafts.

Marksman pointed to a fast rope, a thick braided mass fastened to the ceiling near the rear of the craft, hanging and coiled on the ramp like a cobra.

Lanyard held up bare hands, fingers splayed. "I didn't bring my leather gloves." He glanced at the rest of the team. "Neither did you guys."

Marksman lifted a fist, then the other, in a reverse hand-over-hand motion. "This ain't an insertion. It's an oyster roast. We're not in a hurry, so use your arms."

Lanyard gave a thumbs-up.

Red gripped a handrail and made his way to the rear of the aircraft, next to the fifty cal, then peered over the edge. Because they were in flight, the ramp wasn't lowered all the way. Thus even he had to duck to keep from smacking his head on the ceiling. Lanyard gripped the fast rope and joined him, studying the suburban streets as the chopper flew toward the Chesapeake Bay. The roads melted into wintry brown park, which faded to stripped hardwood forest, then dark green salt marsh, and finally into a long tan beach.

The pilot, keeping the helicopter two hundred feet above the deck, passed over the site of the beach party. Several civilian four-wheel-drives were parked at odd angles around a bonfire, and metal racks held oysters baking over beds of hot coals. Behind an eighties blue Ford pickup with dropped tailgate stood a keg with a pump valve and several filler hoses stretching from it. The contraption always reminded Red of a diving respirator. The craft flew through the fire's column of white smoke, chopping it in turbulence, filling the interior with hickory, beech, and saltwater scents.

Lanyard turned toward Red. "Why's the pilot passing by?"

Red quenched a smile, forcing his lips tight in one of Jim's more common expressions. "Probably just lining up for an approach."

218 • *David McCaleb*

A minute later, from her seat the copilot stuck a fist into the aisle. *Quarter mile out.* Good to go. The craft slowed and settled into a shallow hover and frigid salt spray washed into the cargo bay. Red nodded to Marksman. He and Crawler had snuck close, pretending to peer out the opening. Each grabbed one of Lanyard's shoulders and slammed him to the ramp.

"What the hell!" the Marine yelled.

Richards yanked off the soldier's sneakers and pants. His feet flailed as if he was trying to take off the captain's head. Maybe he was. Marksman and Crawler managed to strip off the sweatshirt, but had to tear loose a waffle patterned thermal underwear jersey. Crawler took an elbow to the chin, but it didn't shift his smile. The bullet bruises on Lanyard's bare stomach had faded, but one still appeared deep purple and sore. With bandage scissors, Ali cut off the man's underwear and the operator stopped struggling. His entire body was goose pimpled in the cold.

"A little tradition we have in the Det," Red hollered, vapor swirling about his head, misting his beard. "After your first op, a naked ocean swim back to the party. In summer it's a mile, but since the water's only forty-eight degrees, we've cut it down to a quarter that." With two fingers he pointed over the ramp's edge. Marksman and Crawler pitched him ass over heels into the air. Lanyard tucked himself into a tight ball as he fell forty feet into the water.

A second later, his head bobbed up, barely visible above the whirl of rotor-washed spray. Red pointed toward the beach to give the man his bearings.

Crawler leaned over the ramp, fingers gripping a rib on the ceiling like a mountain climber wedging digits into a crack. For the last week the man had boasted about how the explosion of the VEVAK warehouse had been such a work of art, going so far as to liken it to the *Mona Lisa*. Could the man could even spell her name? He told how he'd splashed a MIG 29, as if he'd done it by himself. "Enjoy your swim, jarhead!" Crawler called down to Lanyard as the helicopter drifted away. "Gonna need tweezers to take a piss!"

Red locked Marksman's gaze, then shot his eyes to Lanyard in the water. Marksman beamed and gave Crawler a firm shove in his back. The chunky grunt tumbled down, not tucking tight like Lanyard had done, and splashed flat on his back. He bobbed up like a buoy, shock on his face, held up a fist, and hollered something indecipherable over the pulsing slap of the rotors.

Ali had set up a green tent with propane heater on the beach in anticipation of the event. Red had instructed it to be stocked with a six pack of Bud Light to appease Crawler. He'd come out of the water an angry bear, but once the man was full of his favorite brew, his character mellowed.

Red tightened his grip on the handrail. You never know if some other joker was going to get an idea to toss him out as well. The Sikorsky shuddered for a few seconds, then smoothed. Red sensed the old girl didn't like leaving any of her team in the water, but obeyed the pilot's command. Glancing around the group, he saw that everyone wore broad smiles. Richards slapped Red on the back, waving to Lanyard and Crawler in the water. The team was tight. A woven sheet of fibers, like the hardened skin of a cloak, cemented into place, formed for a purpose, a function, each strand lending its particular strength, all forming a greater whole.

Yes, for Jim, he'd hold the Det together. They'd done so much good. Such a team should be protected.

As the Sikorsky approached the beach, his mouth watered at the scent of roasting oysters.

Penny, Nick, and Jackson shuffled in front of the chrome-wire shopping cart. A wheel with a flat spot clacked a steady cadence on a vinyl-tiled floor. Just Red's luck, another broken cart. And no matter how many times the kids got their feet run over, they'd still stop randomly when different toys caught their attention.

The family was walking through Gloucester's Walmart, only one county over from their old one. The CIA had insisted a move and a new identity would help ensure the family's safety. In an area with over 1.6 million people, even a short hop from one county to another was significant, though not nearly as thorough as the Witness Protection Program.

Jackson jerked to a halt again, reached out and grabbed a package off a hangar. Lori leaned over him. "What does David like?" she asked. Red hated venturing down the toy aisles, but his son was on the hunt for a birthday present. He'd been in his new kindergarten class for three days and had come home with a birthday party invitation for a new friend, David.

Jackson rubbed the shiny clear package. "He likes Legos and *Star Wars*."

Funny. They hadn't made it to the Lego aisle yet. "What you holding there, buddy?" Red asked.

The boy turned and held the package over his head. It was a black pistol, a three-quarter-size model Colt 1911 with orange-tipped barrel. Except for STINGER stamped on the side, it appeared relatively anatomically correct, down to the beavertail grip safety.

"I don't think David's mother would appreciate that. What do you think?" Lori glanced at Red, eyebrows high, her *agree with me or die* expression.

Red stepped around the cart and took the package. Squatting down next to his son, he rubbed fingers across the clear plastic. "You mother is right. This is a cool sidearm but—" a knee smacked his back. "It's a nice weapon—" another jab. "A good toy, but it's for older kids. And some parents don't like pistols."

Jackson's feet marched in place, as if jogging. "It's not for him. *I* wanna buy it. How much money do I have?"

Red glanced at Lori. She held up a palm, eyes narrowed, *Not on your life* written in her face. Red placed the package back on its hanger, in front of three identical boxes. "I don't think you have enough saved up yet, buddy."

"But Nana gave me ten dollars for my birthday." *$9.89* was written in black on the orange price tag.

Red tousled his son's hair. "Maybe next time. This one shoots plastic bullets. When you're older." He pointed to a yellow Nerf revolver that shot foam darts. "Maybe that one would be better."

Jackson hopped, pointing to the 1911's box. "But this one looks like yours." He pushed on Red's chest, beside where his Det Sig Saur sidearm was strapped beneath his shoulder. How'd he know Red was carrying? "You've got one. Why can't I?"

A tall brunette in tight black sweats stepped behind Lori, towing a chubby girl gripping a green-taffeta-clad party-Barbie by the hair. The woman glanced at the bulge under Red's arm, then yanked her child down the aisle.

Once the woman had stepped around the corner, Red tapped the 1911's package. "This one says you have to be ten years old to buy it. The store won't let us. In a couple years, maybe."

They strolled to the Lego aisle without further protests. The far end was dedicated to pink toys.

The brunette glared at Red and jerked her daughter's hand as the girl held a huge box. "That's a good one. Mommy will get it for you." Then they scurried around the end.

Outside, making their way across the parking lot, bright sun warmed Red's face. Lori held Nick's hand this time, her hips rocking in the same graceful sway. "A little different than last visit to Walmart."

Lori smiled back. They hadn't spoken much of the op. Just letting things calm a bit first. One night after a glass of wine she'd confessed she was in the employ of the CIA, but assured him it was only as an analyst, more administrative than anything. Not an executive at Merkel Research, a high-powered think tank. That was a cover. But the conversation hadn't gone any further, and Red wasn't inclined to force it. *Not yet,* he thought. So often Jim had said, *Always trust your team. Like family.* But why had she helped keep his past hidden under recall for six years? How'd she know how to incapacitate Amin so skillfully? Could he trust her? His wife?

She lifted Jackson's arm high, helping him jump over a pothole as deep as his knee. Blond hair fell across her face. She lifted her head and brushed bangs behind an ear. A glance at Red, and she grinned, puckering lips for a split second.

To hell with doubt. *Always trust your team.*

ACKNOWLEDGMENTS

I owe a huge debt of thanks to my mother and late father for encouraging creativity in our family, and so many others beyond. To my wife and kids, for pretending to enjoy black ops thrillers. To Dorie, for letting me know when I get too dark. To Abigail, for that neat twist about Mossad. To Jesse, for helping this Type A laugh. To Troy Farlow, for your brutally honest feedback. Sorry, but I'll never be Proust.

I cannot express sufficient gratitude to my writers' workshop. To Lenore Hart and David Poyer, for endless wisdom, willingness to teach, and that cursed red pen. To my partners in crime, Frances Williams, Mark Nuckols, Ken Sutton, and Joan La Blanc, for your endurance, insight, skill, and criticism.

To my editor, Michaela Hamilton, for catching the vision and believing in the manuscript. To my agent, Anne Hawkins, for working so hard on my behalf.

Thank you to the entire thriller community of authors. You have been supportive, open, and willing to share. To my readers, you rock! Thank you for your comments, feedback, and suggestions on my website, DavidMcCaleb.com, and on Facebook (McCalebBooks) and Twitter (@McCalebBooks). They are always welcome.

Ready for more Red?
Turn the page to enjoy an exciting preview
of the next Red Harmon thriller by David McCaleb!

RELOAD

Coming soon from Lyrical Underground, an imprint of
Kensington Publishing Corp.

Chapter 1
Baseball

Tony "Red" Harmon glanced at unrepaired holes from automatic weapons fire that had stitched a neat line in beige siding beneath his neighbor's second-story window. The wet team had hit three weeks ago. You'd think the Cutlers could have gotten a contractor to patch up the five-five-six millimeter perforations by now. Considering how many times the covenant committee had told Red to cut his own grass, surely they'd be hot to get the punctures fixed so the place didn't look like a Beirut slum. He could imagine the blond witch from the homeowners' association visiting Mr. Cutler now, tossing her head. *Bullet holes and unkempt yards bring down property values*, she'd say.

Red stepped on to the pitcher's mound centered in his cramped backyard and flipped a Wiffle ball from palm to back of hand. He smiled as he waited for his four-year-old son, Nick, kneeling in the batter's box, to tie mismatched laces. No matter. His kid would be tripping over them again in minutes. But his boy just had to have real sneakers. The ones without Velcro. Nick switched to the other foot, fingers gripping 550 paracord. Red could almost read Nick's mind as he made the loop. *Around the tree and through the—*

Something moved off to the side. Another neighbor snapping shut white-lined curtains, blue scalloped hem, then tugging the edges so they sealed tight. The night of the attack, their home had escaped with only a single hole punched through the garage door. The projectile had been 9mm, copper with a hardened tungsten steel core, coated with polytetrafluoroethylene.

Red and his family hadn't been back since armor-piercing bullets had flown through their middle-class neighborhood by the magful. But he'd promised the kids a good-bye to their home, because that's what this house had been called for the last six years.

He stepped off the mound toward second base. It was Sunday, but no one was outside except them. He shouldn't have brought the family back here, not even for this quick last visit.

A white Chevy Suburban parked out front weighed almost twice what it had coming off the assembly line, heavy now with bulletproof glass and armor plates hidden inside the doors. The engine had been supercharged to compensate, the drivetrain beefed up as well. The driver had a Glock 17 beneath a shoulder, an MP5 in the center console. A single day in this vehicle and Nick had already managed to empty a juice box into the adjoining leather seat, while Penny had dropped her bubble gum on the carpet.

Penny wound up and threw a second Wiffle ball back to Red, this time necessitating a jog outside third base. He stifled a contented laugh as he stooped and picked it up. She had been all ballet and Barbie dolls for years, but now had a 50-cal for an arm. Get some accuracy and college was paid. Jackson and Nick were still too young to predict.

"Okay, kids. We need to go."

Penny's shoulders slumped. "Dad-de-e-e! We just got here. You *promised*."

"I promised you could say good-bye, not play a whole baseball game. One more pitch."

Red planted a boot atop the brown spot where the dog had peed and burned the grass—now his pitcher's mound. Nick stood in the batter's box, thick orange plastic bat slung atop a shoulder like a hobo's satchel. This would be quick.

Red's arm drew a slow arc back, giving the boy plenty of forewarning. Nick pounded home plate with the bat like Bam-Bam from the Flintstones, closed his eyes, and swung. A hollow *tunk* and the ball flew between first and second. He stood there, motionless.

Penny slapped his calf. "Run, dork!"

Nick hesitated, then turned toward third base. His older brother, Jackson, shoved him at first. The boy looked down at his feet as if expecting them to decide, then started pumping in a half-trot, flinging the bat back toward Penny's head. The ball smashed into a holly hedge against a gray-patinaed privacy fence and dropped out of sight in the prickly green shrub.

Red raised arms and shouted, "Home run! We're done. Inside."

"But what about my ball?" whined Nick.

"I'll get you another."

"But it won't be a home run ball!"

Red stomped over to the bushes. Dandelions rubbed his cheek as he searched under the branches on hands and knees. Dandelions that wouldn't die no matter what chemical he sprayed. Dandelions he no longer gave a damn about, now that *new identity* had landed atop the family's to-do list. Their home was property of the CIA. In fact, county tax records showed it had never been their own. Someone by the name of Marsha Peekly was listed on the trumped-up deed. Ms. Peekly was selling it because a new job was sending her to Arizona, or Alabama, or one of those other A states.

"I can't see it," he said. "It's not under here."

"There it is!" Nick exclaimed, kneeling beside him. He pointed toward the back of the holly row, near the bottom of the fence.

Red followed the line of Nick's index finger. His hand still held the scent of citrus from the orange Lori had given him in the Suburban. It was the two boys' favorite treat. "Come on. Not even Br'er Rabbit could wiggle in there."

Penny's nose wrinkled. "Who's Briar Rabbit?"

Red gasped. "You mean, I never—we've never . . . Oh, forget it." He lay on his belly and stretched an arm under the hedge. Stiff twigs pushed up his sleeve and leaf barbs clawed at his wrist. His hand was still a couple of feet short. Muttering low curses, he ducked again and low-crawled underneath, breathing in damp partially decayed leaves. A brown wolf spider sprinted out, just below his forehead. He closed his eyes and shoved in a few more inches, the sharp leaves now scoring his neck. His fingers landed upon the plastic orb. He hooked two fingers into the holes and wriggled out backward.

The ball caught on a branch and popped off. He shoved a hand back in after it and hit something else—something cold, hard, like metal. Maybe a beer can from a summer barbeque? No, heavier. The ratchet he'd lost two years ago? How'd it get way out here?

He wrapped his fingers around the thing and it fell knowingly into his palm, like the familiar tool it was. No, not a ratchet.

* * *

A light turned green and the supercharger gulped air, force-feeding the engine, singing a muffled high note. The driver of the Suburban rolled a shoulder back, as if his holster was chafing. He pressed a phone to one ear and spoke in low tones, probably to another CIA goon, about a UPS shipment, tracking numbers, arrival dates, and other drivel. Red sat in the seat behind him, jacket folded across his lap. He lifted the corner toward Lori, next to him.

"What is it?" she asked, glancing down.

He turned to look at the third seat. All three kids were strapped in, heads down, each thumbing some small electronic gadget. The driver was still mumbling something in code. "A pistol," Red whispered.

She rolled her eyes. "Of course. I meant where'd you get it?"

"Under the hedge out back."

She held a breath. "What type?"

"Holly."

The tendons between her jaw and temple stretched tight. She was gorgeous when angry. "Not in the mood, dammit."

That was Lori's warning to get serious, quit kidding, or otherwise straighten up. He whispered, "German, P-08 Luger Mauser, I think. Stamped 1941 on the barrel."

A clump of her blond bangs hung over an eye. The visible one was rimmed in red, dark flesh puffy beneath it.

"Wasn't trying to piss you off."

"Just comes naturally." She leaned back but kept her voice low. "We'll talk about it later. Not in front of the kids."

Jackson made *boom-boom-boom* gun noises behind them. Both flinched when he yelled, "Got 'em!" His gaze never left the gadget in his hands.

Red inched closer to Lori. "It needs to get to your guys."

She frowned. "Then you should've left it under the hedge and called forensics." She glanced up at the distracted driver.

"Forensics missed it the first time. Haven't turned up anything for three weeks. No one is getting it. The more time passes, the longer whoever took a shot at us the first time has for a second chance. I'm tired of waiting. We've got to get this to someone who knows what to do with it."

Her nostrils flared and she shoved a hand beneath the weapon.

"See this scar?" She tapped an indentation at the bottom of the grip. "This was shot out of the guy's hand. A round hit there."

"A *guy*. How do you know it was a man?"

"Right-handed one, at that."

His forehead knitted. "Seriously, how you figure?"

A glow of interest lit her eyes. "The slide is locked open. He emptied the entire clip. More concerned with quantity than quality." An accusatory glance. "A guy thing, obviously."

"You're straying from the subject."

Lori held the handle toward him, displaying a brown crust across the butt. "Also, it hit near the bottom, yet the round drew blood. It's stained into the wood. So the shooter had a big hand. Again, probably male."

"But why right-handed?"

"Look at the scar. The round hit and ricocheted that way. If he'd been left-handed, the projectile probably would've hit him square in the chest. Then you'd have found a body instead of just the gun."

Red squinted. "How do you know all this?"

She glanced at the kids. "Not now, dear."

Married for ten years—or so he'd been told—he knew less about the woman sitting next to him today than on their honeymoon. He'd thought his life was relatively normal, till the kidnapping, then recall. The realization his past wasn't . . . just wasn't. Memory had been artificially suppressed. The doctors never gave a satisfactory answer as to method, and Red held doubts that even they understood, but they'd cleared him for duty. "You've got full recall," Dr. Genova had said.

Bullshit. What about the nagging feeling something important wasn't back yet? Something else obscured by fog. A shadow still indecipherable. Maybe it was sitting next to him, palming a Luger, saying *Not now, dear*. Even so, the scent of Extatic drew his nose closer to her neck, and he left a kiss there.

"I've gotta do something with it," Red whispered. "Your folks are the cleanup crew. Get it to someone who will know what the hell it means. Your side deals with it."

She leaned close. "They won't care. They've already closed the file, reassigned personnel. In their minds, taking us off the grid will fix all this. They'll run forensics, then stick it in an evidence warehouse. The weapon won't be traceable. They never are."

"Then what?"

She looked him in the eye, as if resigned to discussing this now, after all. "You do it."

"The Det?"

"You guys have access to the same intel, maybe even more."

"We're operational. That's part of the deal. Someone else figures out who owns the thing. We just, you know—kill 'em."

"Just?" she snorted. "What if he's on our side?"

"Above my pay grade, honey. We stick this Luger in his mouth and he talks. We're the gorillas. Someone else plays detective. Give me an investigation and I'll screw it up."

The Suburban slowed at a stoplight, pausing next to a green Honda Odyssey. Paint peeling on the hood. The wife yawning, husband's cheek pushed against the passenger window, breath fogging it in rhythm, eyes closed. Two car seats with snoozing toddlers in back.

"That'll be us in another week," she said. "No more escort. Be nice to get back to normal."

"Hmm," he breathed. In whose world is this normal? Being an operative felt as natural as an alpha wolf leading a pack, marking territory, sniffing out rivals, hunting mule deer. But when the op's over, you're safe. Obscured by the Det, a fusion cell, a non-organization held together by a thousand handshake agreements. Now someone had cut through that nicely painted top-secret canvas, ripped it open to look behind. How much had they seen? This constant worry about who's behind you, remembering faces, doubling back to take a pretend second look at a store window, trying to shake a tail while shopping with your kids for size-three sneakers—no. All this spook stuff was crap. "You think this guy is a danger to us? Or the kids?"

Lori tucked the weapon into his jacket pocket and crossed her arms. "Don't need that to know *someone's* after at least one of us. Or who we work for. Reinserting us on the grid will only delay them discovering us again. Maybe not even much."

"So, I'd better figure it out."

She threw up her hands. "Red, it's only one piece of a puzzle! One in a box on a shelf in a warehouse full of a million others. The only way it'll get opened again is if something actionable comes up. That's not gonna happen, not with the agency spread as thin as it is. *This* is our new reality, even in a new home. We've got to accept it."

"But if something actionable turned up?"

"Then maybe the powers that be would let your gorillas out of the cage." Her slender fingers brushed his cheek, pulling his face to her. "Honey, look. This may be something we just can't fix. You've got to be okay with that. Once information is out, it's like a virus. It spreads, fast. Secrecy is our only ally. We may even have to hop the grid again sometime."

Red pulled the jacket close to his belly and leaned in to her ear. "But intel is always stored. Maybe on a computer—or on paper. Or just in someone's head. I have *fixed* all that stuff before. Sniff out the trail, back to the source, then kill the source." He winked. "I'll take it. Our kids may have a normal life yet."

She gaped. "What're you saying?"

"I'm going to bend the rules. I know a bloodhound."

ABOUT THE AUTHOR

DAVID MCCALEB was raised on a farm on the Eastern Shore of Virginia. He attended Valley Forge Military College, graduated from the United States Air Force Academy, and served his country as a finance officer. He also founded a bullet-manufacturing operation, patented his own invention, and established several businesses. He returned to the Eastern Shore, where he currently resides with his wife and two children. Though he enjoys drawing, painting, and any project involving the work of hands, his chosen tool is the pen.

Recall is the first novel in the Red Ops series. Many more are planned. Please visit David McCaleb on Facebook or at www.davidmccaleb.com.

CPSIA information can be obtained
at www.ICGtesting.com
Printed in the USA
LVOW07s1712300117

522613LV00001B/253/P